KGB KILL

KGB KILL

by

James Mitchell

Hamish Hamilton · London

HAMISH HAMILTON LTD

Penguin Books Ltd, 27 Wrights Lane, London W8 5TZ (Publishing & Editorial)
and Harmondsworth, Middlesex, England (Distribution & Warehouse)
Viking Penguin Inc., 40 West 23rd Street, New York, New York 10010, U.S.A.
Penguin Books Australia Ltd, Ringwood, Victoria, Australia
Penguin Books Canada Limited, 2801 John Street, Markham, Ontario, Canada L3R 1B4
Penguin Books (N.Z.) Ltd, 182–190 Wairau Road, Auckland 10, New Zealand

First published in Great Britain 1987 by
Hamish Hamilton Ltd

British Library Cataloguing in Publication Data

Mitchell, James, *1926–*
KGB kill.
I. Title
823′.914 [F]   PR6063.I793

ISBN 0-241-12365-8

Typeset in Great Britain by
Tradespools Ltd., Frome, Somerset
Printed in Great Britain by
Richard Clay Ltd, Bungay, Suffolk

Chapter 1

JASON BIRD looked out of the window of his hotel suite in Saint Petersburg, Florida, and thought that, all things considered, life was pretty good. It would be no exaggeration to say that life for Jason Bird had often been pretty bad. His time in the Siberian gulag, for example, or his time at the Lumumba University in Moscow, worrying about whether or not he was going to be sent to the Siberian gulag, on so many of those little jobs that the K.G.B. had dreamed up for him in the past. Often there had been danger, mostly there had been discomfort, and all too few the times when he had shown any profit on what he had had to do.

That was Jason Bird's problem. As a Russian, he was far too interested in profit, and far too appalled by lack of it. It had been something thrust upon him, in his genes, and there was nothing he could do about it. Jason Bird was not just an ambitious man, he was a financially ambitious man, and for a man like that, the K.G.B. was of very little use.

His name had not always been Jason Bird. He had chosen it not long after his defection, because it seemed to him to sum up the things that fascinated him most. Jason, after all, was a Greek hero who had found the Golden Fleece, and that was something to be proud of after all. To find something of such enormous value, and to be able to hang on to it. And the Bird, why not? After the plastic surgery operation and the new identity, he was as free as one after all. Free to go where he wanted, to do what he wanted, and to be paid for it. Free even to take the money that was given him and invest it and maybe show a profit. Life was pretty good for Jason Bird, and in his opinion, it could only get better, provided the Dow-Jones index behaved as it should.

And that very day another way of making money had suggested itself to him. He'd gone down to the coffee shop to have lunch and stopped in the foyer and looked around. The news-stand, as usual, was a riot of paperbacks, and for once he'd gone over to take a look. Jason Bird had been amazed at the number of books about spies there were to buy in the United States of America. And not all of them fiction, either. By no means all. Memoirs galore. Big spies, little spies, some who weren't even spies at all, not as an ex-K.G.B. operative understood the word. And yet there they were, all on display, $2.50 a throw at least. And, he had been told, some of these books had prints round a quarter of a million, or even more. Jason Bird pondered for a second the facts of his own life and knew that if only he handled it right, he was very close to very large sums of money indeed, sums of money that could be invested in the boom that he knew was coming.

He got up to go to the bar and pour himself a drink of the kind of vodka that was made in Russia, and almost impossible to buy there, unless you knew somebody important, and yet was available in every liquor store in the United States. Then he switched on the television, because television was a useful, almost meaningless background to his thinking. That was another thing that he liked so much about the United States of America. Nobody thought very much... He took his drink back to his chair, and used the remote control button to switch from a news programme to a quiz programme, to a chat show, to an old movie. All were too stimulating for the kind of thought he was about to indulge: thought about his past and the dangerous, dreadful, fascinating people he had known, and how to convert them into the kind of money he would get from an American paperback publisher. He pushed another button, and was rewarded at once by a roaring sound. He was, it appeared, in Detroit, and was about to watch a motor race.

Yelling above the appalling noise of Formula One racing engines revving up, a commentator was telling anybody who could hear that this was a crucial stage in the world championship, and that a man called Sandy Keith, a red-haired Britisher who crowded his luck more than any sane person would ever do, seemed about to become world champion.

Jason Bird looked at the television set, appalled. Sandy Keith was the worst news that he could possibly hope for, worse even than Lumumba University, because Sandy Keith was where all his troubles had begun. Sandy Keith hadn't known him at the time, of course – in fact he didn't really know him even now – but nonetheless Sandy Keith was responsible for every wretched moment in Jason Bird's life until that very day, and for an awful lot of people at Lumumba University, too.

Jason Bird found himself thinking of the class of '81. There had been a good bunch of students, that year, at Lumumba University. They had been a weird bunch too, but then Lumumba was a weird university. There weren't all that many institutes of learning outside Moscow whose specialities were murder, arson, misinformation, subversion of established governments, and things of that sort. Lumumba could give you a graduate course in all of them, and if you were good, a post-graduate course to follow. Lumumba U could teach you almost everything there was about murder, assassination, the vilification of decent human beings, the destruction of a house, a street, even a city. Rare,

3

fatal, and appalling were the skills you learned at Lumumba.

Its graduates were for the most part from what is called the Third World, but now and again a space was found for prominent people from the East or even the West. In the year of '81, as Jason Bird remembered, there had been a South American, and a Chinese – that was normal – but there had also been a girl who was almost certainly Austrian or German, a man he could have sworn was Australian, and others too, who belonged to the world of shadows so dark that nobody was quite sure who they were, not even Jason Bird.

What they were taught of course was killing: the gun, the knife, their hands if necessary, a brick, a broken bottle, anything at all that was within range and would serve its purpose. They were wellnigh perfect students, as eager as they were dedicated, and the K.G.B. were very pleased, delighted even – until the incident of the man they called Sanchez. Despite himself, and hating himself too because there was no money in it, Jason Bird began to remember Sandy Keith and that damned elephant, and once he did that it was impossible not to remember Joe Cave...

You could say it all began on the day that Sir Roderick Finlay took his nephew Sandy Keith out to lunch.

Alexander Keith, who nobody, not even his mother, had ever called anything but Sandy, was a mild young man despite his red hair, but he was also potentially the greatest racing driver around. In his own mind he had long since decided that only death would ever prevent him from becoming world champion.

On the day that his uncle decided to feed him, he should in fact have been lunching in Belgium, but an accident had resulted in broken bones which had still not perfectly healed, so he found himself restless and in London, instead of at Zandvoort and behind the wheel of a racing car.

Sir Roderick spread his napkin over his lap, looked

4

with distaste at the menu – the prices quoted in this particular restaurant always appalled him – then turned to his guest.

'I trust you're keeping fit?' he said.

'You know perfectly well I'm not', said Sandy Keith, and glowered.

Mildness had its limits after all, and Sandy Keith felt entitled to glower. That last crash has resulted not only in two broken ribs but a broken collar bone also, and it hadn't even been his fault – he was far too good a driver for that. Yet even so the bones still ached on dull, wet days. And even though it is July, it's dull and wet today, he thought.

'You know perfectly well I'm not fit', he said. 'Not after that last shunt.'

Sir Roderick gestured dismissively. 'That was two weeks ago', he said. 'You young men heal quickly. I know I always did.'

Sandy Keith sighed, and took a sip of wine. It was difficult, it was downright impossible, to persuade Sir Roderick to accept what he didn't want to accept. And perhaps that was just as well for him. Sir Roderick was the head of a very special section of British Intelligence, a section whose concerns were danger and death, and now and again he had need of a driver, and now and again that driver was his nephew. 'I'm well enough, I suppose', said Keith, then added warily, 'but I wouldn't call myself fit, exactly.'

'You're fine', Sir Roderick said. 'Couple of fractured ribs – broken collar bone – happens every day on the hunting field.'

How the hell did he get hold of my medical report? Keith wondered. He sipped his claret.

'And just what is it you want me to do?' he asked.

'I want you to serve your country', Sir Roderick said.

He spoke the words simply, as he would say 'It's a cold, wet day' but he meant every word.

'There's a race at Zandvoort very soon', said Keith.

'You just told me you're not fit', said Sir Roderick, then added illogically, 'and anyway – Zandvoort isn't for another couple of weeks, and it's next week you'll be serving your country.'

Keith wished for the hundredth time that a man might be given the right to pick and choose his relatives at birth. 'Someone's going to die I suppose', he said.

'Of course', Sir Roderick said, and ticked the names off on his fingers. 'Sanchez, Boldini, Costas, da Silva, Ben Bakr. And – oh yes – Ovchenko.'

'For God's sake', said Keith. 'I never said I'd take part in a massacre.'

Sir Roderick glanced around the restaurant. 'This restaurant is secure', he said. 'That is why I invited you here – despite the extortionate prices it charges. All the same, there's no need to shout.'

'Sorry, uncle', said Keith. 'But I mean – you say you want me to help you knock off all those fellers –'

'You're quite wrong', said Sir Roderick. 'All I want you to do is drive to the place of execution – and then away from it after it happens.'

'All the same', said Keith, 'four or five fellers.'

'Six', said Sir Roderick. 'But you're still wrong. They're aliases. They're all the same man.'

Keith relaxed.

'Who'll do the rough work?' he asked. 'Joe Cave?'

Keith's uncle sliced into his tournedos. 'Joe will be present of course', he said. 'But the actual execution will be carried out by the K.G.B.'

And that was all that Sir Roderick was prepared to tell him. It was all he needed to know, it seemed, until it was time to liaise with Joe Cave.

Joe Cave was a craftsman whose craft was killing, and he was a master of it: a tall, lean man with sleek, dark hair and the most expressionless eyes that Keith had ever seen. No matter what he was doing Cave's eyes, grey as northern seas, would tell nothing. Nothing at all. He was a strong, fit man, even by Keith's standards, and Keith valued his fitness as he valued his flawless reflexes, his muscular co-ordination. Fitness was a part of what would make Keith world

6

champion, but for Joe Cave it was the difference between life and death.

They met in Keith's house in Sussex, four hundred thousand pounds' worth of converted millhouse, a paddock full of horses. Soon, Cave thought, Keith would make so much money he'd have to live in tax exile, and then where would Sir Roderick find a driver even as half as good as Sandy?

Keith greeted him rather crustily, he thought, but even so, Cave was glad to see him. The Filipino couple who looked after Keith prepared marvellous meals, and the place was quiet – you could sleep all day if you wanted to – and between jobs Joe Cave slept whenever he could. When a job was on there were times when it seemed he might never sleep again – or else never wake. And then there was Keith's sauna – Cave adored Keith's sauna. He could sleep there indefinitely if he got the chance – and if he were awake and talking he knew he would be totally secure. He'd been over it himself, every inch.

They went there that afternoon, and at once Cave turned up the heat, stretched out on the high bench. Cautiously, Keith sat on the lowest.

'Nice to be working together again', said Cave.

Keith grunted: already he felt more liquid than solid.

'We're going to Spain', said Cave. 'Up in the north – San Sebastian. Should be nice this time of year.'

'It'll probably be raining', said Keith.

'Nonsense', said Cave. 'Sunshine and señoritas, roses and wine. You'll love it there.'

'Why do you need a driver?' Keith asked. 'You can fly to Spain these days – or hadn't you heard?'

'Certainly I can fly', said Cave. 'But there's a chance San Sebastian airport will be watched.'

'Especially for you?'

'For blokes like me', said Cave. 'No, old son. We fly to Bordeaux instead – pick up a car –'

'What sort of a car?'

'Nothing flashy. Couple of lads on holiday, you and me. We don't want to be conspicuous. Then across the Pyrenees and away we go.'

'To find this Sanchez?'

'Alias Boldini, alias Costas, alias da Silva, alias Ben Bakr, alias Ovchenko.'

'That's a lot of names', said Keith.

'He's done a lot of things', said Cave.

'Such as?'

'Assassination, political kidnapping, urban terrorism, bank robbery, murder, bombing.'

'He doesn't sound very nice', said Keith.

'He's not', said Cave. 'He's nasty... We think he's an Argentinian, but we're not sure. We're almost sure he's South American. But he can pass as a Greek – or an Arab – or a Russian.'

'Versatile sort of a chap', said Keith.

'You'd better believe it', said Cave. 'Educated in Paris... Spoiled brat. Rich man's son playing at being a student. But he's dead keen on Communism. They took him off to Moscow – sent him to Lumumba University.'

'What happens there?' Keith asked.

'Crash course for Reds in emergent nations', said Cave. 'How to overthrow non-Communist governments in twelve easy lessons. Then off to the K.G.B. Headquarters in Dzerzhinski Street to see if he was any good at killing people.'

'I gather he is?'

'He's superb', said Cave. 'Best pupil Kalkov ever had.'

'Kalkov?'

'Pavel Ivanovich Kalkov, K.G.B. Colonel. Their top killer. He taught Sanchez personally. After that Sanchez was sent to the guerrilla school in the Lebanon for the post-graduate course there.'

He leaned back, sweat cascading from his body.

'He must be about the most efficient killer the Ivans ever produced', he said. 'And God knows he's done

enough jobs for them. Thirty-seven that we know of –
maybe half as many again that we don't.'

'If he's so ruddy marvellous', said Keith, 'why does
Uncle Roderick say the K.G.B. will kill him?'

'Because that's what your uncle's decided should
happen', said Cave.

'But why should they kill him? – I mean if he's their
star pupil –'

Cave said, 'The most likely reason will be that they
can't trust him any more. Upset his pals no end, that
will.'

'What pals?'

'The P.L.O. – the Cubans – some blokes in the
Congo, Red guerrillas in Italy, a lot of blokes in Libya.
It will upset all the bad lads when they hear the Ivans
have knocked off Sanchez.'

'But why are *we* going there anyway?' Keith asked.
'The way you tell it he could be as good as you.'

'He could be better', said Cave. In anywhere else but
a sauna Keith would have shivered.

'I wish to God I'd turned the job down', he said.

'We're very grumpy today', said Cave. 'What happened to my smiling little champion?'

'I drive for Charlie Morton these days', said Keith.
'He's the one who designed the car. He's the one I
belong to, really. I like Charlie Morton.'

'Why shouldn't you?' said Cave.

'I'm going to have to tell him a lie', said Keith. 'He
expects me to be ready for Zandvoort tomorrow. Now
that won't be possible.'

'So tell him a lie', said Cave.

'I'm going to have to', Keith said again. 'But you're
going to have to come along and help me tell it.'

He'd never felt more angry towards Joe Cave, but to
attack him would be a form of suicide, and anyway Joe
had become as insulated as a man can be from
compassion and regret. He couldn't function otherwise.

'What kind of a car will I be driving?' he asked.

There was no answer. Joe Cave was asleep.

Chapter 2

CHARLIE MORTON gave his party in Chelsea
because that was where he lived and also because that
was where he liked to give parties. Like all Charlie
Morton's parties, it was a good one, because there was
enough champagne and more than enough pretty girls.
Joe Cave felt happy as soon as he walked into the
room, but Sandy Keith did not. He was about to make
excuses, even tell lies, and he did not like doing that to
Charlie Morton, who was just inside the door of the
drawing room with his wife by his side, and the butler
with an enormous tray of glasses of champagne
immediately behind him. As soon as one entered one
got an enormous smile from Charlie, a kiss from his
wife, and a glass of champagne. No wonder his parties
were successful.

Not that there were any kisses for Cave, nor should
there have been, he thought. After all it was the first
time that he had met Mrs Morton, and even so, she had
taken one look at him and realised, like the good wife
she was, that he brought no advantages to her
husband. But he did get a glass of champagne.

Cave wandered around the party and marvelled at
the number of people he knew, almost as if it were a

10

party to which all the invitations had been sent out by gossip columnists. And that of course was because of the racing drivers. They were there in large quantities, and their very presence had brought out the crowd of beautiful, silken groupies who always follow racing drivers. Not that Cave was complaining. He looked around him, and sipped champagne, and admired the pretty women, and all the time kept an eye on Sandy Keith. Sandy Keith had an eye for only one pretty woman. She wasn't really pretty, at that, Cave thought. She was beautiful: a blonde, as tall as Keith, elegant, smiling, sophisticated.

Unfortunately she herself had eyes only for one man, and it was not Sandy. It was her husband, Pierre Jannot. Pierre Jannot was a racing driver too, and one who was not nearly as successful as Sandy Keith. He had nevertheless managed to win the love of Trudi, a beautiful, vulnerable blonde, and Cave guessed that Sandy would have given anything in the world, literally anything, except his racing skills, to have her.

Cave looked away to another bird, a shy, worried little bird standing in a corner, all by herself. Charlie Morton's daughter. She had a hungry, anxious look, that would if it were not satisfied soon develop into one of screaming need. Joe Cave had no doubt at all that when he looked at Jane Morton he was looking at an addict, but it was none of his business, and Sir Roderick Finlay would be furious if he made it his business. He turned away to eavesdrop on her father.

'I've seen the doctor's report', Charlie Morton was saying. 'You're not all that ill, and you need the practice. You should be going to Zandvoort as soon as possible.'

Charlie Morton was small and plump and smiling, and usually he looked like Mr Pickwick's younger brother. But he was now talking about motor racing, and all he looked was good and mad.

'I *will* be there as soon as possible', said Keith. 'I promise you Charlie. It's just that I have a little personal business to attend to.'

11

'You can't tell me what it is?' Charlie Morton asked.

'As I said', said Keith, 'it's personal. But it'll only take a day or two. I promise you I'll be ready in time for Zandvoort, and provided another loony doesn't bump into me, I promise you I'll win.'

'You'd better', Charlie Morton said, then added: 'I'm disappointed in you, Sandy. I never thought that you would behave to me like this.'

On her way out, Elsie Morton didn't kiss Sandy Keith once. She didn't even notice that Joe Cave was leaving.

As they waited for a taxi, Keith said, 'I really like Charlie Morton.'

Joe Cave said, 'I can understand that.'

'Can you?' Sandy Keith said. 'Then why do you and Uncle Roderick insist that I keep letting him down?'

They flew to Bordeaux, two happy holiday-makers without a care in the world, provided that at the airport a car would be waiting for them, and indeed a car was waiting in the car park, a Ford Escort with a left-hand drive, just as Sir Roderick had predicted. And yet Joe Cave wasn't happy and said so. Sandy Keith couldn't understand it. A girl was standing by the car: a tall brunette who leaned against the near door as composed and beautiful as a pedigree cat.

'You're getting awfully choosy these days', said Keith.

'My gun's in my suitcase', said Cave.

'Gun? What do you need a gun for? She's on our side.'

'Is she?' said Cave. 'The one we're supposed to collect the car from is called Bernard. Now I ask you. Does she look like a Bernard?'

'What do we do?' Keith asked.

'We need wheels', said Cave. 'So we talk to her.'

Keith started forward, but Cave's hand reached out, pulled him back.

'No', he said. 'Me first. You wait till I signal. Run if you have to.'

12

'I don't think so. My ribs hurt when I run', said Keith.

Cave grinned.

'Thanks', he said. 'But run anyway.'

He picked up his suitcase and walked, taking his time, towards the girl, who continued to lean against the car, her right hand thrust into the pocket of her driving coat. When he was just short of an arm's length from her she called out to him: 'Don't come any closer. We haven't been introduced.' Her voice was low pitched and gentle to the ear, but she meant precisely what she said.

'I expected to meet a man called Bernard', said Cave. 'I have a message for him.'

'I'll take it', said the woman.

'*You?*'

'I'm Bernadette.' Her English was almost without accent but it was not, Cave was sure, her first language.

He shrugged. There was no Bernadette in his script but he needed the car. 'When the market closed Old Oak Preferred stood at forty-two pence', he said. 'We advise against buying until they're down to thirty-five.'

The girl nodded, then said carefully: 'I was told thirty-seven would be a good price, but I don't think I'll bother. The Stock Market bores me.'

She moved away from the car, but Cave stood still.

'What's wrong?' she said. 'I know I got it right.'

'If you'd just take your hand from your pocket', said Cave.

She laughed: a very pleasant noise.

'Sorry', she said, and suddenly both her hands were visible. Cave waved to Sandy Keith, who came over at a trot. The girl smiled at him. But at her height her eyes looked straight into his.

'This is Bernadette', said Cave.

'How do you do, Bernadette?' said Keith.

'How do you do, Mr Keith?' said Bernadette.

Cave said at once, 'You've got the name wrong.'

13

'Have I?' she said. 'He looks so like the famous Mr Keith. I'm sorry you're not the one I thought... Who are you please?'

'He's Alec', said Cave, 'and I'm Joe. And what we want to know is – what happened to Bernard?'

'He had an accident', the girl said.

'A shooting accident?'

'He broke his ankle. He was very sorry.'

'Why'd he get you to drive the car here?' Joe asked.

'Because I *can* drive it. You think this is an easy car to drive?' She smiled at Keith. 'It is a pity you aren't Sandy Keith', she said. 'This one really is not easy to drive.'

She tried to move away, but Cave stood in her path.

'How do you get back?' he asked.

'I'll hire a car', she said. 'Something easy.' Then she smiled at him. 'Gentlemen.'

The two men watched her go, and Cave let out his breath in a sigh.

'I don't like it', he said.

'I do', said Keith, and kept on watching as Cave took out car keys, opened up the car and inspected it; engine and body work, then underneath. There was nothing: or at least there was nothing he'd been trained to find. And all the time he worked, Sandy Keith watched the brunette called Bernadette walk away, and Joe Cave didn't blame him. Trudi Jannot might be the love of Sandy's life, he thought, but she was not only unattainable, she was in London, and this girl was no more than a hundred yards away.

At last he said: 'Ready when you are.'

Keith got behind the wheel and switched on the ignition, then his hands suddenly clenched as he felt the engine's response. 'What on earth have they done to this car?' he said.

'Just about everything', Cave commented and stowed their suitcases on the back seat, opened his, and took from it a neat wooden box. In it were a Smith and Wesson 357 magnum and a handful of rounds. Cave loaded the gun and slipped it into his pocket,

14

then returned the box to his case.

'Happy holiday', he said.

Sandy Keith backed out the car and took the road to Bordeaux.

Bernadette was right: it wasn't an easy car. It was magnificent: a clone from the works' Ford Escorts which had dominated so many rallies in his early days. It could claw round corners and accelerate with all the grace of a charging rhino – but with all the power too.

'She brought you a good 'un', he said.

'She was supposed to be a he', said Cave.

They reached Bordeaux.

Bordeaux is a spacious and elegant city, and Joe Cave and Sandy Keith took their time looking at it: the medieval cathedral, the university, the Bourse and the quais that thrust deep into the centre of the town, bearing the names of wines that are among the glories of France: Margaux, Lafite, Montrose, and Pape Clément... The two men gawped as tourists should, and Joe Cave worried about the girl who'd met them, worried too about whether they were being followed. With Bordeaux's traffic seething about them it was impossible to tell, but he didn't feel good. When they left the town and reached the motorway he still didn't feel good. It was all very well for Sandy Keith. Sandy Keith had a fascinating new car to drive and a pretty girl had told him Sandy Keith was famous: but there shouldn't have been a girl... And yet she'd known the password, known it perfectly: and the car hadn't blown up: worked a treat in fact... Yet maybe he should have abandoned the job. Walked right past her: taken his little racing driver back to Sussex and a sauna... And what would Sir Roderick have said about that? This, Cave's chief had made clear, was probably the only chance they'd ever get at Sanchez, with or without K.G.B. involvement, and Sanchez had to die.

15

Jason Bird stared at the television set. They were showing a recording of the Japanese Grand Prix, Sandy Keith's car threading its way through the opposition, like a shuttle on a loom. But even so, the only car he could see was in his mind's eye: a Ford Escort on its way from Bordeaux to Spain, carrying a hard man on his way to a kill. This was the beginning of the bad times for Jason Bird, and even worse times for Sandy Keith and Joe Cave. The elephant would have its work cut out, all right.

The Escort roared on down the autoroute, the only car that could live with it a BMW whose driver was not long for this world, thought Cave; not unless he changed his style of driving. He became aware of the speed they were doing.

'Slow down', he said. 'This isn't Le Mans.'

'There's nothing here to touch us', said Keith.

'Slow down.'

Keith sighed and moved into the slow lane, the BMW flashed by in triumph, and a Merc and a Peugeot, an ageing Facel-Vega and a couple of leather clad blokes on motor bikes with pillion passengers. 'I hate being passed', said Keith.

They drove sedately down the autoroute, crossed the River Adour, then on to Navarre, and left it before Biarritz. Joe Cave had his own instructions on how to go to Spain... The road they took after the autoroute was a problem for anyone but a very good driver. It twisted, snaked, chicaned, widened and narrowed, its surface uneven, every straight stretch a trap for the unwary because of the corkscrew bend that inevitably followed... But Sandy Keith was a superb driver and welcomed the road as a grand master might welcome a new problem at chess.

The motorbike riders with the pillion passengers welcomed it too. Keith saw them first, in his rear view mirror, and recognised them at once. They were the ones who had annoyed him by passing him on the autoroute.

'We've got company', he said to Cave.

Cave looked behind him and swore.

'Remember them?' Keith asked.

'Yes', said Cave. 'They've passed us once before.'

'Why would they do that?'

'To make us feel secure. Then all they had to do was wait for us on the exit road.'

'They must know where we're going', said Keith.

'Looks that way', said Cave. 'You'd better lose them, old son.' Then he added unfairly: 'You and your blasted brunette.'

Keith's left hand quitted the wheel briefly, felt inside his shirt for the little silver elephant on its silver chain, rubbed it as his father had once done when he piloted a Spitfire, then did his best to lose the motorbikes. It was a remarkable best, but whoever had set up the trap had chosen both men and machines well. Even with two men up, the bikes were faster than the car, and just as roadworthy.

The only advantage Keith had was the road's twisting, slithering turns. On the straight the bikes moved up on him, but on the turns he stole back distance, banging the car into the bends at speeds that made Cave close his eyes and wish he'd become a solicitor after all, as his mother had always wanted...

But even with the risks Keith took, the motorbikes gained. Their riders had chosen the killing ground well. The countryside the road traversed was deserted: not a farmhouse, not a cottage in sight; only scrubland and sheep and goats, corn restlessly rustling, the inevitable vines...

Keith came into a long straight stretch and groaned. The car was doing its best, but that was the point. It *was* its best and the bikes were gaining. In the mirror he watched them grow, one on each side of the road, precisely apart. Each passenger now held a short, stubby gun, resting on the driver in front of him.

'For what we are about to receive', said Keith.

A blast of fire raked the road, a ricochet spanged off the rear bumper and Keith leapt into the next bend

17

like a salmon leaping back into the stream, the bullets scything into the vines as he swerved. Into a turn. Right hand down. Brake. Left hand down. Into second. Foot ready to hit the accelerator – and only a short straight stretch ahead of them. That was the good news. The bad news was that somebody had abandoned an ancient tractor broadside on across the road.

Cave flicked a glance behind him at the black clad figures – black leather overalls, black helmets, tinted glass, sinister as the wicked knights of medieval tournaments. They came on confidently now, their passengers holding their fire for the kill... Cave yelled instructions at Keith, who nodded and kept on going.

When he reached the tractor he swerved round it into a vineyard, and the left hand motorbike wriggled around the tractor's other side to cut him off. The right hand motorbike followed him, then, as Keith regained the road, he braked the car.

It was so totally the wrong thing to do that the bike behind him swerved, and was broadside on: the passenger unable to bring his machine pistol to bear. The bike in front braked too, and as it did so, Joe Cave leapt from the car, grasped the magnum two handed and shot first the passenger, then the driver.

As he did so, Keith slammed the gears into reverse and put his foot down hard, hit the bike before it could come out of its swerve: its passenger's last act a blast of fire into the sky, like a volley fired over his own grave. Keith stopped the car, then eased it forward, switched off the engine. He was trembling so violently it took him three tries to do it.

Joe Cave came towards him, still holding the magnum, and walked on past the car, looked down at the bike, then knelt beside the driver and his passenger. Not looking round, Keith called out to him.

'Are they –? Are they –?'

'You got them both', said Cave. 'Nice going.'

Sandy Keith was sick.

They found a culvert not far away, just big enough to contain four dead men and two bikes. Unless it rained.

Sandy Keith tried hard not to imagine what it would be like if it rained. But Joe Cave was happy now to the point of cautious optimism.

'So long as they're not found we're in with a chance', he said. 'Whoever's in control will think they're still after us... Or the car.'

'I don't follow', said Keith.

'I don't believe whoever is after us knew what we looked like. It was the car they were after. Until your girlfriend turned up and knew who you were. Now they'll all know. We'll have to get rid of the car.'

'But I like the car', said Keith.

'Who wouldn't?' said Cave. 'All the same I think it's earned a rest.'

They drove by highways and byways back to Biarritz, found a garage where Cave produced money and was welcome at once, and swapped the Escort for a Peugeot 304. While Keith kept watch, Cave took a shallow metal box from his suitcase and pressed it, lidside up, to the bottom of the Peugeot. Its magnetised lid clung on, and Cave got back into the car, guided Keith to a village on the Spanish border and to a little hotel where food and wine were good and the armagnac superb. Keith found he needed it.

'We go to Spain tomorrow?' he asked. Cave nodded. 'To kill Sanchez?'

'More or less.'

Sandy Keith didn't bother trying to figure out the ramifications of that one. He ordered another round of armagnac instead.

'I can't understand what a bloke like that would be doing here anyway', he said. 'Surely he belongs in South America or the Middle East – or maybe Africa.' He looked around the restaurant that was full of solid bourgeois French eating solid bourgeois meals.

'He's been to all these places and created all kinds of hell', said Cave. 'Now he's going to do it here.'

'Here?'

'Here is the Basque country', Joe Cave said. 'This is the French side – and just now it's quiet. But tomorrow we go in among the Spanish Basques, and they're not quiet at all.'

'They want a separate state', said Keith.

'They do indeed', Cave said. 'There's a group called E.T.A. wants it so badly they blow up admirals and generals every chance they get. They blew one geezer's car up onto the roof of a three-storey building.'

'But what's that got to do with Sanchez?' said Keith. 'They're not Communists.'

'They're urban guerrillas making war on established authority. So they take help wherever they can get it.'

'But why should Sanchez help them?'

'Two reasons', Cave said. 'First because he's told to. The Ivans always enjoy a bit of unrest in a capitalist state – and they wouldn't mind E.T.A. owing them a favour.'

'And the other reason?'

'Sanchez enjoys it', said Cave. 'It's the biggest turn on he can get.'

And you don't? Keith wondered. But he kept the question to himself...

He awoke next morning, vaguely hungover, to the sound of men's feet on gravel, and a steady, rhythmic clunking sound. He went to the window and looked out. Two young men were playing pelota against the wall of the village church. The basketwork gloves used instead of bats were like an extension of their hands and they played fiercely, intensely, intent on winning. They would make formidable opponents in peace or war, thought Keith, and went down to breakfast. Joe Cave poured coffee.

'How do we get to him?' asked Keith.

'He's a Red', said Cave. 'They don't come much Redder. But he likes the rich full life. Good food. Good wine. Bad girls.'

'And you know one of the bad girls, I suppose?' said Keith.

'No I don't', said Cave, '– but I phoned your uncle

20

last night. He knows one.'

Her name was Amparo, and she sang in a club in one of the maze of streets behind San Sebastian's seafront. And Sanchez was mad about her, but she, Cave said, had spurned his advances, not so much because of virtue, but because Sir Roderick was paying her to do so. It was a very expensive operation, Sir Roderick had said...

Sandy Keith discovered that he liked San Sebastian: he liked the drive through the mountains to get to it, no matter how demure the drive had been; he liked the solid rampart of hotels looking out on the Bay of Biscay, the long, roller-coasting waves that for once held back their strength and slapped at bathers gently, almost playfully. He liked the huge, elegant room that Joe Cave had booked in a huge, elegant hotel. He liked the cafés and the bars and the casino. San Sebastian was a place where you could enjoy youself. It was also a place where a man was about to die.

Chapter 3

THE CLUB was for the most part a disco, where the drinks were expensive but drinkable, the lighting psychedelic but not mind-blowing: but now and again, when the dancer needed a rest, between rounds as it were, they brought on a singer and guitarist. Amparo was the singer.

She was by any standards a gorgeous girl, thought Keith, and yet she was almost *too* gorgeous: the hair almost too red, the dark eyes too flashing, the figure too ripe. Mind you, thought Keith fair-mindedly, that depended on how you liked girls' figures – but no matter how big you liked them, for Amparo a diet was only a matter of ounces away. Put her alongside Trudi Jannot, he thought, and Amparo would be altogether too much.

But she could sing, or rather Keith assumed she could. The songs she sang were flamenco, the folk music of Andalusia, and to Keith quite meaningless – but it seemed the other customers enjoyed them. It seemed that Joe Cave enjoyed them too, if the rapture of his applause was anything to go by – and then at the end of her last song Amparo bowed to the audience and blew a kiss to Joe Cave – and as Cave scribbled a note

22

and handed it to the waiter, Sandy Keith realised that
Sanchez had moved one step nearer to death, as Cave
ordered champagne and waited for Amparo to join him.

Keith looked away towards the bar. There was a
brunette there and she was smiling at him, raising her
glass in a toast.

'Bernadette at the bar', said Keith. Cave's glance
flicked towards her, then away, and the brunette
began blowing kisses.

'What on earth are we going to do?' said Keith.

'Soldier on', said Cave. 'What else can we do?' Then
he rose to welcome Amparo.

Close to, she was even more opulent than when seen
from a distance, but her smile still dazzled, her eyes
still flashed, and she extended her hand to be kissed by
Keith with a gesture so regal that he found himself
bowing as he took it.

'Is e-very nice to meet you', she said and yawned,
and added: 'Excuse me please. But is always the same
when I work. I become e-sleepy.' Then she turned to
Joe Cave and switched to Spanish. Keith, whose
Spanish was limited to 'gracias' and 'adios', spent his
time pouring champagne and drinking as much of it as
Amparo and Cave could spare. It wasn't a lot...

Then the house lights went down, the psychedelic
lights took over, and the music began once more. A
squat, muscular man came over to Amparo and said
something curt and abrupt in machine-gun Spanish.
Amparo yawned once more and left reluctantly, and
Keith grabbed what was left of the champagne.

'You shouldn't take too much of that', said Cave.
'You're driving.'

'You didn't leave too much', said Keith. 'What's
happening?'

'It's like I told you', said Cave. 'Sanchez wants her –
but she doesn't want him – or she didn't till tonight. So
Sanchez has taken steps to see that people like you and
me keep our distance.'

'The muscular gentleman who came up and was
rude to her?' said Keith.

'He's one of the club's bouncers', said Cave. 'Sanchez pays him to keep away the boyfriends.'

'A very puritanical attitude.'

'It has its compensations', said Cave. 'He gives her the occasional diamond. He's giving her one tonight as a matter of fact. Up at her place – outside town.'

'So Amparo's finally giving in?' said Keith.

'He thinks she is', said Cave. He looked round the club. 'Your girlfriend's gone', he said. Keith looked. There were lots of brunettes, but no Bernadette. 'Time we were off, too', said Cave.

Time to fetch the car, that was parked in the square by the club. They had almost reached the Peugeot when a car horn sounded, blasting the night air in warning. But Joe Cave was already swerving round, moving into a fighter's crouch, facing the club's bouncer, and another one who could have been his twin. The bouncer spoke in Spanish to Cave, and as he did so his mate jumped at him. Cave swayed away from the roundhouse swing the other man aimed at him, and his right hand shot out, right forearm rigid, as his spear strike aimed just below the rib cage. The other man seemed to collapse standing up. There was no other way of putting it, thought Keith. He stayed vertical, but there was no force left in him, almost no life.

Then the bouncer moved in, as fast as his friend, and he too threw a fist, a professional boxer's blow that Cave couldn't quite duck, a bolo punch that hit the muscle on Cave's shoulder hard enough to numb. Cave gasped aloud, and the bouncer moved in closer, aiming for Cave's face. Cave swerved away and swung his right hand, using the hard edge this time as though it were an axe blade, smashing into the bouncer's arm. The bouncer yelled, and then the yell died, chopped off by that axe blade hand as it swung again, smashed into the side of the bouncer's neck. He crashed against his friend, together the two men fell.

Perhaps ten seconds had elapsed since the car horn had sounded, thought Keith, and here I am still

24

wondering what to do. 'Why don't they like us?' he said.

'It's like I told you', said Cave. 'We drank champagne with Amparo. It seems the price of that is a hiding.'

'Well you certainly gave them one', said Keith.

Cave got into the car.

Amparo's place had been chosen carefully for the task that Cave – and the K.G.B. – had to perform. It was at the top of a quiet street, and there was an olive grove fifty yards from the house and a lay-by beside the olive grove. There was also a very bright porch light and a garden that was either flower beds or raked gravel: no cover at all.

Keith ran the car into the lay-by and switched off, and Cave slipped on a pair of gloves, then disappeared under the car to reappear with the box with the magnetised lid. From it he produced the three parts of what Keith guessed was an automatic rifle, and snapped them together.

'The AK 47 assault rifle', Cave said. 'The guerrilla's best friend. The Kalashnikov.'

'So that's where the K.G.B. comes in', said Keith.

'That's where', said Cave, and vanished into the olive grove.

They had less than an hour to wait. A big Seat drove up to the house, and the driver and another man, both obviously bodyguards, got out: a slim, dark young man followed them, a dapper, elegant man who smiled as he left the car. He was still smiling as Cave shot him, firing on single rounds, head and heart. The bodyguards grabbed their guns and spun round firing, and Cave shot them too – Keith saw it all – then stepped out of the olive grove, laid the Kalashnikov on the ground and ran back to the car. They were away before the first neighbour's light was switched on.

'I would have thought Sanchez would have had better bodyguards than that', said Keith.

Cave pulled off his gloves. 'He used to', he said, 'but I killed two of them. As a matter of fact so did you.'

Sandy Keith made his own way back to London – Joe Cave it seemed had one more job to do – and went to see his uncle in his office. Very elegant, Sir Roderick Finlay's office. A classic Persian carpet, an Irish Sheraton sofa-table which he used as a desk, a William IV carver chair at the desk, a little Degas of a dancer tying her shoe, and an old Georgian decanter full of single malt at his elbow. For as long as Sandy Keith could remember, where his uncle was, there had been a decanter of single malt. Sir Roderick pushed it towards Keith but Sandy Keith shook his head. 'No thanks.'

'Not sulking, I trust?' Sir Roderick said.

'I might be', said Keith. 'I saw the three of them die. Those bullets were appalling.'

'Lead body with a copper shield', said Sir Roderick.

'They made holes the size of teacups', said Keith.

'That's the hollow nose', said Sir Roderick. 'It squashes on contact to a thing like a mushroom and just keeps on going.'

'Did Joe have to use that kind of bullet?' Keith asked.

'It's what Sanchez and his pals always used', said Roderick. 'As a matter of fact it's what the Russians are using in Afghanistan.'

'Oh', said Keith. 'I see. – All the same, I don't understand how you hope to blame the K.G.B. just because Joe used a Kalashnikov.'

'It's got prints on it', Sir Roderick said. 'Colonel Kalkov's prints.'

'But why would he kill his own best pupil?'

'For the only reason he ever does anything', said Sir Roderick. 'Because the K.G.B. told him to do it.' He sighed. 'You wouldn't believe how much it cost just to find out where the Kalashnikov was, never mind get my hands on it.'

'I hope it's worth it', said Keith.

'Of course it's worth it.' Sir Roderick was testy as he often was about money.

'Will the Spanish police know they're Kalkov's prints?'

26

'They will by now', said Sir Roderick. 'I sent them a complete set – off the record of course... By now E.T.A. will know', he added, 'and soon the P.L.O. and the Red Brigade and the Libyans and all the urban guerrillas will know that too – that the K.G.B. murdered their particular hero.'

'Won't they want to know why?'

'Of course they will', said Sir Roderick, 'and there isn't a reason, as you and I know perfectly well – and that will worry them even more... Dissension in the ranks of the ungodly. Enjoy it while it lasts, Sandy boy. It doesn't happen often.'

'What about Bernadette?' said Keith. 'She got away – and she was among the ungodly.'

'What nonsense', said Sir Roderick. 'She was the one who sounded the car horn when those two thugs jumped you. She works for French Security. Ungodly indeed!'

'But didn't she tip off those motor cyclists?'

'No', Sir Roderick said, and sighed. 'The feller who supplied your car did that. The chap I sent to arrange the deal got a bit too talkative – the chap with the car put a little something in his drink, I suppose – and sold us out to Sanchez for cash. It's the thing freelancers do. Lucky I asked Bernadette to keep an eye on you.'

'You mean the man who broke his ankle?'

'It was his neck that was broken as a matter of fact', Sir Roderick said.

Sandy Keith said, 'Perhaps I will take a drink after all', and Sir Roderick poured. 'Why did you let the French in on it?' Keith asked.

'No option', Sir Roderick said. 'They had the Kalashnikov.' He sighed. 'They drove a hard bargain... Oh by the way – Bernadette wants to see you.'

'What about?'

'Don't be absurd', Sir Roderick said. 'She's over in Paris and she wants you to join her there. But you have to pay your own fare. This job's cost a fortune already.'

'There won't be any problem', said Keith. 'I shan't be able to go.'

27

'Why ever not?' Sir Roderick asked.

'I haven't got time. I'm due at Zandvoort', Sandy Keith said.

'Extraordinary', said Sir Roderick.

'What is?'

'That a nephew of mine should utter such words', said Sir Roderick and poured himself another single malt. There was no more for Sandy Keith...

Joe Cave parked his hire car and walked to the block of flats that was a long way from San Sebastian. In his briefcase was the equivalent of ten thousand pounds in Swiss francs – Amparo had been most insistent on Swiss francs – and Sir Roderick had groaned aloud. But it had been worth it, Cave thought, and went into the block, pushed an elevator button. Nice to be doing something pleasant for a change, like giving a pretty girl her hard-earned reward – and it had been hard earned considering the risks she had run. She was big, O.K., but if there was a good thing why shouldn't there be lots of it? And he admired the way she looked sleepy when she was working... Joe Cave wondered if she was fond of saunas.

The Sanchez killing caused instant uproar in Dzerzhinski Street, Jason Bird remembered. In the beginning there was no talk of revenge. For the K.G.B. revenge was always considered as stupid, useless, even counter-productive, reprisal for reprisal's sake. But nonetheless Sanchez should not have died, and a lot of heads rolled – metaphorically at least – because Sanchez had died. There had been more than one operative sentenced to the Gulag Archipelago too, and Jason Bird could still remember his own fear, as for quite a while he imagined himself to be on that list. But somehow he had wriggled off that particular hook, and fulfilled the rôle of denunciator rather than become a victim. He could still remember it. The checking and cross-checking, the fever of investigation, the massive authorisation of funds, the saturation of agents all over Western Europe with but one object in mind: to find out who had done it. And it didn't take all that long. Amparo in particular had been stupid. Ten thousand pounds in Swiss francs was nowhere near enough money on which to disappear. And sooner or later she had had to go back to work. And there weren't that many red-headed flamenco singers around. For a brief while she was allowed to live, but when the revenge policy changed there had been very little difficulty in killing her.

Joe Cave now, he was another matter. Killing Cave was a problem of enormous difficulty, and one at which the K.G.B.'s Wet Job specialists laboured for years. And in the end, they found that the only possible approach to Cave was Sandy Keith... But all this was for the future. Immediately after Sanchez's death, their principal concern was information: on Cave, on Keith, on Sir Roderick Finlay. The kind of information that would help to ensure that something like this would never happen again.

Cave was a problem, Sir Roderick an even bigger problem, as he rarely left the shelter of his own unit of Intelligence, and that left Sandy Keith. Keith at least was vulnerable. Once he'd gone back to England, he'd hung around briefly in London attending the same parties as Trudi Jannot, but that soon palled, and he'd gone back to his home in Sussex to superintend the activities that he'd talked about with his uncle. Activities was perhaps a rather grand word for the installation of a flag staff, but at least it was something to do, Keith thought, after he'd won at Zandvoort. The flag staff marked a point in his life, and, Keith liked to think, marked it wittily.

The flag it was to support consisted of a background of the old British racing green, and on it the silvery white portrait of an elephant. The information, when they obtained it, interested the K.G.B., just as the information that he went to the same parties as Trudi

Jannot interested them. There was a lot to be learned from both of them, the woman and the elephant.

The elephant's name was Ganesh, which is the name of the Hindu elephant god who brings good luck, and was a large scale copy of the little silver elephant on the silver chain which Keith at all times wore round his neck, just as his father had done before him.

His father, the K.G.B. knew, had been a Spitfire pilot in the Battle of Britain, and for him at least the elephant's charm had worked: he survived the war, and even got a D.F.C. and bar out of it. It seemed as if it was going to work for Keith too, after he'd won at Zandvoort, and as a result went to the top of the table in the world championships.

He didn't do quite so well though in the Brazilian Grand Prix: he broke his leg in the fifth lap. But as he wrote to Joe Cave, 'You can't win 'em all, old son. Except that I believe I ought to win 'em all.' So he was out of racing for a while, and Charlie Morton was devastated. For Charlie Morton there was no one in the world who could drive a Morton car like Sandy Keith.

But Keith healed quickly, as young, fit men usually do, and after a while was limping, and cautiously driving a Jaguar XJS, as being the only safe car he knew. There was time for parties too, but not much time for Trudi Jannot, because Pierre Jannot was now driving Morton's second car and she went with him from circuit to circuit and Sandy Keith stayed at home and moped and flew his elephant flag.

When he went off to London to see his doctor he invariably saw Charlie Morton too, because Morton was a very obsessive person about all the things he valued, and of the things he valued Sandy Keith reckoned that he, Keith, came fourth. First was either his wife or his daughter; second was either his daughter or his wife; third was the car he had designed, the Morton car; and fourth was Sandy Keith. For Morton, Keith felt an enormous respect, almost a kind of filial love, and knew very well how much Morton suffered

30

when those he loved were in trouble. Not that he
suffered too much for Sandy Keith. Soon he would be
driving again. What worried Morton was his daughter,
Jane, and Keith felt that he knew why. Jane Morton
was on drugs, and far down the road on which there is
no turning back, and both Keith and Morton knew it,
though neither ever discussed the matter.

As he became able to limp about more easily, it was
inevitable that Sandy Keith received another invitation to lunch with his uncle. It was inevitable because
his uncle liked to keep an eye on his nephew in case he
should need him for something, as he put it. What that
meant, as Keith well knew, was that he might be
obliged to drive a car for Uncle Roderick, something he
detested doing, and yet something he never managed
to avoid doing.

On the day that the invitation, which was rather
more like a summons, came, Keith received a brochure
in the post from a travel agency. Why not get away
from it all? the headline said, and went on to talk
about the joys of the Far East, of Singapore, Bangkok,
Pattaya and Hong Kong, how far away they were, and
how blissful. Sandy Keith thought of his uncle and
signed up at once.

When they met for lunch Uncle Roderick as always
provided impeccable wines and a very expensive meal,
and as always talked about the necessity of serving
one's country, then moved on to the joys of Finland as a
place to visit in the summer. Keith knew at once that
there was a driving job to be done in Finland, but this
time he was ready for Uncle Roderick.

'I'm sorry, uncle', he said, 'but I'm afraid I shan't be
able to manage it. I've already signed up to go to Hong
Kong.'

Uncle Roderick was displeased and said so at great
length, but for once Sandy Keith managed to be firm,
and held out even until the coffee and brandy. He and
his uncle parted rather less than friends, but he was
still going to the Far East.

Chapter 4

THE FAR EAST proved to be every bit as relaxing and peaceful as the brochure had said it would be. In Singapore, Malaysia, Bangkok and Pattaya, Sandy Keith swam, ate exotic food, drank exotic drinks, and from time to time even forgot about Trudi Jannot. Hong Kong was different. Hong Kong was alive with busy people, the last bastion of capitalism before mainland China, each one striving to make two Hong Kong dollars where only one had been before, and Sandy Keith was fascinated by it, but it was not a place to relax. It was in fact one of the most unrelaxing places that Sandy Keith had ever come across. It was no surprise really then, that one day when he returned to his hotel suite, he found Uncle Roderick waiting for him.

For once in his life Uncle Roderick looked furtive, even shifty, and seemed to find it difficult to begin the conversation. Things became a little easier when Keith phoned down to room service and ordered up single malt. Single malt made everything easier for Uncle Roderick.

'Just happened to be passing', Sir Roderick said, 'so I thought I'd look you up.'

Sandy Keith pondered the vast ineptitude of that staggering lie.

'Come off it, uncle', he said at last. 'You sent me here.'

'How could I possibly do that?' Sir Roderick asked.

'By sending me that brochure', said Sandy Keith, 'then threatening to pack me off to Finland. That's how you sent me here.'

Sir Roderick stopped looking shifty, and looked cunning instead.

'Be that as it may', he said, 'you're here now, and that's all that really matters.'

'No!' said Sandy Keith.

'What do you mean, "No"?'

'What ever it is you want me to do', said Sandy Keith, 'I'm not going to do it.'

'I've already told you', said Sir Roderick, 'I've just looked in for a chat. Came to ask how you were enjoying yourself.'

'Very well – until now.'

Sir Roderick ceased to look cunning and looked hurt instead. 'You can be very wounding', he said. 'All you young people can be very wounding. Just because I came to ask how you're enjoying your trip, there's no need –'

'There's every need', said Keith. 'I'm supposed to be relaxing. Getting fit for my next race.'

'Pshaw!' Sir Roderick said. 'You *are* fit. What's a broken leg at your age?'

'You said the same thing when I broke my ribs and collar bone', said Keith.

'It was just as true', said Sir Roderick. 'You look jolly fine to me, old chap.'

These mild terms of endearment were an even greater danger signal, and Keith knew it.

'I wonder', said Sir Roderick, looking shifty again, 'whether you'd thought of visiting Macao while you're here?'

Sandy Keith laid back in his chair, looked out of the window at Hong Kong harbour's incomparable view.

'I don't think there's much there for me', he said.

'Only take you an hour and a quarter by hydrofoil', his uncle said, and struggled out of the comfort of his chair to pour out a single malt.

'I don't think so', said Keith. 'It's mostly casinos, isn't it? I don't go much on gambling ... Monte Carlo bored me rigid.'

'Lots of pretty girls there', said Sir Roderick.

'Lots of pretty girls here', said his nephew.

Sir Roderick sighed. He was a patient man, not so much by nature as by necessity. As head of his particular branch of British Intelligence, patience had been a virtue he was forced to acquire. But somehow he never found it easy to be patient with his nephew, even though this time he had arrived determined to try.

The reason for this was that Sandy had escaped his clutches. Sir Roderick admitted it to himself freely. Only a few years ago the boy had been hard up and desperate with a need to drive a car – any car – that would further his single-minded ambition to be the best racing driver in the world. And his uncle had helped him. Cars whenever needed: even money – in doses as carefully measured as the single malt (Her Majesty's Secret Service was as hard up as every other service) – and in turn all the boy had been asked to do was drive a car, which he did superbly, and keep his eyes and ears open, and generally to do what he was told.

Sir Roderick felt very strongly about young people doing what they were told. He'd been young himself once: in Dunkirk, in El Alamein and Normandy, and done what he was told for the good of his country.

But Sandy didn't see it like that. The trouble was the boy had done well – too well, the way Sir Roderick saw it. Half a million in the bank, and on the way to the world motor racing championship before he'd broken his leg in the Brazilian Grand Prix, but even that accident had only served to bring him more fame, more fortune. Really it was too bad.

34

'I don't think I'll bother with Macao', said Sandy Keith.

Very carefully Sir Roderick put down his glass. Patience, he told himself. Patience and sweet reason. Remember what the doctors said about your blood pressure.

'Sandy, my boy', he said at last, 'we both know that you're playing games – now don't we?'

'I don't *want* to go to Macao', said Keith.

Still patient, still reasonable, Sir Roderick said, 'But what you want to do isn't really the point, surely?'

'Isn't it?' said Keith.

'No it damned well isn't', Sir Roderick yelled, and ruined the whole effect. But he plunged on anyway.

'You've *got* to go to Macao', he said.

'Are you going to tell me why?' Keith asked. 'I thought I was supposed to be on holiday.'

'You're going to Macao because I have a contact there and I can't send anybody else', said his uncle.

'Are you trying to tell me you've run out of agents?'

'I'm trying to tell you', said Sir Roderick, 'that my contact believes that any local agent that I send over from Hong Kong would be blown before he arrives. And he could well be right.'

'But I wouldn't be blown?' asked Keith.

'Well, of course not', Sir Roderick said. 'You're not a pro, are you?'

'Just a chap on holiday who's popped over to do a spot of gambling? Is that what you're saying?'

Sir Roderick looked furtive again. 'Well no', he said. 'Not quite that precisely.'

'Why wouldn't I be blown then?' Keith asked.

'There's a car race in Macao soon', his uncle said. 'Bit of luck, really. Absolutely the best cover we could wish for.'

Sandy Keith ran his hand across his hair. At once it turned from a mild auburn to a flaming, furious red.

'I might have known it', he said. 'If there's a way of making my life miserable, you'll find it.'

'I thought you liked car racing?' Sir Roderick said.

35

'You spend enough of your time doing it.'

'Well of course I like car racing', said Keith. 'It's what I'm *for*. One day soon I'm going to be world champion – if you'll leave me alone long enough to race.'

'But that's just the point', Sir Roderick said. 'I *want* you to race. In Macao.'

Sandy Keith stayed calm, but his hair glowed more furiously than ever.

'Uncle', he said, 'are you trying to kid me you didn't know Macao was a Formula Two race?'

'You make it sound as if it was motor-bikes', Sir Roderick said.

'It might as well be', said Keith. 'I'm a Formula One man. I have to be. Formula One's the only one that counts towards the championship.'

Sir Roderick said, 'You're terribly grand these days.'

'Grand?' Keith yelled. *'Grand?'*

'Certainly grand', said Sir Roderick. 'In Formula Two they drive the same kind of cars you do. And a lot of Formula One drivers enter. I've checked.'

'Not the ones who want to be world champion', said Keith.

Despite himself, Sir Roderick was impressed. Single-mindedness on that scale was admirable, even enviable. But all the same he couldn't give way. The boy had to go to Macao.

'You'll have to make an exception', he said.

Keith grinned. 'I can't make an exception', he said. 'I'm under contract. Didn't you know that? The only car I'm allowed to drive is the Morton – and I can't see Charlie Morton flying a car out here for a Formula Two race and even if he did – I can't see him giving me permission to drive it.'

'Ah', said Sir Roderick. 'I think I may be able to help you there.'

'Help me?... *Help me?*' This time Keith was screaming.

Sir Roderick hurried on: the boy was becoming hysterical.

36

'I've had a word with Morton', he said. 'Or rather Joe Cave has ... explained the whole thing. Morton says it's perfectly all right for you to drive in a Formula Two race.'

'He's gone off his nut', said Keith. It was the only conceivable explanation.

'Joe explained why you had to go', said Sir Roderick. 'He thought Morton quite sane, I believe.'

'Uncle', said Keith. 'Will you listen?... Will you please listen? Just once? Charlie Morton isn't interested in Red Chinese or Green Chinese or even Yellow Chinese. He's interested in cars.'

'This isn't just political', Sir Roderick said. 'This is drugs.'

'Oh', said Keith. 'I see.'

'I don't think you do', Sir Roderick said.

'Oh yes I do', Keith said. 'It's Charlie's daughter. She's on heroin, poor kid.'

'Not any more', Sir Roderick said. 'Jane Morton's dead.'

Keith looked at him. 'An overdose?'

'Infective hepatitis', Sir Roderick said. 'She was living in a squat in Hackney, and contracted the hepatitis by using a dirty needle for injecting heroin into herself. It happened six days ago. The injection was supposed to be a birthday celebration, poor soul. She was exactly nineteen on the day she died... Charlie Morton cared about her more than he ever dared to admit.'

'So that's why he says I can take part in the race?' said Keith.

'That's why.'

'I'd better do it then', said Keith, and Sir Roderick sighed his relief. Getting his nephew to agree to go to work could often be the worst part of the job.

'It's really quite simple', he said. 'Burma's still the place for raw opium. Worth about ten times as much as anything else they grow. But raw opium's bulky ... awkward stuff to carry... True, it's worth a lot, but heroin's worth a hell of a sight more. Better if you

37

could process your opium – turn it into heroin. A fraction the size and a hundred times the value.'

'They're doing that in Burma?'

'They're doing it on a ship', said Sir Roderick. 'Sort of floating laboratory or processing plant or whatever... Trouble is we don't know which ship... Still – you see the beauty of it? The heroin's being processed on its way to its delivery point. Cuts down the waiting time to a minimum. And it can make its delivery in international waters – and nobody can do a thing about it.'

'Delivery? To another ship?' asked Keith.

'In this case to a fishing boat', said Sir Roderick. 'The Burmese slip the stuff across the frontier into Thailand, then they load up the laboratory ship and it heads off into the South China Sea to meet a fishing boat from Macao.'

'That must be over a thousand miles', said Keith.

'More like two thousand', said Sir Roderick. 'But the fishermen don't mind. They live on their boats anyway – and the money is good.'

Keith said, 'I'm not trying to duck out or anything, uncle, but I honestly don't see where you fit me into this. I mean isn't this a job for the Macao police?'

'The Macao police have only one job in the summer', said Sir Roderick. 'To keep the traffic flowing on the way to the casinos... This is rather more tricky. Besides – Hong Kong's involved. There isn't a market for heroin in Macao. If there were the Red Chinese would be in there by teatime. The Reds don't like drugs... Unfortunately they can't stop them in Hong Kong any more than we can. They realise it's an impossible job – in Hong Kong. But not in Macao.'

'Technically Macao's administered by Portugal – but in fact it's part of China. Much more so than Hong Kong. The Reds let it go on as it is because it earns foreign currency and they get their share – but as I say they don't like drugs... They won't like us either – if they ever found out we knew what was going on and failed to stop it.' He sipped at his drink. 'Well, my

38

boy... That's the job. How soon can you start?'

'I'd better start now', said Keith. 'My leg's still not a hundred per cent, you know. I'll have to give it some exercise.'

'In a gym?' asked Sir Roderick.

'In a car', said Keith. 'And where would I have to go to get one? Japan?'

'We're having one air freighted', said Sir Roderick, 'from Australia. Quite a decent little bus so they tell me.'

'You take an awful lot for granted', said his nephew.

'I know what a good friend of yours Charlie Morton is', said Sir Roderick. 'I know how much he's done for you... It never occurred to me you'd be ungrateful.' His nephew winced.

Chapter 5

BEFORE 'the decent little bus' arrived Keith hired
himself a practise car. It took the best part of a day to
find it, but the walking was good for his leg and the car
itself was exactly what he needed – a vintage E-type
which seemed to be held together mostly by an act of
faith on the part of its owner... But it could still go:
even now the engine remembered what it was made for
– and the brakes sometimes worked quite well.

Keith took the fast road out of Kowloon, bypassed
the film studios and headed on for Tsuen Yan Town.
There were still too many tourist buses, too many
lorries and bikes and cars for him really to let go. He
pushed on along the coast road, past the reservoir, and
still the road was true and fast – and – at last – almost
empty. His foot went down, squeezing out the speed
and the Jaguar moved. Keith eased her up and down
the gears as he passed the farming villages, the
vegetable fields, the ponds full of ducks. Children
waved at him, a truck load of Gurkhas cheered, an
ancient farmer gave him a blessing worthy of an
archbishop, and Keith raced on, working the car,
testing it to its limits. On towards China, where the
road ran almost parallel to the Canton railway line

and a chance came to race the Canton Express. No contest... No contest at all. The old E-type was going like a racehorse fed on oats all winter on the first day of spring.

On and up towards Li Wu, and Communist China only a stroll away. It wouldn't do to upset the Red Chinese, his uncle had said, and Keith eased and slowed, and found a place to turn, and took the car up the gears as he headed back to Kowloon. He felt good: in fact he felt better than good. His leg hadn't bothered him at all. Just let him settle this business for Uncle Roderick, he thought, and he could go back to Europe and some serious racing...

It was no surprise to Keith to find that Joe Cave was waiting for him when he got back to the hotel. Sir Roderick knew as well as Keith himself that his nephew's expertise wasn't fighting; it was driving, but the fact that Joe Cave was there told Keith that there would be fighting involved in this assignment somewhere.

Typically, Cave was asleep in a deep and comfortable chair in the hotel's lounge: equally typical, he came awake as soon as Keith stood over him.

'Sandy', he said, and stood up at once. Cave had as much faith in Keith as in any man living: all the same you're better off on your feet. 'How are you, old son?'

'Fit enough to drive', said Keith. 'Are you going to help me?'

'I'm handling the P.R. end', said Cave.

Among Cave's many and varied skills, as Keith well knew, was an ability to handle P.R. – and an excellent cover it made. All the same...

'I hope Charlie Morton won't mind', said Keith.

'It was his idea', said Cave.

'You sure?'

'Ask him yourself', said Cave.

'You mean he's here?'

'He's here all right.' Cave's voice was bitter. 'That was his idea, too... I couldn't keep him away... But try telling your uncle that.'

41

'Try telling my uncle anything', said Sandy Keith.

They dined together in a Cantonese restaurant in
Hanoi Road, then walked back to their hotel. All
around them were nightclubs, and in all the nightclubs there'd be girls, but jet lag had caught up with
Joe Cave at last.

Hong Kong never slept. The streets were still
jam-packed with people, the traffic endlessly flowed,
kerbside vendors still frantically sold, and they left
the throbbing street at last, turned into a side street,
enjoying the quiet, the absence of strip lighting. Cave
woke up.

'We're being followed', he said.

Keith strained his ears: he could hear no footsteps
but their own.

'What do we do?' he asked.

Cave nodded towards a dark alley ahead.

'We stroll as far as that – then we run', he said.

Here we go again, thought Keith. Even so he felt
glad that his leg was better.

They reached the alley and ran for it, and Keith
stumbled in the dark, almost tripped, and swore aloud.
Then there was a soft, popping sound, which once he
might have mistaken for a cork leaving a champagne
bottle, but not since he'd met Joe Cave. He kept on
running until there was nowhere else to run. They'd
reached a high and unscaleable wall lit by one dim
light. The alley was a cul-de-sac.

'Sorry', said Cave. Keith noticed without surprise
that there was a gun in his hand, as he listened with
an animal's straining concentration.

'No more company', he said. 'Unless it's an ambush.
I'd better go and see.'

'Must you?'

'Nothing else for it', said Cave. 'Except wait for
daylight. And I'm bushed.'

He went off into the darkness, as silent as grass
growing, and Sandy Keith waited because it was the

42

most useful thing he could do... Then suddenly Cave was back beside him.

'Something you ought to see', he said, and led Keith back up the alley to the spot where empty cartons were stacked. Behind the cartons was a dark and huddled mass. Cave took a pencil thin torch from his pocket and switched it on. Keith found that he was looking at a slim, tough-looking Chinese with a gun in his hand, a Chinese who might have been quite handsome if a bullet had not done such things to his head.

'Recognise him?' asked Cave.

'Why on earth should I?'

'Because it says on his passport he's a motor mechanic called Shan, and in his pocket there's a key to the Hotel Coimbra in Macao. You sure your uncle didn't say anything about a mechanic?'

'Of course I'm sure', said Keith.

Cave switched off his torch and yawned. 'My God I'm whacked', he said.

Next morning, Keith had breakfast with Charlie Morton. Usually it was fun to have a meal with Charlie, who knew and understood food the way he knew and understood cars. But that day there was neither joy nor wit in the meal they shared together. Charlie Morton was still enduring his daughter's loss. Keith told him how sorry he was to have learned the sad news, and Morton accepted it because he knew the sympathy was real, but even so he was not ready to discuss it. Not yet. What he wanted to discuss was another matter entirely.

'It was good of you to agree to help us, Sandy', he said, and Keith blinked. Sir Roderick wouldn't see it like that at all. For Sir Roderick there was never any 'us': only Sir Roderick in charge and everybody else doing as they were told. All the same, Charlie was in no state to be warned off.

'Least I could do', Keith said. 'I've always hated drugs.'

'Jane was nineteen when drugs killed her', said Charlie. 'It nearly killed her mother, too. Gave her a heart condition. We're going to catch these bastards, Sandy.'

First 'us' now 'we', thought Keith.

Aloud he said, 'I hope so, Charlie.'

'Oh, we're going to catch them', Charlie Morton said. 'I wish we could kill them.' He finished his coffee and got to his feet. 'Now let's go and look at this circuit in Macao.'

They took the hydrofoil. The saloon of the craft was packed, mostly with Chinese men, and most of the men carried briefcases. If what Sir Roderick had told Keith was right, what the briefcases contained was money. Hong Kong dollars, U.S. dollars, and pounds sterling for the most part. To Hong Kong Chinese there was only one good reason to visit Macao and that was to gamble. In Hong Kong the only legitimate ways of gambling were horse racing and mah-jong. Macao was as wide open as Las Vegas. The casinos offered every possible way of gambling from roulette to Chinese dominoes, and if you preferred the open air life there were greyhounds to bet on flown in from Australia.

But Sandy Keith and Charlie Morton had come to see about racing of their own. They'd disembarked, paid a fee, and were provided with a form, then met by a racing official who proceeded to drive them around the circuit.

Keith found Macao a distressing place. The hill country was pleasant, like a Chinese landscape painted on silk, and the view across the Pearl river estuary to China was spectacular enough, but the old town was drab and dirty, its people poor, its goods shoddy. After Hong Kong it was a sad place to be. The only signs of true vitality were the casinos and fishing boats. They were the only signs of money, too.

The casinos were open round the clock, and never empty. The fishermen too had wealth. Looking at their strong, traditionally built craft, huddled together like

44

seagulls on a rock, it was hard to imagine it was so, but their guide assured them it was true enough. The fishermen worked hard and lived poor and the profit from every catch was converted into gold. A tempting target for robbers, or even pirates you would think, their guide said, and there are still far too many pirates in the South China Sea – but nobody ever attacks fishermen. These, said the guide, were real tough guys.

'Some of them had better be', said Morton, and Sandy Keith rushed in with a string of questions about the circuit and their guide drove on. Really, Charlie Morton was the wrong man to be on this assignment. His grief and outrage were getting in the way of his commonsense... The circuit would do: not too big and not too tricky, but then he wouldn't be hitting Formula One speeds either. What speeds he would hit would depend on the quiet decent little bus from the Land of Oz... Keith looked at the circuit and made notes and wished that the Macanese would spend a little money on road maintenance. At last it was time for lunch and a mandatory visit to a casino.

To Keith it looked like hell: a hell of punters, who were mostly men, whose money was systematically taken from them by croupiers, who were mostly women. The noise was deafening, the heat from the artificial lights tremendous, despite the air conditioning. There were, of course, no windows. In casinos like that there never are. There must be no reminder of day or night.

Scattered about the high stools throughout the gaming room were look-outs. Not that the casino owners were afraid of robbery. Where could a success- ful robber go – except Red China – and what robber, successful or not, would want to go there? The men on high stools, it seemed, were there to guard against cheating. And the temptation to cheat must be pretty strong at that, Keith thought. All over the room men with briefcases took out dollars and pounds by the fistfuls. Keith yawned and fidgeted with the fruit machines until it was time to go.

When they returned to the Hong Kong hotel, Joe Cave was waiting with a summons to Sir Roderick, and Charlie Morton went along too, without being asked. That won't go down well, thought Keith, nor did it, but all the same Morton settled himself in his chair with the air of a man who intends to stay comfortable, no matter how long the meeting lasts.

'This really doesn't concern you', Sir Roderick said at once.

'Oh but it does', said Morton. 'Drugs always concern me.'

'The things we have to discuss are top secret.'

'They'll be safe with me', Morton said.

Sir Roderick sighed. 'Very well. Since you force me to, I'll say it. I don't want you here.'

'In that case I'll go', said Morton, not moving. 'But if I do, I'll take Sandy with me. After all he's on my team – not yours.'

Sandy Keith thought it might turn out to be quite a decent sort of a day after all, and watched with interest as Sir Roderick fought for and finally achieved control.

'Very well', he said at last. 'I hope to heaven you know what you're getting into.' He turned to Keith. 'That feller Shan – the chap who was following you. He was chief mechanic of our Macao contact.'

'Our man's a *driver*?' asked Keith.

'Among other things,' Sir Roderick said. 'Harry Lo. Calls himself Hank... Blessed if I know why. Playboy millionaire. His father died a few weeks ago ... left him that casino you visited. That's where the heroin's handed over as a matter of fact.'

'And this Lo chap's shopping his own men?' Morton asked.

'He'd better be', said Sir Roderick.

'How do they transfer the stuff?' Keith asked. 'In a briefcase?'

'Who the devil told you that?'

'The place is full of them. A switch would be dead easy', said Keith.

46

'Let's hope so', said Sir Roderick. 'Hank Lo will tell you when it's going to be and you'll tell your P.R. man' – he nodded at Cave – 'and he'll follow him back to Hong Kong on the hydrofoil and we'll have him picked up. And you, Mr Morton, will mind your own business.'

Morton gave a grunt that could have meant anything.

'At least that's the theory of it', Sir Roderick said. 'But that chap Shan being killed – that's a piece that doesn't fit. Joe here thinks he must have been trying to reach you for some reason, and some unpleasant person who knew what he was doing got there first and killed him, poor soul. That could mean that they're on to you, Joe. Or you, Sandy. Or both of you. You were followed after all.'

'What do you propose to do about it?' Morton asked.

'Nothing', said Sir Roderick. 'Not a damn thing. We go ahead as planned. What else can we do?'

'Won't that be dangerous?' asked Morton.

'Certainly it will', said Sir Roderick, not without satisfaction. 'But I did warn you.'

The decent little bus from Australia arrived at Kai Tak airport, and was shipped, still crated, to Macao. Morton and Keith went to look at it and took their P.R. man with them to visit the improvised pits.

The car was not what Keith had been used to for a long time, but then neither were his fellow competitors who clustered round it. Flanked by Cave and Morton, Sandy went up to the car and one by one the other drivers fell away; he could hear the whisper of his name over and over, Sandy Keith, Sandy Keith, Sandy Keith; sometimes in envy, sometimes in anger, but all he needed was the car.

Beside him Morton murmured, 'Does it go, I wonder?'

'I can't wait to find out', said Keith.

It was a Special, a one off, and once it had been somebody's darling, but that had been a long time ago.

It still sparkled on the surface, still looked good to the unskilled eye – but Keith's eyes, and Morton's, were skilled indeed. The decent little bus had had more than its share of shunts.

The chief of the team of Chinese mechanics Sir Roderick had found for them looked at the two-litre engine and turned to Keith, astonished.

'Maybe it does work,' he said. And in fact it did, Keith found. It worked very well. That is the engine did. The chassis was quite another matter: the chassis seemed to have been cannibalised out of at least four different bodies, and handled like it. All the same he did a very fast trial lap, almost as fast as Hank Lo's. But then Hank Lo was driving a spanking new Ferrari – and driving it pretty well.

He came over to Keith by the pits, watched as the mechanics checked his car.

'You did well', he said. 'Congratulations. But then we amateurs expect you to do well... Especially when we have lost our best mechanic.' He smiled. 'It is safe to talk, for the moment,' he said. 'Perhaps it will not be safe again. Pretend we talk about cars please.'

Keith smiled back and gestured to Lo's Ferrari. 'When and where? That's all I need to know.'

'My casino, as usual', said Lo. 'After the race a man called Chen will exchange briefcases with a man called Tang. Chen is a fisherman here. Big. Scar on forehead. The briefcase is brown pigskin. Tang has a moustache. He is small, wears a deaf aid. He will register at the Hotel Lisboa.'

'Thanks', said Keith. 'I'll pass it on.'

And then because he couldn't help it, he asked, 'How on earth did you get into this?'

'I'm a Hong Kong millionaire', said Hank Lo, 'and therefore I'm a crook and a friend of crooks. But my father died because of heroin. Because of a man like Chen and Tang.' He smiled again, clapped Keith on the shoulder, and walked away.

You too, thought Keith, you and Charlie Morton.

He went to find Joe Cave, who was busy being a P.R.

48

man in the cocktail bar of Lo's casino; telling the press what a good sport Keith was: using the opportunity to test out his injured leg and so adding lustre to Macao's big day. He did it quite well too, thought Keith, making it sound like an exhibition bout. But they'd never get that from him. When the race started, all he'd be concerned with was winning.

It took a while for Cave to ditch the press and Keith to avoid Morton, but they managed to meet at last, and Keith passed on his news. Then Cave disappeared to pass it on in his turn, Keith joined Morton to drink champagne and talk about his next day's chances, then more champagne for his competitors. Still there was the envy, still the anger that a pike should have invaded the minnows' pond – but they accepted his champagne even so. Hank Lo took a glass and then offered a bottle of his own, but they exchanged no more words. Hank Lo was no fool, thought Keith.

Later on, Cave, Keith and Morton dined together in the hotel restaurant, a quiet, early dinner, and then back up to bed. Before a race Sandy Keith found he could and must sleep for ten hours at least, and Morton and Cave, too, were glad of the chance to relax.

All three men had rooms on the same floor, and as they walked along the corridor, Keith found that his chances of sleep would be very slim indeed. On one side of him someone appeared to be playing the world's most powerful radio, on the other they were giving a party a pools' winner could have envied...

'I'd better ask for a little silence', said Keith, and headed for the party.

'Wait', said Cave, and took Keith's key in his left hand, took out a Smith and Wesson magnum with his right. Morton's eyes projected as if on stalks. Cave went to Keith's door, turned the key, then kicked the door open and dived through. Morton made as if to follow, but Keith held him back. In the confined space of the room their presence would only increase Cave's problems...

Cave landed flat by the bed and a man crouched

49

behind it loosed off a shot that hit the wall. Cave fired back and hit the other man in the leg, then squirmed round on his stomach to face a second man hidden in the angle behind the door, pinned down by the door's sudden, violent opening, but now free and holding a knife, hurling himself at Cave. There was no time to loose off a shot: the knife man came at him like a missile. All Cave could do was swerve away from the knife's thrust before the knife man landed on top of him, pinning him down, raising the knife for a second try.

The three middle fingers of Cave's left hand formed themself into a spear point, slammed into the knife man's ribs, and the knife man groaned, his lunge went wide. Cave put his left hand under the man's chin. He had to be free of him before his friend with the gun could try another shot, which was why he was limping towards them, still hanging on to his gun.

Cave levered and heaved, and the knife man went up in the air just as his mate pulled the trigger, and Cave wriggled free, loosed off another shot, and broke the gun man's arm. The gun man screamed aloud, but the knife was silent. The gun man had just shot him dead.

Wearily Cave climbed to his feet to face another onrush of Chinamen, jammed into the doorway – but these were Keith's mechanics.

'Sorry', the chief mechanic said. 'But we didn't realise you'd go to bed so early. Extremely sorry.'

'That's O.K.', said Cave. 'Only what do we do now? Call the coppers?'

'Better not', said the chief mechanic. 'Better Mr Keith shares your room. We make all tidy... No problem.'

Cave left them to it and looked into the two rooms on either side of Keith's. Both were empty: in one of them was a radio turned on full, in the other a video cassette of a movie tuned to the part where World War Two had just ended and everyone in the world was celebrating. He turned them off and yawned.

'Bedtime', he said.

Morton still stared at him, eyes protruding even further.

'I never met a P.R. man who could fight like you before', he said.

'You're lucky', said Sandy Keith.

Chapter 6

KEITH RACED. Joe Cave was against it, but Keith raced because it was impossible for him to do anything else. Hank Lo had the pole position, an Italian in a Chevron was next, but Keith had number three. The old Billabong Special – or whatever it was – was full of surprises. Keith took care to rub the little silver elephant on the chain round his neck, just in case, but even after patting it he wouldn't have that much of a chance, he thought. Though if he'd forgotten, he'd have had no chance at all.

The flag went down and the Ferrari took off the way a Ferrari should, and the Chevron did its best to follow. Despite the fact that Keith was prepared to swear that some parts of his car were going faster than others the Billabong hung on to third place. It was a nice, easy circuit: no dramas, no wall of death, just a pleasant little afternoon spin – and not even all that much effort when he managed to slipstream the Italian, work up to within six feet of him and let the Chevron do all the work.

The Italian was driving very prettily too, until they went into the chicane by the reservoir for the seventeenth time, and the Italian suddenly got the idea that

52

he could take a particular kink in the road in top gear, and found that he couldn't. Cave saw him leave the road and hit a barrier. It didn't look as if he'd hurt much more than his feelings. Now, Keith thought, all I have to do is coax this jet propelled crab into catching a Ferrari.

He was still trying on the twenty-fourth lap – was even creeping up on it a little – when the Ferrari ceased to exist, became instead mere assorted bits of flaming metal flying, burning into the road. Keith put his foot down – it was the only possible thing to do – and drove on through. It was spilled oil that got him. The car, crablike to the last, hit a slick and decided to go sideways instead – at ninety miles an hour – and yards away from the pits. It hit the barrier and Keith waited for death, but it was the car that died, as Joe Cave raced up to him to grab him free.

'You're hurt', said Cave.

'Oh no, I'm not', said Keith.

'Oh yes you are', said Cave, and knocked him cold. Then he yelled for a doctor.

Keith came to on a hired motorboat. Every part of him that could take a splint felt as if it had received one. He opened his eyes and found that Morton was looking at him.

'What on earth's going on, Charlie?' Sandy Keith asked.

'That P.R. man hit you', said Morton. 'He was afraid that you might get killed.'

'That's ridiculous', said Keith.

'Hank Lo was killed', said Morton. 'Cave was afraid they'd have another try at you – so he issued a statement that you're dying without regaining consciousness.'

'That's too much', said Keith.

'No', said Morton. 'I don't think it is. He reckons that way those heroin pushers may still try to bring that filth into Hong Kong.'

53

'I hope so', said Keith. 'I really do.' He wriggled in discomfort. Time to change the subject. 'You know, Charlie', he said, 'that Aussie bus was the weirdest thing I ever drove.'

Chen looked nervous until the switch was made, and then it was Tang's turn. Joe Cave left the casino as soon as the moustached man with the deaf aid took the case. It was Keith's mechanics, working as a team, who tailed Tang to the car.

No hydrofoils after sunset, so they had to take the ferry, but at least there were fruit machines to help pass the time. The man with the deaf aid didn't use them. He needed both hands to hang on to his briefcase...

As the ferry prepared to dock, Cave positioned himself to leave first. The mechanics were still the back-up team. They'd follow Tang from behind as they'd done in Macao... Cave looked ashore as the ferry moved cautiously in. Beyond the wharf there was a blaze of hard, white light: hundreds of acetylene lamps lighting up what was by day a car park, but was now a night market where hundreds, maybe thousands of people haggled and bargained and bought.

Morton liked the night market. He'd seen Sandy Keith on to an ambulance and declined the offer of a lift. From what Sandy had reluctantly told him it would be here that that mad P.R. man would grab the heroin pusher, and he wanted to see that. In the meantime the market was a good place to be: the pots and pans and shoes and shirts for sale; the food stores and quack doctors and the fortune tellers. It was a nice market – and these were nice people. They knew nothing about drugs...

Tang knew all about drugs: he'd trafficked in them all his adult life. It had made him as wary as a cat at Cruft's. And somehow, as he moved into the night market, his instincts told him that something had gone wrong, badly wrong. And without a second's

54

hesitation he ran for it, veering away from where Cave waited for him. Cave swore. His back-up team were still leaving the wharf. All he could do was to take off in pursuit, but Tang was moving like a wing three-quarter – running straight at a European whose features stood out clearly in the hard, white light.

'Morton', Cave yelled. 'Stop that man with the briefcase. It's full of heroin.'

Morton acted on reflex. His arms clamped round the man with the deaf aid, pinning one of his. The Chinaman used the free arm to hit Morton. The Chinaman had been kung-fu trained, and even his first blow could have killed Morton. The second one was bound to. And yet Morton's arms clung on as the Chinaman struck him, blow after blow, till Joe Cave reached them and struck at the Chinaman – and Joe Cave too had been kung-fu trained.

'I'm sorry it had to end like this', said Sir Roderick.

'It's not your fault Charlie died', said Keith.

Sir Roderick sighed. Amateurs have a habit of dying.

'What will you do now?' he asked.

'It's time I got back to England', said Keith. 'There'll be a lot of sorting out to do, and Mrs Morton is going to need help.' He sipped at his drink.

'They're a ruthless lot, aren't they?' he said. 'Poor old Charlie, Hank Lo, his mechanic.'

'They didn't kill the mechanic', said Sir Roderick. 'He was being bribed by the fishermen in Macao... As a matter of fact he was following you when he – died.'

'Me? What on earth for?'

'Because you'd entered for the Macao race I gather – and he'd heard Lo say he'd like a chat with you.'

'You had him killed just for that?' asked Keith.

'As you said yourself they were a ruthless bunch', said Sir Roderick. 'The mechanic designed a booby trap that wrecked Lo's car. Somebody else planted it of course – but you don't often come across a posthumous murderer. He carried a gun, too, that night he followed you. He might have used it. On you – or the chaps who were looking after you. I told them not to take any chances.'

'Does Joe Cave know you supplied us with body-guards?'

'Good Lord no', said Sir Roderick. 'Joe hates people interfering.'

'So do I', said Keith. 'You should have left us alone, uncle. Joe wouldn't have killed that feller. We'd have learned something from him. Maybe Charlie and Hank would still be alive... We might even have found out about that factory ship.'

'I still have hopes', Sir Roderick said, and it was true enough. The man Joe Cave had shot was still alive, because of the orders Cave had received, and already he was being questioned...

A week later, when Sir Roderick had returned to London, and Joe Cave was issuing statements to say that Sandy Keith was making a miraculous recovery, Sir Roderick received a cutting from the *Hong Kong Morning Post*. It informed him that the motor vessel *Délice* (Lichtenstein owned, Liberian registered) had blown up in the South China Sea. A Macanese fishing boat, which for some reason had been moored to the *Délice* at the time, had sunk without a trace.

Sir Roderick burned the cutting in his ashtray, and poured a single malt, and drank to the memory of Charlie Morton and Hank Lo.

Somehow life went on, even without Charlie Morton. His widow had made up her mind to go on, and Penelope Morton making her mind up was like an elephant sitting down. There wasn't much you could do to stop her... But when Keith returned he found she'd taken on a partner. Once Charlie died there was just no way of raising the kind of money that Formula One guzzles as a Hooray Henry swills champagne...

It was fortunate that Iskandar Nadir had the money

to guzzle, and a passion for racing cars. He had left Iran with a pocketful of industrial diamonds, one jump ahead of the Ayatollah, and converted the diamonds into a carpet business, a chain of petrol stations, and California real estate. Keith liked him very much...

The man who didn't like Keith was Pierre Jannot, because as long as Keith was around Jannot was second driver, and he hated it, so therefore he hated Keith. Trudi Jannot did not, Keith thought. Judging by her smile she might even have liked him, but there was no more for Keith than a smile... He loved her, but she didn't love him, and so being the kind of man he was, Keith kept away from her. It didn't stop Jannot from hating him, though. Not until he died...

Ironic, the way Pierre Jannot had died, Jason Bird thought. Keith had caught mumps at twenty-seven years of age; a grotesque experience that was as painful as it was humiliating.

And while he hid himself, Jannot had become Number One driver of the Morton-Nadir, and come fifth at Monaco, and third at Nurburgring... The press took notice of the fact that Sandy Keith had a rival, and Pierre Jannot took notice of it too, and went to Rio de Janeiro with a Keith-like determination to come first, and accelerated in the rain, and killed himself.

Jannot's death, Jason Bird thought, had been a beginning, rather than an end. Until Jannot had died none of the other things, the terrible, disastrous, appalling things, could have happened, and he, Jason Bird, would not have been sitting in Florida, remembering. Jason Bird was sorry that Jannot had died, but by no means sorry about the chain of events which that death had triggered, not now when he was sitting safe in Florida...

Sandy Keith looked round the smoking room of Sir Roderick's club, and sighed. Why on earth had he bothered to come? he wondered. Sir Roderick's club always depressed him, and Sir Roderick always ordered him a single malt when he knew his nephew much preferred a Campari and soda. But then Sir Roderick held strong views on the kinds of alcohol a Scottish gentleman might drink. What it amounted to was malt whisky and claret, and not all that much claret, not if Uncle Roderick was pouring...

'I hear you're going to Las Vegas', Sir Roderick said.

'It's been in all the papers', said Keith.

'I'd no idea they raced cars there', said Sir Roderick. 'I thought all one did there was gambling.'

'I'll be gambling', said Keith. 'In a car ... it's a newish circuit, Uncle Roderick, and as circuits go it's reasonable – not all that dangerous. But my car's just had a refit... I'll be gambling all right.'

As he spoke Sandy Keith found himself wondering why he had even bothered to accept his uncle's invitation for a drink and a chat, and then suddenly he realised the answer. The old boy had to be warned off. Best get on with it. He had a party to go to once he'd finished his whisky.

'I may as well tell you now, uncle', said Keith, 'I'm going to be awfully busy in Las Vegas. There just won't be time to do any of those little extra jobs you keep finding me.'

Sir Roderick looked pained.

'The thought never crossed my mind', he said.

'Didn't it?' said Keith. 'Then this'll be the first time you ever stood me a drink just for the pleasure of my company.'

And it was true, he thought. His uncle could always find him a job to do. But then Sir Roderick Finlay was head of a department of British Intelligence that needed all the recruits it could get: danger, violence, death – most men didn't exactly rush to meet them, and the ones who did rarely measured up to the tasks Sir Roderick had in mind. Keith's ability and freedom of movement as a racing driver were assets that Sir Roderick had not hesitated to use, ever. But not this time, thought Keith. The Las Vegas race was a gamble, as he'd said, but with luck he could win: come out so far ahead on points that the world championship would be his. And winning a Grand Prix is a full-time job. He said so.

'My dear boy', Sir Roderick said, 'you've grown very excitable lately. I've often noticed it. Where do you get it from, I wonder? Not from my side of the family... And I wish you wouldn't call them jobs... They're your patriotic duty.' He sipped his malt. 'My only reason for bringing you here – apart from the pleasure of your company as you so aptly put it – was to tell you that Joe Cave is also going to Las Vegas. I thought it would be as well to warn you. You might say something out of turn.'

'Joe?' said Keith. 'Going to watch a Grand Prix?'

'Going to perform his patriotic duty.'

Sandy Keith was enjoying the party. It was a good one: lots of pretty girls, lots of champagne, lots of blokes who knew about motor racing. The very best sort of party in fact, and yet Keith found himself thinking about Joe Cave. Joe was something to think about, all right. The hardest of all the hard pros in Uncle Roderick's little army. Deadly with a gun, a knife, or just his hands. Literally deadly... Keith had seen Joe Cave in action often enough to know. So why the hell was he going to Las Vegas?

The thought nagged at him so much that it began to spoil his enjoyment. The silken groupies who hang around racing drivers are rich, pretty and willing, else why would racing drivers encourage them? thought Keith. And there was he, poised to become world champion, so naturally they clustered round – yet he just couldn't get interested... Damn Joe Cave anyway, he thought. But it wasn't all Joe Cave. He turned away from a particularly luscious redhead and found himself look-ing at the man who was giving the party – the current world champion, a neat and smiling Venezuelan.

59

'Now I know you are determined to be world champion', the Venezuelan said.

'I've always been determined', said Keith. 'Why now in particular, Luis?'

'Because you turned down all the girls I invited', said Luis. 'You think they are not good enough for the next world champion.'

'It isn't that', said Keith. Luis reached out an arm, procured a bottle, topped up Keith's glass and his own. 'What then?' he said.

'These girls are only interested in one thing.'

'Sure', said Luis, and laughed.

Keith ran a hand over his hair, and it changed at once from copper colour to a glowing fiery red.

'Don't laugh, please', he said. 'I'm serious.'

'O.K.', said Luis. 'Then I am serious too.'

Keith looked at the girls once more. The best girls in the best suite in the best hotel in London. And yet –

'They want us because we may die', he said. 'It isn't us they love. It's death.'

The Venezuelan shrugged. 'What you say may well be true', he said. 'But does it matter?'

'It does to me', said Keith.

'But not to me', said Luis, and smiled. 'I too intend to win at Las Vegas. I might just as well celebrate in advance.'

He picked up his bottle and went to talk to the redhead, who smiled at him at once. Sandy Keith wondered if he were perhaps a little tight: malt whisky topped up with champagne made a pretty volatile sort of mixture. And then three more people joined the party, and Keith knew he couldn't possibly leave.

The man was Iskandar Nadir: chubby, cheerful and as rich as ever. Not for the first time Keith felt grateful for the fact that Nadir's one abiding passion was Formula One racing. Without him, Keith had no hope of becoming world champion, or even of going to Las Vegas.

The Morton part of the Morton-Nadir car was one of the women with him – Penelope Morton, always known as Penny; sturdy, untidy, endlessly optimistic, the widow of the car's designer. The other woman who was with them was also a widow, but there the resemblance ended.

Trudi Jannot was blonde; elegant, slender, the black she wore symbolic more of chic than of bereavement. Yet, Keith knew, she had been bereaved when Pierre Jannot died. He had died because he didn't have the skills to achieve his goal, but even so she had mourned for him deeply and passionately. She had loved him, Keith thought, because he had lived, and not because he might die. There was nothing of the groupie about her. Nadir couldn't keep his eyes off her, and Keith didn't blame him. Neither could any other man in the room. He obeyed as always the magnetic tug of his need for her and went to join them. At once she looked up and smiled.

'Sandy', she said. 'It's good to see you.'

'You too', said Keith, and found that he had nothing more to say once she smiled like that and the merest hint of a German accent showed in the soft, low voice.

'Are you all ready for Las Vegas?' she asked.

'Doing my best', said Keith.

'I certainly hope so', said Nadir.

'My God yes', said Penny Morton. 'Oh I wish I was going to be there.'

'Why won't you?' said Keith. Penny Morton was always there when he raced, the absolute epitome of mumhood. Without her, driving the Morton-Nadir could never be the same.

'Blasted heart murmur', Penny Morton said. 'Why in hell did it have to happen now? But don't worry, Sandy darling. Iskandar's nephew will take care of you.'

Keith was quite sure she was laughing at him. 'Luis reckons he's going to beat me', said Keith.

'And you?' said Nadir.

'I reckon he's not', said Keith and Nadir grinned, and clapped him on the back, and said he didn't reckon so either, but that it had been nice of Luis to invite his enemy to his party. And then another man joined

61

them, a man who was a smaller, younger version of Iskandar Nadir.

'I'm sorry to be so long, uncle', he said. 'It took me all of five minutes to find a parking space.'

'That's all right, Rafi,' said his uncle. 'You're driving – you drink lemonade. So you don't miss much anyway.'

The young man's glance showed that he missed Trudi Jannot.

'This is my nephew, Rafi Firdousi', Nadir said. 'Been making his fortune in Europe, he tells me – but just for now he's taking a rest and working for his uncle – eh Rafi? He's going to look after you in Las Vegas, Sandy – just like Penny says.'

He turned to his nephew and put an arm round his shoulder. There was affection in the gesture and also an unmistakable air of possession. Sandy Keith was now quite sure that Penny Morton had been laughing at him. Nadir gestured to Keith.

'This is Sandy Keith', he said. 'The best racing driver in the world – and do you know something? He drives for me.'

'He drives for us', Penny Morton said.

Nadir made a gesture that said quite clearly: Women must be indulged because they are women, but I'm the one with the money – then turned back to his nephew and spoke to him tersely. Penny Morton took herself off to be gracious to Luis.

'Alone at last', said Keith.

'Not very', Trudi Jannot said, and glanced at Nadir, then away.

'I wish we could be', said Keith.

'Why do you?'

'I want to talk to you', said Keith. 'No... I need to talk to you.'

'I work for Nadir', she said.

'I know you do', said Keith, 'but –'

'Let me finish. I work for Iskandar Nadir Enterprises Ltd, I handle a little, little bit of his P.R. for him. But he doesn't own me. Nobody does. And it's time I clocked off anyway. So why shouldn't we be alone together? . . . Just wait there till I tell him.'

And she did tell him, at once, quickly and firmly, and Nadir was not happy, nor was any other man in the room – except for Sandy Keith.

He took her to a restaurant where he was known and the food was good. The staff without exception approved of his choice of girl and left them alone, but somehow Keith was able to overcome his shyness at being with her, not least because she seemed pleased to be with him.

At last she said, 'You told me you need to talk to me.'

'I do', said Keith.

'Tell me about this need.'

'I think I'm in love with you', said Keith.

She smiled. 'It is difficult for me to believe that', she said.

'I know I haven't said it before', said Keith. 'Since Pierre – had his accident, I haven't –'

'Since Pierre was *killed*', Trudi said, 'you have said nothing to me at all. Until tonight.'

'Well I mean how could I?'

'You mean because I was so new a widow?' She sipped her wine. 'I loved Pierre, truly I did. But he was a difficult man and a complicated man and sometimes I loved him more than other times. You are not like that.' Keith's face fell, and she smiled once more. 'Oh Sandy, my dear', she said. 'How easy it is to hurt you. What I mean is that I love you too – but with you my love is always the same. Shall we go back to your place? It would be bad for your P.R. image – believe me I am a P.R. expert and I know – if you were to seduce me in a public restaurant – or if I were to seduce you, come to that.'

Keith hesitated.

'You do *want* to seduce me?' she said.

'Oh yes', said Keith, and instantly blushed scarlet. It was such a feeble thing to say.

'Well then?'

'Couldn't we go to your place?' he asked.

'My dear, I share with two other girls', she said. 'Both of them stayed home tonight. You would not find it amusing but what is wrong with your place? Is it so awful?'

'My place is in Sussex', said Keith. 'When I'm up in London I stay in Nadir's company flat. It's a bit awkward.'

'Not in the least', said Trudi Jannot. 'We won't tell him.'

Chapter 7

IT WAS in fact she who seduced him – he was far too
nervous for it to be otherwise – but she behaved
beautifully to him, blending passion with a kind of
sexual elegance that made him at last respond.
Together they found delight, and afterwards, as they
lay together, he asked her to marry him.

She smiled, and stroked his hair, turning its sleek
auburn to fire.

'You are going too fast, my dear', she said.

'It's the way I earn my living', said Keith.

'No.' Her voice was serious. 'Pierre went too fast.
That was why he crashed – but not you. You earn your
living by going just fast enough.' Her fingers hooked
into the silver chain around his neck, tugged gently at
the little silver elephant. 'Let us just enjoy what we
have for now', she said. 'Isn't it enough?'

'Not for me', said Keith.

'Wait', said Trudi. 'Best to wait.' She looked at the
little elephant. 'And who is this splendid fellow?'

'His name is Ganesh', said Keith. 'He's the elephant
god who brings good luck.'

'He does indeed', said Trudi. 'He's going to make you
world champion.'

'He brought me you', said Keith.

'He's nice', said Trudi. 'Have you had him long?'

'He belonged to my father', said Keith. 'He was a Spitfire pilot.'

'He was successful – your father?'

'He did all right', said Keith. How could he tell this enchanting German how many of her countrymen his father had killed?

'He is a very good, kind elephant', said Trudi. 'He brought you to me – but also he hurt me a little.' She put her hand just below her left breast. 'Here. But my dear I was so busy I didn't even notice. It is good to be busy.' She embraced him again.

A man as totally in love as Sandy Keith was, is aware of nothing but the time when he is with his beloved. Everything else is a matter of going through the motions, no more; of keeping appointments, attending meetings, driving cars, and thinking as he does so how good it was to be with her.

Nadir kept him busy: out at Brand's Hatch practising with the new car, learning its new tricks, talking tactics with the new second driver Penny had found to replace Pierre – a briskly enthusiastic New Zealander called Bill Speers. Then there were dates with the firms for whom he sponsored: the tyre firm, the car wax firm, and for reasons best known to his business manager, the firm that made meat pies: still, his not to reason why. All three paid well and a man in love needs all the money he can get: for emerald bracelets set in platinum, caviar, Dom Pérignon. Trudi scolded him but he bought them anyway. He was entitled to, he told her. He was in love with her...

The day before he flew to Las Vegas was their last chance to be together. He had one more meeting with his meat pie man, but it did go on a bit: a dinner that lingered over the oysters and salmon – and positively dawdled over the profiteroles. The pie man didn't believe in eating the product when he wasn't in his factory, but he did enjoy telling Keith how to drive. But after all, thought Keith fairmindedly, why shouldn't he? He paid enough for the privilege... If only Trudi hadn't got bored with waiting and gone home...

But the meal ended at last, even if it did take the pie man another five minutes to add up the bill, and Keith declined the offer of a lift – he'd been driven by the pie man before – and set off almost at a trot for the company flat that was tucked away discreetly in a mews in the maze of streets behind Shepherd's Market.

The trouble was it was too discreet. As he turned into the street that led to the mews, two figures moved out of the shadows, stood by the one dim light, blocking his path. Keith spun round, looked behind him – and there was another figure moving towards him, slow, unhurried, herding him towards the two who waited. Punks, thought Keith. No – skinheads. Bald, gleaming skulls, heavy Doc Martens boots, deliberately ugly clothes. Never mind the clothes – it was the boots he had to worry about. Those boots could maim, break bones, even kill, and here he was on his own, no talent for fighting, no talent at all.

And yet the thought of surrender didn't occur to him. Instead he dashed at the young man who stood alone, aimed a blow that was haphazard to the point of vagueness, and the skinhead replied with an accurate right to the face that sent Keith reeling, as the other two came running to share the kill.

The skinhead on his own aimed another blow, and Keith lurched across the street once more, fighting to keep his feet, for he knew that whatever happened he must not go down. Once he fell his hopes of Las Vegas were over: he might never see the company flat again... And then the other two came up, the gang stood about him; he was encircled by boots and fists and he knew that he was finished, except that the Seventh Cavalry arrived – or maybe it was his guardian angel.

Later he thought it was more like a jack-in-the-box, a tall, lean figure who came sailing through the air in a flying leap, knocked Keith deftly out of the way and kicked one of the skinheads in the side of the neck, landed and hit one of the other two in the stomach, while the third one did his best to disentangle himself from the one he'd kicked, who had fallen on number three, just as the tall, lean man had intended.

The one he'd hit retched and sagged forward, and the tall, lean man kicked out once more, then turned to face number three, who had freed himself at last, and lashed out with a kick of his own. The steel-shod boot aimed straight for the groin, but his opponent knew that one, stuck out his leg, rigid as an iron bar, so that the skinhead's shin crashed hard against his calf muscle and the skinhead howled, and hopped one-footed, nursing his shin's agony, and the tall, lean man had all the time in the world to pivot and kick for the third time, clipping the skinhead under the chin so that he fell on top of the other two, and turned to the man he had rescued.

'Hello Joe', said Sandy Keith.

'Hello Sandy', said Joe Cave.

'With legs like that you ought to be in the chorus line', said Keith.

'These blokes are so fond of kicking I thought I'd show them some new ones', said Cave.

Keith's smile faded.

'Were you following me by any chance?' he asked.

'What an idea', said Cave. 'I was coming to see you.'

'What about?'

'I'm going to Las Vegas.'

'Yes', said Keith. 'Uncle Roderick told me.'

'Well now he thinks I ought to tell you I'm going as a photographer, and the odds are you'll be seeing me quite a lot – only you don't know me.'

'Why will I be seeing you?'

'I'll be working for Nadir.'

'Oh come on', said Keith.

'Not the racing car bit', said Cave. 'He's just bought a

68

factory – what the Americans call a plant – in Santa Monica, in California, that makes rocket fuel.'

'Oh', said Keith.

'Oh is right', said Cave.

'But shouldn't the C.I.A. take care of that?'

'The F.B.I. actually', said Cave. 'They're the ones who take care of internal security in the States. But you know what your uncle is – never could stay in his own back yard.' He added hastily, 'So from now on we're strangers, O.K.?'

'Couldn't you have phoned?' said Keith.

'What a suspicious feller you are', said Cave. 'I just thought it might be nice to come and see you – have a chat about old times.'

'Oh', said Keith again.

'You don't want a chat?'

'You see there's this girl', said Keith.

'What girl?'

'Trudi Jannot', said Keith. 'Pierre's widow. Did you know Pierre?'

'We ran a check on him once', said Cave.

'On *Pierre*?'

'He was a Red', said Cave.

'He talked a lot of nonsense', said Keith. 'It made Trudi very unhappy – but I honestly don't believe he'd ever have *done* anything.'

'Neither did we', said Cave. 'Is she nice? – His widow?'

'She's wonderful', said Keith, and Cave had no doubt that he meant it. Behind them a skinhead groaned.

'Shouldn't we call the police or something?' said Keith.

'I'd rather you didn't', said Cave. 'Be a bit tricky for me.'

'Yes of course', said Keith. 'Maybe I'd better not tell Trudi either.'

'She'll only worry', Cave agreed.

Keith looked at the huge Doc Martens boots the bald young men wore.

'She'd have reason to be', he said. The skinhead

69

groaned again. 'You won't mind if I rush off, will you Joe? I'm late as it is.'

'I won't mind', said Cave, and Sandy Keith rushed.

Cave watched him go as a small, battered van came round the corner and pulled up beside him. He gestured at the skinheads, and a large man got out of the cab and stacked them in the back of the van as if they were logs of wood, and Joe Cave yawned, stretched and got into the cab. The name on the side of the van was 'Oddjobs Ltd'. Cave hoped they'd never come any odder than the one he'd just done.

'What did you get?' asked Sir Roderick.

'Not much', said Cave. 'The geezer who hired them picked them up in a pub.'

'Description?'

'Twenty-eight to thirty-five, brown hair, muscular build, smartly dressed.'

'What does that mean?'

'Dark suit, umbrella, striped tie.'

'The voice?'

'Posh geezer. At least two said he was posh. The third one thought he was foreign.'

'Colour of eyes?'

'One said brown, one said blue, one said grey.'

Sir Roderick sighed. 'Do you think he is known to us?'

'I doubt it', said Cave. 'This one'll be a cut-out – told to do just this one job and then get lost.'

'Were they paid?'

'Certainly', said Cave. 'He told them Sandy Keith was making a pass at his wife and he wanted him taught a lesson. He paid them a hundred quid apiece.' He hesitated, then added, 'Of course it could be true, sir. Not that she's somebody's wife – but Sandy could have a rival and he could be jealous.'

'Rafi Firdousi', said Sir Roderick. 'I suppose it's possible –'

'What other reason could there be?'

70

'That's what worries me', Sir Roderick said, and then: 'What happened to the money you took from them?'

'I burned it', said Cave. 'In front of their eyes. One of them broke down and cried. The other two couldn't believe what was happening. Once they saw it all go up in smoke they would have told me anything I wanted.' He thought a moment and then added, 'They were promised another hundred quid apiece if they did a good job.'

'Payable at the pub, no doubt', Sir Roderick said. Cave nodded. 'Did you go?'

'Yeah', said Cave. 'Nobody there who answered to that description.'

'Of course not', said Sir Roderick. 'If this man's a pro he'd be hiding somewhere nearby to watch the assault. It's just as well I told you to keep an eye on Sandy.'

'They'll know we're on to them now.'

'If it's anything more serious than jealousy', Sir Roderick said, 'that knowledge won't stop them. What did you do with the delinquents?'

'Taught them some more dance steps then let them go', said Cave. 'They'll stay quiet.'

'You treated them roughly?'

'Well, of course', said Cave. 'Sandy's a friend of mine.'

'You'd better continue to keep an eye on him, at least until you leave', Sir Roderick said. 'I don't want the boy to be hurt.'

'I don't see how you can avoid it', said Joe Cave.

The flight across the Pole to Los Angeles had shown him a scene of amazing beauty – if you like tundra. But he'd seen the movie, and was too tensed up to read, and he couldn't drink because he was in training. Then he'd transferred to the Vegas flight and the first person he'd seen when he left it was Joe Cave, taking pictures – of him, of Iskandar Nadir, of Rafi Firdousi and Bill Speers. And they'd be good pictures, Sandy knew,

71

because Joe was a good photographer, could have made his living at it – but he didn't want to see Joe. Not just then. Joe reminded him of jobs for Uncle Roderick, patriotic duty – and it worried him to know that there *was* a job even if he wasn't involved. Winning the world championship was worry enough. Not that he wasn't grateful to Joe – of course he was – but now there was no room in his life for anything but the Grand Prix and Trudi Jannot. She tugged at his arm. 'You're so far away', she said.

'I was thinking.'

'About us?'

'I always think about us', said Keith. 'This time I was thinking about winning as well.'

'Thinking what?'

'Thinking I'm going to win', said Sandy Keith.

Then they went to the V.I.P. lounge to face the press.

They were in a hotel on the Strip. All the drivers were in hotels on the Strip, and very nice hotels they were: good room service, good air conditioning, and the opportunity to place a bet should the need come upon you. In Las Vegas you can gamble almost anywhere you go, from the airport lounge to the general stores, if fruit machines fulfil your need. Keith had heard they had them even in doctors' waiting rooms. But in the hotels you could place a bet on anything you liked: craps, black jack, roulette, chemin-der-fer, and the bet could be any size you liked, from one dollar to a thousand.

And there were places like this all over Vegas, Keith knew: from the cheap tawdry glitter of Fremont Street to the Strip, where the tawdry glitter was very expensive indeed.

The trouble was he hated the place. Gambling with money was just silly when you gambled with your life, and the round the clock idiocy of it appalled him. And there was no Trudi any more to take his mind off things: she was out in Santa Monica helping Iskandar

72

Nadir with his supersonic fireworks...

Keith spent as much time as he could at the circuit with Bill Speers and the car. It really was a good car now. All the modifications had worked, and yet the car was still rugged, durable, the kind that goes on, keeps on going until the very last lap: racehorse performance, carthorse strength. The car was good and everybody knew it, including Luis. Luis continued to smile – Luis always smiled – but he was worried.

To Keith the trouble was the nights. There was nothing to keep him at the circuit at night time, and he avoided the other drivers. For once their mood wasn't his: he wanted Trudi and she wasn't there. And so, he told himself, he was sulking, which was childish, but it was also inevitable. Not that he lacked for company. Iskandar had left Rafi Firdousi in charge, and Firdousi seemed to have made up his mind that Sandy Keith needed his company, which was absurd. Firdousi quite obviously disliked Sandy Keith intensely, and yet here they sat in the cocktail lounge and bawled thinly veiled insults at each other above the uproar of a Rockabilly group that had just made number one. Firdousi, Keith thought, must really be afraid of his uncle. For himself he preferred the noise of the fruit machines, and it seemed Firdousi did, too. He nudged Keith's arm, and made a pumping motion with his hand as if he were pulling a pint of beer... Keith followed him out.

The gaming room has no windows or clocks – no gaming rooms in Vegas have windows or clocks – and in that respect it was just like Macao, Keith thought, and for the same reason: that way you didn't notice the passage of time. There were one-arm bandits wall-to-wall, and all of them in use. The gaming room throbbed and crashed like a boiler factory. Almost every one of the gamblers carried a paper cup to catch their winnings, if winnings there were, and they fed the machines eagerly, devotedly, like worshippers at a ritual.

Firdousi chose a dollar machine and got lucky

73

almost at once. A stream of dollar plaques flowed into his cup but even so he left it and went over to roulette, and Keith was delighted. Roulette was much quieter. Firdousi put chips on numbers, apparently at random.

'Have a good day?' he asked.

'Yes', said Keith.

One of Firdousi's numbers came up. 'I hope so', said Firdousi. 'It's important to Uncle Iskandar that you win.'

'It's important to me, too', said Keith.

'Such a small thing for my uncle to worry about.'

'Small?' said Keith. 'It's the world championship.'

'But of what?' Firdousi said. 'It is such a bourgeois sport.'

'You don't like things to be bourgeois?'

'It is not the way of the future', said Firdousi.

'Have you told your uncle so?'

'My uncle is not a serious person', said Firdousi. 'He laughs.'

'Pierre Jannot used to talk like you', said Keith.

'How do you know?'

'Trudi Jannot told me.'

Firdousi looked up from the roulette table to Keith, and Keith realised then that the Iranian didn't just dislike him, he hated him.

Chapter 8

THE NEXT DAY was good. The next day he did the fastest lap of the circuit, which meant he had the pole position. The best on the starting grid. Next day too Iskandar Nadir flew in from Santa Monica, which put an end to the little chats with his nephew. It put an end to Keith's loneliness, too. Trudi Jannot flew in also. So did Joe Cave, but he kept out of Keith's way. Nobody had the right to butt in on such happiness.

On the day of the race, at three in the morning, Trudi Jannot said that she would marry Keith after it was over, and he reached for her again. When it was time to get up she had to shake him awake.

'You certainly know how to relax a chap', he said...

Cave didn't like car races. In his more honest moments he admitted that it was because the drivers were doing something he could do himself, only they could do it a hundred times better, even the worst of them. But in Las Vegas it wasn't so bad. First of all he and Canovan, the F.B.I. man working with him, had plugged the leak at Nadir's factory. It had been a fast and tricky operation, but the secret of the rocket fuel at the end of the day remained a Western secret. They hadn't yet got the K.G.B. agent responsible for the operation, but that was only a matter of time. It would happen, and soon, Cave was sure. Russia was desperate for that particular secret. And Nadir had been warned. He'd yelped a bit – who wouldn't? – but he was a realist. He'd accepted what must be.

For the moment all that Cave had to do was enjoy the race, and it was pleasant enough: Nevada sunshine, Las Vegas razzamatazz, and pretty girls wherever you looked, Trudi Jannot not least, down by the Morton-Nadir pits, talking to a couple of tall, chunky fellers who had Security written all over them. When Firdousi tried to draw her away she just looked at him, and it was enough. He wilted... The power some women had, thought Cave, and vowed they would never have it over him.

The race was Sandy's, right from the start. The Morton-Nadir behaved exactly as it had done at practice, and as Keith had the pole position he got out in front and stayed there, heading the procession, thought Cave, as inevitably as the drum major heads the band. First at the chicanes, taking his own line round the bends, easing away so fast in the straight that only Luis in second place was worried, less about catching him than avoiding Bill Speers, who was third.

The laps clicked by like beads across an abacus. It was the race every driver dreams of and few drivers have. Love and marriage and success thought Keith, and he owed it all to Ganesh. He drove into the straight one handed, eased a gloved finger beneath his overalls to pull out the little elephant's chain... It wasn't there. His hand was still off the wheel when the explosion came, a small, thin crack like a revolver shot, but it was enough to send the Morton-Nadir spinning like a dodgem, ramming into the next chicane. And after that came the fire.

Cave saw it all because he was fifty yards away from where it happened. He cursed and leapt the barrier and started running, and Canovan, the F.B.I. man,

76

whose orders were never to let Cave out of his sight, because the F.B.I. never ever trusts British Intelligence, started running too. Cave fought his way through marshals and officials as the crash wagon arrived and then the ambulance, and the Morton-Nadir was doused in foam. Then the F.B.I. man bulldozed his way alongside Cave and flourished a badge, and they were let through. Cave walked up to whatever was left of Sandy Keith. Incredibly he was not only still alive, he was conscious.

'Oh my God', said Cave.

'It was bound to happen', Keith whispered. 'No Ganesh.' Then he fainted.

'No what?' Canovan asked.

'Come on', said Cave, and started running. The F.B.I. man sighed and followed.

The ones Cave sought had a Nadir Cadillac, but Canovan had managed to extract a Corvette Stingray from the F.B.I. On the road back into Vegas they didn't try to overtake – the desert road was no place for a gunfight – but then in Vegas the people in the Cadillac saw that they were followed and kept on going, down the Strip, past the temperature clock that told them it was 4.37 and 91°, then on into Fremont Street, the Cadillac breaking every traffic law and the Stingray ignoring their existence – then the man driving the Caddy made a mistake. Perhaps it was ignorance, perhaps it was panic. Whatever it was he doubled back, turned west on Sahara Boulevard, and kept on going till he reached the sign that said 'Pavement Ends. Road Closed. Travel At Own Risk.'

And the pavement did end. Ahead of them was nothing but a sort of unofficial city dump, acres and acres of it, cars and T.V. sets, sofas and refrigerators, radios and ironing boards, as far as the eye could reach. The consumer society's last stand. The three people in the Caddy got out and ran, and Cave got out and followed as if following them were a reflex. Canovan, the F.B.I. man, sighed once more, and once more joined in the running...

77

Cave killed the first man before he could gain the shelter of the cooking stove he was heading for, killed him almost casually, on the run. He was a man between twenty-eight and thirty-five years of age, brown hair, muscular build, smartly dressed. The sort of posh geezer who might well have bribed three skinheads to rough up a racing driver, then got out of town, but to Cave he was of no importance. He kept on going.

The two in front of him ducked down behind the chassis of an aged Buick and began firing. Canovan dropped down behind an air conditioning unit and opened up with all he'd got, which was considerable. Amongst his car's equipment was a Sterling machine pistol.

But the crazy Englishman just kept on running, then made a flying leap on to the top of a refrigerator, fired down at the two behind the Buick. The F.B.I. man came running for the third time. He was beginning to feel very tired. The man behind the Buick was dead, but the woman lived, was conscious.

'You going to finish her?' Canovan asked.

'She has to tell me things', said Cave.

Canovan sighed a third time and trudged back to the road's end, where what looked like half the Las Vegas police force was waiting to ask him questions.

'She'd been with East German Intelligence since she was seventeen', said Cave. 'They let her marry Jannot because he was a loud mouth who never did anything – except preach the left wing gospel. The perfect cover for a lady who said nothing and did everything. But she married Jannot because she loved him.'

'How do you know this?' Sir Roderick asked.

'She told me', said Cave.

Sir Roderick grunted, but let it lie. 'Firdousi's clean, I take it?' he asked.

'Just another Jannot', said Cave.

'And the leak at Nadir's factory?'

78

'There is no leak. Not any more', said Cave. 'The F.B.I. says thank you kindly.'

Sir Roderick reached for his whisky. It was a relief to find that one could get a decent malt in Las Vegas.

'We thought it might be her', he said, 'ever since the F.B.I. asked us to keep an eye on Nadir. Her connection as P.R. representative was just a little bit obvious. All the same it's a bitter way to find that we were right... Tell me, Joe – why did she pick on Sandy?'

'Because she hated him', said Cave. 'Sandy was a winner – Jannot was a loser. She couldn't stand that. So she asked East German Intelligence if she could destroy him and they must have thought why not? It's cheaper than a bonus, and he'd been a damn nuisance in the past after all. So they set up that little incident in Shepherds' Market and when it failed they tried again in Vegas. They even supplied the little bomb that wrecked his car.'

Cave poured himself a drink, unasked. An unheard of thing, Sir Roderick thought, but I doubt if he even knows he's done it.

'She even said that she'd marry him', said Cave. 'She even stole Ganesh.' He took the little elephant from his pocket.

'For God's sake why?' Sir Roderick asked.

'To make sure she'd destroy him', said Cave. 'Saying she'd marry him made him so happy he got careless. Stealing Ganesh made him lose his luck. And you know what happens when you think your luck's gone... God knows I do.' He gulped his whisky. 'Do me a favour.'

'If I can.'

'You must', said Cave. 'Let me take Ganesh back to him. Tell him we found it in his overalls. Tell him the chain broke.'

'Very well', said Sir Roderick and then: 'What are his chances?'

'The doctors are amazed he's still breathing', said Cave. 'But I'm not. He hasn't won the world championship yet.'

79

In the lethal game of chess which he had once played, Jason Bird thought, Sanchez had been a major piece – a knight perhaps, or a bishop – whereas the distinguished looking feller who had hired the three punks had been no more than a pawn at best. But even so it was the destruction of that pawn and his assistant, together with the immobilisation of Trudi Jannot, that had influenced the decision made at the top, the very top, of the K.G.B.; the decision that it was time to eliminate Joe Cave. It was because he was becoming far too expensive in terms of the lives of those against whom he was matched. Normally the K.G.B. in its present state preferred simply to accept its losses: part of the profit and loss account which every business, no matter how efficient, must endure. But Joe Cave, those at the top thought, was becoming altogether too much of a bad thing, and it was time for him to go. A meeting was set up almost immediately with Department V, the 'wet job' department that handled all the really nasty ones, including the assassinations. Joe Cave's file was marked from that moment: 'Most Urgent'. To begin with, Jason Bird remembered, they began to bug the office of that intern with the literary pretentions...

'He lived because he refused to die.' The intern read the sentence over again, and decided he liked it. It was going to introduce the most dramatic chapter of his memoirs, and an intern in the best and busiest hospital in Las Vegas surely *had* to write his memoirs. They were bound to be a runaway best seller. He already had a title for them: *Leave Them in Stitches*, and now he had high drama, too.

He'd been the first doctor to look at Sandy Keith after his car exploded at the Las Vegas Grand Prix. That had been some sight all right. The woman who had said she loved him, who was herself loved by him, had planted a bomb in his car and done her best to kill him, and a pretty good best it had been. When the

80

intern had got to Keith he was prepared to declare him clinically dead, but after three minutes a heart beat had showed, tentative at first, but almost at once growing stronger, so that all Keith had to recover from were a broken leg, a broken arm, a fractured pelvis, a punctured lung, and first and second degree burns. And shock on a gigantic scale. Refused to die just about summed it up.

The guy had no right to be alive, and yet he was. And he was big news, too. The biggest. On top of everything else his car had been leading when the explosion came; he himself had been about to become world champion... And instead his woman had reduced him to the wreck of humanity the intern had tended: hardly a man at all: more like the bits and pieces from which a man might be assembled.

But his heart had resumed beating, and the assembly had begun. First a lean, dark man had come into the room where Keith lay unconscious, and put a little silver elephant on a silver chain into his hand, and Keith's hand had closed round it tight, and his heartbeat had grown stronger, and how about that for significant detail?

And after the lean, dark man, the specialists came flying in from California and New York and London, and the intern's day was over, but even so he'd got the material for his chapter.

Sometimes he wondered about the lean, dark man, who'd been warned to be quiet, and made no more noise than an empty room. Only once had he looked at the intern, when he'd asked if Keith was a friend of his, and the look had frightened the intern more than anything else he'd ever undergone, and he hadn't pressed for an answer... Then the specialists had arrived and the process of assembly began, and the intern had gone back to traffic accidents and gunshot wounds – much too dull for his book, apart from the really luscious blonde he'd picked up in a bar who had listened to everything he had to say. For a couple of days. Then she had disappeared.

Joe Cave had returned to London when at last the experts had assured him that Keith would not die. He took the news to Sir Roderick Finlay, who had also flown out to Las Vegas for a while, but had been recalled almost at once. There had been an emergency. Sir Roderick's life was one long series of emergencies, and he was glad to see Joe Cave back in London where he belonged.

'How is he?' he asked, and pushed a glass of single malt over to Cave.

'A mess', said Cave. 'All wire and plaster like a piece of modern sculpture.'

'Did you speak to him?'

'The doctors won't let him speak', said Cave. 'It tires him too much. But they let me in the room where he was.'

In his mind's eye he could see it. The aseptic room all white and washed-out blue, and the clinically white bed, Keith's shock of red hair the only visible bright colour. He could hear his own voice stumbling over hackneyed phrases of sorrow and condolence, while Keith's face told him of nothing but pain: pain of the body, pain of the spirit, and then –

'He's incredible', said Cave. 'You know what he did? He winked at me.'

'There aren't many like him, I agree', said Sir Roderick. 'He'll be difficult to replace.'

'He'll be impossible to replace', said Cave.

Sir Roderick finished his whisky and got down to business. He had no time to waste on regrets; there was too much to do.

'There's a chap in Rome on his way to the Gulf', he said. 'He claims to be a Saudi but actually he's Lebanese. Been on that K.G.B. course at Lumumba University as a matter of fact.'

'Like Sanchez?' Cave asked.

'Pretty much', said Roderick. 'He's not as good as Sanchez – I doubt if anybody could be, thank God – but all the same he's good enough.'

'He took the assassination course then?' Cave asked.

'He did indeed', said Sir Roderick.

Cave grew thoughtful. The Ivans ran a very good assassination course indeed at good old Lumumba U.

'Who's this chap going to kill?'

'My information is that it's a couple of our best friends in Saudi Arabia', said Sir Roderick, then added: 'Unless you stop him.'

'How am I going to do that?'

'Any way you can', said Sir Roderick, 'so long as it's final. We really can't allow our best friends to be badgered like this.'

He handed a file to Cave.

'Get on to it at once, will you?' he said. 'Take whatever action you consider appropriate.'

On a street near the Spanish Steps an Arab fell in front of a Volvo bus full of Swedish tourists and was killed outright. If a lean, dark man was near him when he fell nobody remarked on the fact, and in any case Rome is full of lean, dark men... The corpse was found to possess a Saudi passport, but the Saudi ambassador took no action...

At number 2 Dzerzhinski Street, Kalkov, the controller of the dead graduate of Lumumba University, was far from happy. In the first place he had had high hopes of the dead man, but that was the least of it. When the news of the death had been received, Kalkov had at once been appointed chairman of the committee which had been formed to take remedial action against Joe Cave. It was an important position, and on the face of it a gratifying one, but there was one major snag: the penalty for failure would be appalling. Nevertheless it had never occurred to Kalkov to refuse the appointment. The penalty for refusal would have been even worse. But killing Cave would not be easy: it wouldn't be easy at all...

Joe Cave had killed the Lebanese just before midday. That night he dined in Amalfi with a lady advertising copywriter who'd picked him up the night before. She'd been looking forward to it all day, and indeed he proved to be as passionate and macho as even a lady advertising copywriter could wish for. If only, she found herself thinking, his mind hadn't been on something else all the time. And if only he hadn't left next day.

Chapter 9

'A NICE, neat job', Sir Roderick said. The words didn't
come easily: praise was something he rarely gave.

'Thanks', said Cave. 'Any more news of Sandy?'

'Still making progress', Sir Roderick said.

'Still in Vegas?' Sir Roderick nodded.

'I think I'll go and see him.'

'I'd rather you didn't.' The words were bland but
what they meant was no and Cave knew it.

'Why ever not?'

'You've just done a job', said Sir Roderick. 'The place
for you now is somewhere out of sight.'

'Sandy's the one who's news', said Cave. 'Who's
going to bother about me?'

'The hospital is up to its hocks in reporters', said Sir
Roderick. 'Papers, magazines, agencies, T.V., radio.
Don't you see? He was about to be world champion and
he came back from the dead. Everything about him is
news – including his visitors. I'm sorry, Joe.'

Cave thought it over, and it made sense. 'O.K.', he
said. 'Give him my regards when you see him.'

Sir Roderick nodded once more. It would have been
churlish to say he had no intention of visiting his
nephew; churlish, and what was the phrase they used

nowadays? – counter-productive. It would upset Joe Cave, and that would never do.

Kalkov considered what facts he had on Cave. There weren't a lot. He was a very able killer, but then the controller knew that already. He liked women and champagne. Most men did. He changed his address frequently, and it was always a furnished flat in or around London, with space to park a car so that he could leave in a hurry. There couldn't be more than nine or ten thousand places like that in Greater London, Kalkov thought. He read on. A keen amateur photographer, he learned, and fond of taking sauna baths. And that was it. From what he learned from this vast dossier, he was supposed to track down one man among London's millions (always supposing the one man wasn't somewhere else at the time) and have him killed, despite the fact that the man himself was one of the ablest and wariest killers in the Western world.

It couldn't be done, Kalkov thought. But it had to be done. It wasn't just that his chances of promotion depended on it. Maybe even his life depended on it. From the moment he received the appointment, the thought had depressed him, but that day it depressed him even more. He had just been told that people very high up indeed were concerned about this one, including a member of the Central Committee... To fail would be a form of suicide.

And all he had to go on was saunas and furnished lodgings. Kalkov and his agents grew fitter and leaner by the day as they tramped round Earl's Court, Kensington, Chelsea, and soaked up Health Club heat. But Cave remained invisible, and time was moving much too fast.

For Sandy Keith time ceased to exist. It had been supplanted by pain. All day, every day, he lay in his cool clean room and his body punished him because he would not let it die... The specialists came and went, the drips were changed, his body was cleansed, and all the time his thoughts were of the woman who had so nearly killed him... That blonde and lovely widow who had hated him because in motor racing he had been an inevitable winner, and her late husband had been a loser every time. He had loved her so much. Even now he could feel her weight within his arms, smell her hair, her perfume, her skin. It hurt him very much to remember, but he knew no way to stop himself...

One day the specialist from London said, 'You're getting better, Mr Keith.' He sounded surprised.

'Lucky old me', said Keith.

'You're unique. I suppose you know that?' the specialist said. 'People aren't supposed to be able to stay alive by willpower alone.'

Keith's left hand, the one whose fingers were not broken, stroked the little silver elephant called Ganesh. It had kept his father alive during the war, so it had done its job once. Maybe it was still doing it, he thought. After all I *am* still alive. If you can call it living.

'For a man to survive as you have done there has to be a driving force. Something to motivate the will', the specialist said.

'Quite right', said Keith.

'Do you mind telling me what it is?'

'I still haven't been Grand Prix champion', said Keith.

The surgeon looked at him. Keith was perfectly serious.

Kalkov was ordered back to Moscow: a standard Aeroflot flight, no caviar, no special vodka, no V.I.P. status. In Dzerzhinski Street, it was a full general who interviewed him. The K.G.B. must have had as high hopes of that Lebanese as I had, Kalkov thought.

The Lebanese had had friends at Lumumba University and they too were doing the assassination course, but they wouldn't be too keen on taking the Lebanese's place if his killer was still around, still able to kill. And that was reason enough, more than enough.

'This is a very negative report', the general said. 'Too negative.'

'I am sorry, comrade general.'

'Naturally', the general said. 'It is your responsibility. Of course you are sorry. You have one more week.'

Kalkov sighed. It seemed to him that these days he did very little else. 'Without further information it will be useless', he said. 'You may as well arrest me now.'

The general, whose name was Malkovsky, considered it. The member of the Central Committee very much wanted a scapegoat. Using the Lebanese had been his idea. On the other hand there was no one who could do a better job than the man in front of him. 'What do you suggest?' the general asked.

'I have to consult with the computer again.'

'Very well', the general said at once, and Kalkov realised yet again how very important his task was. What he didn't realise was that the member of the Central Committee held the comrade general personally responsible.

The computer told him about Sandy Keith. He and Joe Cave were friends as well as colleagues, the computer said: had been working on a job together in Las Vegas until the moment of the accident. Cave had pursued the woman Trudi Jannot, killed her bodyguard, handed her over to the F.B.I. after he had conducted his own interrogation, but even so the computer thought he would be racked by guilt. Keith was not like Cave. He needed protection, and it was certain that Cave would see himself as having failed his friend Sandy. Under no circumstances would he ever fail him again...

'Do you think it will work?' the general asked.

'I'll need somebody on the inside', said Kalkov. 'Someone who can stay close to this man Keith.'

'We have had word from Las Vegas', the comrade general said. 'There will be further developments quite

88

soon. I think perhaps that it can be arranged, but for God's sake we must be quick.'

His use of the word 'God' didn't surprise Kalkov. Both men were atheists, but both, Kalkov now realised, were in danger of dying.

'We've decided to move you', the bone specialist said.

'Where am I going?'

'Switzerland – if you'd like that.'

Keith didn't shrug: to do so would have hurt his shoulder. 'If you've seen one hospital room you've seen them all', he said.

'We want you to go to a clinic run by Dr Weiss. He's probably the best bone man there is.'

'Then I'll go', said Keith.

Motor racing, Kalkov learned, paid and paid well to those who were successful. Sandy Keith for instance. Not quite a world champion, and therefore not quite a millionaire, but with a place in Sussex, a converted millhouse with a Filipino couple to look after him, and seventeen acres of land, including a paddock full of horses. One of the glossy monthlies had done a piece on the house and its owner, and made it sound like a very nice house indeed. It even had its own sauna...

That made it a long shot, the controller thought, but even so it might be a winner. And if it were it could be done quickly. No need to worry about getting close to Keith ... it really was worth investigating. The house was little more than an hour's drive from London, where there are women and champagne in abundance, it had a sauna for its occupant's exclusive use, and if Cave had moved in, it was furnished accommodation. And Keith would have no objections, might even have insisted on it. Joe Cave could well be there: the computer had told him that Sandy Keith was as fond of Cave as Cave was of him.

89

The killer he sent was a weapons expert and hunter. Bears and wolves in Siberia or a man in a Sussex village, it was all the same to Pavel Mirsky. He was as patient as he was deadly, could wait for hours motionless, scarcely breathing, to be certain of a kill.

The millhouse was one of the least secure places that Mirsky had ever seen. Too many doors, too many windows, and not nearly enough burglar alarms. But there were the Filipinos. One of them was always in the house, it seemed, together with Keith's dog. A labrador, probably with a friendly nature, Mirsky thought, but he would bark if he were disturbed. Mirsky had no sanction to kill a Filipino, or even a dog. His target was Joe Cave, and he watched the house from a hide in a strip of woodland that was part of Sandy Keith's seventeen acres, from dawn till almost noon. And at last he was rewarded.

A lean, dark man came out onto the lawn in front of the house, sprawled in a deckchair, and squinted up at the sun. Mirsky reached into the zip bag on his shoulder and took out a pair of binoculars, looked at the lounging man, and knew it was Cave. So there was work to be done.

His instructions had been precise. Cave was to die, of course, but if possible he was to be killed in a way both nasty and frightening to read about, a wet job way, a way that would rejoice the hearts of the Lebanese's friends in Lumumba University. Pavel Mirsky and Kalkov had spent a lot of time thinking about the way Joe Cave should die, and in the end they had decided on the shotgun, but not the usual kind.

What Mirsky had shipped over in the diplomatic bag was an American 20-gauge pump action shotgun with a sawn-off barrel using specially made shot. If you got close enough, Mirsky knew, it would turn a man into meat, maybe even cut him in two. It would be an appalling way to die, but it would put fresh heart into the assassination students at Lumumba.

The problem was how to get close enough. Mirsky had been allowed one day from dawn to dusk, but Cave

showed no signs of leaving the house. By mid afternoon Mirsky was considering the possibility of a break
in, when Cave solved his problem for him. He came out
of the house and headed for the woodland, and the
labrador slept in the sun.

Mirsky, not being a member of the Party, thanked
God for his good fortune and reached for the zip bag,
drew out the shotgun, and waited. Cave walked
steadily, the conscientious plod of a man who takes
exercise because he must and not because he loves the
countryside. He wasn't doing a job, and he had no
reason to think that an enemy was even remotely
near, and yet, Mirsky noted, he walked carefully,
every sense active as radar. Not an easy one to kill, but
one who had to die. Mirsky moved to the shelter of an
oak tree twice as thick around as he was, and waited,
making no more noise than the oak as Cave drew
nearer. To achieve the effect Kalkov wanted he would
have to be up very close indeed: six or eight feet, no
more. And Cave came on.

It was a rabbit who saved him, and perhaps a fox as
well. The rabbit became aware that it had scented a fox,
and at once made a run for it, hopping across Cave's path,
so that Cave turned to watch it go, and in doing so tripped
on the tree root and fell to his knees at the precise
moment when Mirsky emerged from behind the oak tree
and began blasting with the 20-gauge.

Cave's hands fell into the sandy soil as the pellets
splattered over his head. He rolled away from the
blast, twisted as he rolled, and hurled a handful of soil
into Mirsky's eyes, blinding him, then springing as a
cat springs, left hand smacking on the shotgun's
barrel, right hand ready for a fist strike. But it wasn't
needed. The shotgun roared once more and Mirsky
took the blast of shot full in the face. Cave would never
know what his attacker had looked like. From that
moment Mirsky's face ceased to exist.

Searching the body was a nasty business, but it had
to be done. But even so Cave learned nothing, which
was what he'd expected to learn. The zip bag was

German, the gun American, the binoculars Japanese, but Cave had no doubt at all that the man was Russian. Neither had Sir Roderick. He'd sent men down as soon as Cave had phoned in, experts who had examined the body and then got rid of it. They too were sure it was the body of a Russian: the dental work proved it.

'That job you did for me in Rome', Sir Roderick said. 'It seems you spoiled their fun and they don't like it.'

Cave thought of what the shotgun had done. 'They didn't like it at all – or me', he said. 'But why should it be just that job? I've done dozens.'

'There's a theory that this one came from the top', Sir Roderick said. 'Normally they exact casualties for the same reason that we do – because they must. But you upset one of their big boys. He doesn't care who dies – so long as you die too. I think you'd better take a holiday, Joe.'

Cave thought so too. The sun was still warm in the South of France, where there were women and champagne and sauna baths.

When Kalkov learned that he had failed, and that his hit-man had died, he thought that it was his time to die too, Jason Bird remembered. But it hadn't worked out like that. For once, and briefly, Kalkov's luck was good. The K.G.B. general had smiled – wryly was the only word, when informed of the loss of his hunter – but had made it clear that he expected very little else from one whose equivalent K.G.B. rank was major. Now it was the time to prove what a general could do.

'This is the doctor who'll go with you to Geneva', the specialist said. Sandy Keith looked at Dr Enescu without enthusiasm. She was dark and golden tanned and beautiful, but she was a woman, and women were

a problem. Not that he was going queer. Nothing like
that, he thought. It was simply that he wouldn't trust a
woman with his loose change let alone his life.

'I thought you were coming with me?' he said.

'I have to operate', said the specialist. 'In Kuwait.
It's an emergency – but Dr Enescu is really good.'

'She won't be treating me in the clinic, will she?'
Keith asked.

'Dr Enescu is right here in the room with you', the
woman said. 'Why don't you ask me?'

'I'm not all that good at talking to ladies', said Keith,
and the specialist cursed his own stupidity. He'd been
so preoccupied with the state of Keith's body he'd
forgotten about the damage to his mind.

'As a matter of fact Dr Enescu is going to join Dr
Weiss's team in Geneva for a while', he said, and added
lamely, 'She really is first rate.'

Keith grunted. He couldn't change it, so he must
accept it, but he'd never trust her. She was a woman.

'How will he get to Geneva?' Dr Enescu asked.

'Private jet', said the specialist.

'How grand,' said Dr Enescu.

Keith looked at her. 'Like you I'm in the room', said
Keith. 'Only unlike you I'm paying for it – and just at
the moment I want it to myself.'

The woman flushed and walked out and Keith lay
back and closed his eyes. It would be a hell of a long
time before he would drive a car again.

In Geneva he drove a wheelchair. It was Dr Weiss's
idea and the press loved it. The almost world champion
driving a battery operated chair. Dr Weiss was keen on
the idea because it helped the urge for mobility as well
as the human need to be *doing*, and not completely
dependent on other human beings. But to the press it
was all pathos. Even so, Keith loved the chair, and
didn't find it the least pathetic.

To begin with it was a beautiful piece of work and its
fingertip control precisely what it said: the fingertips

really did control it. There was the equivalent of a four-wheel drive mechanism too. The thing could turn on a ten penny piece. Top speed was maybe fifteen miles an hour, but Dr Weiss didn't approve of top speed. Speeding, he told Keith gravely, was dangerous, and gravely Keith agreed with him.

What Dr Weiss did approve of was wheelchair dancing. In a vast open space in front of the clinic the patients would line up and spin, reverse, pirouette, drive in formation. Keith found it fascinating, and worked at it obsessively. It was power, it was movement, and it was wheels.

Klaus, his physiotherapist, was impressed by a search for excellence he thought that only the Swiss possessed.

'You go well', he said. 'Very elegant.'

'Thanks', said Keith.

'Five more times with the weights please, Mr Keith.'

Keith pushed on the weights, glanced down at his body. The skin grafts had taken but their colour was still hideous. On the other hand his arm and leg had mended, his pelvis was mending. Working in the gym helped. They'd supplied him with a pair of arm crutches, and that helped too.

'You really know how to treat broken bones here', he said.

'This is Switzerland', said Klaus. 'Where there is plenty of ski-ing there are plenty of broken bones. Another five please, Mr. Keith...'

Dr Irena Enescu didn't approve of the wheelchair. As an idea it was well enough, she said, but too much use of it could increase the risk of a spill. Sandy Keith ignored her: he was mobile.

Around the great open space he drove, down the broad avenue lined with statues, which led to the clinic which had once been an exiled prince's villa, in and out among the statues, and never once did he feel at risk. The risk came when somebody tried to kill him him by loosing off a shot after climbing the wall that surrounded the villa, a shot that slammed through the back of his wheelchair, inches from his head, then wiped the simper off a statue of Venus behind him. Without thinking, on reflex, Keith spun the chair behind the base of a statue of Neptune, and as he did so, another shot ricocheted from it. Keith sat tight, and found that his knees were shaking, though his hands were steady...

Once again he made headlines. Dr Weiss wanted to hush it up – attempted murder was very bad news for his clinic – but of course it was impossible. Keith was too famous. Joe Cave read about it next morning in *Le Figaro*.

It meant, he thought, that for once Sir Roderick was wrong. The attempt on Sandy's life as well as on his own showed that it was the consequence of a job they'd done together. Maybe even the one in Las Vegas. He flew to Paris, changed planes and went on to Geneva, because it was unthinkable he should do anything else.

Sandy Keith told him he was glad to see him, waltzed round him in his electric wheelchair and took him to his room, opened champagne. Cave raised his glass, 'Here's to you', he said. 'You're looking good.' He sounded surprised.

Keith thought: he's far too much of a friend to mention the burn marks and grafts, but he knows they're there. All the same if I'm not looking good at least I'm feeling better.

'You don't look so bad yourself', he said aloud.

'I can't think why', said Cave. 'Somebody's trying to kill us both.' He told Keith about the fight in the woodland, then: 'Any idea who'd try to kill you?' he asked.

'Irena Enescu', said Keith.

'Why on earth should she?'

'Because she's a woman.' For the only time, Cave wasn't sure whether Keith was serious or not. It sounded crazy, but after what he'd undergone, maybe Keith was a little crazy from time to time.

Before he left he checked out Keith's room. No bugs,

no booby traps, a view of the lake from a third-floor window with no adjacent drain pipes or fire escapes.

'Stay here for a few days', he said. 'So long as you keep away from the window you'll be fine.'

Keith shook his head. 'I have to use the chair', he said.

'Then stay with the crowd.'

'Is that what you're going to do?'

'I'm safe for once', said Cave. 'Nobody knows I'm here. Everybody knows you're here.'

He went to his hotel and, because it was for Sandy, phoned on F.B.I. man who owed him a favour. The F.B.I. man cursed, because where he was it was three in the morning, but he had his revenge. When he phoned Cave back it was 4 a.m. in Geneva.

Irena Enescu's parents, he said, were Romanian; she herself had been born in Romania. Her parents had left the country as political refugees. As a scientist, Irena's father had found it hard to get out but he'd managed it at last, and worked first in England, then in the United States. He and his wife had been killed in a car crash in Nevada. It had happened quite near Los Alamos, and there'd been an H-bomb test going on at the time. Irena's father's subject had been nuclear physics.

'So you see', the F.B.I. man said, 'we sort of wonder now and then about the Enescus.'

'The daughter too?'

'Nothing we can put a finger on. She takes care of a lot of V.I.P.s though.'

'Like Sandy?'

'Like politicians.'

'Oh', said Cave.

'Like I say', the F.B.I. man said, 'we sort of wonder about her, too.'

As Cave put down the phone it occurred to him that he hadn't got a gun, and because he was in Geneva it would take him quite a while to get one. Of course he could always phone Sir Roderick, he thought, but Sir Roderick would almost certainly order him to leave, and he couldn't: not with Sandy so vulnerable.

The gun he bought was a Smith and Wesson Chief's Special with the two-inch barrel. If it came to the crunch he'd have to get up really close, he thought. If the Ivans stayed back his best chance would be to throw it at them. All the same he paid four hundred dollars for a gun that cost less than two hundred dollars new. But then his need for the piece was desperate: a fact which its vendor had spotted at once.

When he got back to his hotel there was a message for him. Mr Keith had telephoned, the desk clerk said, and wanted to see him as soon as possible. It was most important that he should go to the clinic right away. 'Phone the clinic and tell him I'm on my way', said Cave, and raced to the Peugeot he'd rented and set off for the clinic, driving well within the law. The Swiss Police could be very tiresome about traffic offences, and very time consuming.

The road to the clinic skirted the lake, then left the town to climb vine covered hills. It was a nice road, and a nice ride, until he turned the corner before the villa's drive, and found that a heavy lorry blocked his way, and Cave knew he'd blundered.

He swung the car round broadside on so that he was farthest from the lorry, hurled open the door, left the driving seat in a running dive. A burst of automatic fire from the lorry cut the air above him, then he leapt for the wall of the clinic and swung himself over. From the lorry four men came running in pursuit...

Chapter 10

DR ENESCU looked at the X-rays. 'You really are doing well', she said. Keith grunted. He found it hard to communicate with a woman, even one who brought good news. Then the phone rang, and both man and woman accepted the interruption with relief. Dr Enescu reached for the phone, and handed it to Keith.

'It's for you', she said. Then watched as Keith listened and suddenly the fear showed in his face.

'You're saying I told Mr Cave to come here?' he said. And then: 'When was this? Ten minutes ago?'

He put the phone down and touched the controls of his chair.

'Mr Keith', Dr Enescu said. 'Where are you —'

But already he had reached the door, swung it open and taken off down the corridor. Dr Enescu said a very unfeminine word and set off in pursuit, but Keith had already increased his speed to zoom down the corridor, and into the open space before the villa.

The wheelchair formation dance was in progress, but Keith eased his way through it, like a shuttle among threads, and reached the avenue lined with statues, and all the time his speed built up and Dr Enescu fell farther behind...

98

Joe Cave resigned himself to the fact that his death when it came would be his own fault. He lay behind the boulder at the base of the villa's rock garden, and patiently, cautiously, his hunters stalked him. Soon, he knew, they would flush him out – and when they did he would die, because he had been too anxious about Sandy Keith to check on whether he had sent a message, or whether it had been sent by someone else. By Dr Enescu, for example. A clump of ferns in front of him moved very softly and Cave rested the revolver on the boulder, grasped it two handed and fired, missed, fired again. A man screamed, then rolled over into the daylight, dead.

'And then there were three', thought Cave, and as a blast of automatic fire raked the boulder he pushed himself even closer to the urn.

His cover was good – better than good. They could reach him only by frontal assault – but the Smith and Wesson was a five shot. He only had three rounds left. And so he crouched and waited.

He didn't have to wait long. Suddenly two men came at him, weaving as they ran. The third, he knew, would be racing round to the path that could bring him behind where Cave crouched, and there wasn't a damn thing he could do about it.

Cave fired at the first man in front of him, missed and fired again, and again he missed. With his last shot he hit the man in the shoulder, but he checked, and kept on coming. Cave threw the revolver at him, then rolled over as a blast of fire from the second man raked the place where he had been. He had no cover now, and the only weapon he had left was his own body. It was time to use it.

He swung himself to the boulder's rim then leapt for his enemies, and a bullet pierced his shoulder, another seared his ribs, but even so his right fist came up from the hip bone into the side of the neck of the man he had wounded, knocking him into the path of the second man, making him hesitate, so that Cave had time and to spare to leap over the first man's body and kick for the side of the head. He landed awkwardly, his ribs and shoulder slowing him. Behind him a voice said, 'It really is time for you to die, Mr Cave.'

Cave turned. On the path, well out of reach of his hands and feet, a man stood facing him, a machine pistol in his hand.

And that was finally that, thought Cave, except that out of nowhere Keith came zooming up the path, the wheelchair bucketing like a dinghy in a gale, an arm crutch held like a lance in front of him. The man with the machine pistol wheeled and the arm crutch slammed into his stomach. He made a noise like wet cement thrown from a shovel, and the war was over. Cave walked up to him.

'Anybody we know?' he asked.

'As a matter of fact it's my physiotherapist', said Keith. 'His name is Klaus.'

'More likely Ivan', said Cave.

Dr Enescu came running and Keith, amazingly, smiled at her.

'I hate to bother you', he said, 'but would you mind taking a look at my friend here? He seems to have had a bit of an accident.'

Of course that wasn't the end of it. There was still Sir Roderick Finlay to be faced, and if Sir Roderick was relieved at the survival of his best agent he showed no sign of it. Indeed, Cave thought, he was hostile from the start, from the very first words he uttered.

'Grossly irresponsible', he said. Cave tried justification. 'Sandy's my friend', he said, 'and anyway we owe him some protection.'

'Don't be more of a fool than God made you', Sir Roderick said. 'Sandy was the decoy. You were the one they wanted. I told you.'

'I see', said Cave. 'So I'm still on their list.'

'You are', Sir Roderick said. 'Would you like to retire?'

'There's nothing I would like better', said Cave. 'But

100

the Ivans won't let me, any more than you will.'

Sir Roderick tried not to look relieved, and Cave returned to the subject of his friend. 'Even if you're right we ought to have someone look after Sandy', said Cave.

'I'm always right', said Sir Roderick. 'I keep telling you. And somebody *is* looking after Sandy. Dr Enescu.'

'She's one of *ours*?' said Cave.

'Like her father before her', Sir Roderick said.

'But he spied on the Yanks', said Cave.

'And they spied on us. It's all in the family. How's she getting on with Sandy?'

'I think she's solving his woman problem', said Cave. 'The last time I saw him he was designing a two-seater wheelchair so that he could take her for a run.'

Dr Enescu had been allowed to live, Jason Bird remembered. In the first place she was not on the target list, and in the second place she operated against the F.B.I. rather than the K.G.B., and in doing so proved a distraction, which enabled the K.G.B. to get on with the job of spying on Nadir. And in any case, Joe Cave was the target, and would remain so until the man from the Central Committee got over his grudge, and the man from the Central Committee was not exactly famous for getting over grudges; in fact, Jason Bird remembered, he'd never given up on a grudge in his life. And in this case, he actually extended the grudge so that it included Sandy Keith as well. By that time, both he and Cave were on the list, and Kalkov was ordered to resume operations.

It wasn't easy, but then Kalkov had never expected it would be. Both Cave and Keith had disappeared, and disappeared separately, which made them doubly hard to trace. Keith by this time was able to walk, and in a sense, a source of pride for those doctors who had, in the intern's words, put him together again, unlike Humpty Dumpty, Jason Bird thought. He had by then become rather a connoisseur of Western nursery rhymes.

101

The doctors who had done the reassembling however had overlooked one thing, a thing which even the bone man had thought of only fleetingly and then ignored. Whilst Sandy Keith was able to walk again, his mind was still not what it had been before the accident. True, Irene Enescu had helped him to readjust once more to the world of the living, but there had been another nightmare lurking in the wings, one that waited only until Keith was well enough before it struck in its turn. Whilst his body had been no more than one agonising pain, his mind had had no room for remembrance, and even his nightmares had consisted only of present agony. But now the pain in his body had dulled, and the thought of fire came roaring back.

Kalkov, at considerable expense, had gained access to Keith's medical files, and noted that the fire had broken out at last. It neither pleased him nor disgusted him: it was simply a fact. It might well be a fact that could be of service.

Joe Cave flew to Cork airport in a Lear jet, the passenger seats like very comfortable thrones, the hostess's service impeccable – as indeed it should have been, thought Cave. He was the only passenger... Cork had the haphazard quality of all Irish airports, which can be either endearing or infuriating, depending on whether or not you're in a hurry – but the Customs officers weren't in the least haphazard. Not that Cave worried: for once in his life he was clean. No gun: not even a knife. But then why should he be carrying a knife? This was one of the rare days when he wasn't working: was in fact as harmless as he was ever likely to be... A spot of leave.

That was what Sir Roderick Finlay had called it when Cave had gone to see him and told him that a friend of his had been in a car crash and needed his company for a while, and Sir Roderick had huffed a bit and puffed a bit and told him he could have a spot of leave, length of the spot unspecified. Which meant that he could be recalled at any time.

In Cork City Cave rented a Ford Granada and set off driving west down the narrow, wandering Irish roads, past bogs and pasture and potatoes, and sudden unexpected fields of wheat. He'd never really expected to get leave, even though his friend was Sandy Keith.

They'd rather lost touch, Cave thought, after what Sandy had called the Battle of Wheelchair Gulch, but now and again, he'd received a postcard, with a picture of Gstaad, or Venice, or Bermuda on the front, and on the back a message saying that he was still healing. Indeed the final one had told him that even the burns had begun to heal enough for him to be finished with doctors and that all the bones had knitted. That had been a couple of months ago, and then suddenly, three days past, the telegram had come: 'Am on Sheep Island. Come to Port Magee and ask for Michael Walsh. Please come Joe. It is important. Regards Sandy.'

So Cave had gone. It was why he was easing the Granada along roads even more haphazard than the airport, past sheep and donkeys and elderly Fords and VWs that looked like survivors.

He spent the night at Kenmare, and dined off mutton chops, cabbage and potatoes and stout, and thought about the obligations of friendship, and the sacrifices that it entailed. He thought about it even more once he had stretched out on the bed in his hotel room... Sandy still had good friends, he thought. The Lear jet for instance had been supplied by Iskandar Nadir, for Nadir too had never shirked the obligations of friendship. True, for him to lend a Lear jet was no more than a lift in a Mini to the rest of us, but it had been done at once, and without complaint, and Nadir had used a scheduled airline instead. Sandy really did have good friends, Cave thought, and he deserved them.

Port Magee was so small he nearly missed it, but he braked just in time, parked by the church, and walked back to the solid, heavy-set, whitewashed building,

part grocer's and part pub, that was the only information service the place possessed. Cave enquired for
Michael Walsh, and found he was the drinker next to
him, and asked to be taken over to Sheep Island.
Walsh took his time thinking about it.

'I wouldn't recommend you going there', he said.
'That's no place for tourists, sir.'

'I'm not a tourist', said Cave. 'I'm a friend of a man
called Keith. He's living on the island. He asked me to
visit him.'

'Is that a fact?' said Walsh.

'Yes', said Cave. 'It is.'

Walsh looked at him. What he saw was a man, lean,
hard and as dangerous as a whip, a man rapidly
running out of patience. He finished his stout.

'I'd better take you there then', he said. 'The cost of
the trip is five pounds.' He paused a moment, then
added: 'English.'

Cave paid in advance and they went to where
Walsh's boat was moored, a beamy, half decked
twenty-footer with a noisy diesel that persistently
smelt of fish, and set off into the Atlantic. It was grey
that day, with no white horses and a heavy swell.
Walsh waited hopefully for Cave to be sick, but Cave
refused to oblige him. It took a lot of willpower,
especially when the smell of diesel fumes allied itself
to the smell of fish.

Sheep Island was about four miles by two, and there
wasn't a sheep on it. Indeed there didn't seem to be a
damned thing on it, thought Cave, apart from about
half a million seabirds, until the rhythmic thumping of
the diesel reached the one house Cave could see;
another squat and white-washed structure built to
withstand the winter gales, and its door opened, and a
man came out, walked down to the miniature beach.

It had to be Sandy, Cave knew that – and the
suggestion of a limp in the left leg confirmed it – but it
didn't look like Sandy: it looked like his elder brother

104

who'd held a clerk's job for twenty years and never once taken exercise, thought Cave.

For Sandy Keith was running to fat, his red hair was matted and un-washed, and he was quite obviously drunk. Cave looked at him, appalled.

Beside him Walsh said, 'You did say you were a friend of his?'

'I am', said Cave.

'I don't know whether it's a friend's business or not, but maybe you'd best give him this.' Walsh nodded towards a carton labelled 'Baked Beans'.

'It's paid for – and he needs it. Just run up the flag when you want to be taken off.'

Cave jumped down onto the sands and Walsh handed down his suitcase and the carton, and then eased off out to sea as Sandy Keith lurched up.

'Joe', he said. 'It's good to see you. Come and have a drink.' He looked out at Walsh's boat. 'Why did Michael clear off so quick?'

'Maybe he wants to go fishing', said Cave. 'How are you?'

'Can't you see how I am?' said Keith, and bent to pick up the carton. 'Let's go and have a drink.'

They squelched across the turf to the cottage, that was not yet quite a ruin because the walls and roof still stood. But the inside was a slum of unwashed dishes and unswept floor, cooked food rotting in cans. Cave thought of the Lear jet, the Las Vegas hotel Keith had stayed in before the car had crashed. He put down his suitcase on the cleanest piece of floor he could find and wondered what his bedroom would be like, while Keith lurched about looking for glasses, then opened the carton, took out bottle after bottle of colourless fluid.

'Poteen', he said. 'A whole gallon of it. I've got some good friends, Joe.'

He pulled a cork and poured, and pushed a glass over to Cave.

'Cheers', he said, and swallowed.

It might have been lemonade, thought Cave. It's the same colour. But he didn't let that fool him, and sipped

105

as primly as a spinster at a sherry party. The stuff seared its way down.

'What the hell are you doing here?' said Cave.

'It's quiet', said Keith.

Cave looked out of the window: nothing but ocean. To the left the first landfall was Port Magee, to the right it was New England.

'I wanted a quiet place, a place to think', said Keith. 'A pal of mine – Lord Munster – he owns this island. The last shepherd left years ago, and took the sheep with him. It's just what I want. Quiet... I can think', he said again, and again poured whisky.

Better talk now before he falls over, Cave thought. 'What about?' he asked.

'Mm?' said Keith.

'What do you think about?'

'Sometimes I think about how rich I am – richer than ever since I wrote my memoirs. I liked that.'

'I thought a ghost wrote it for you', said Cave.

'That's why I liked it. All I did was correct the spelling.' He drank again. 'Sometimes I think about the accident. Not the bones... I didn't mind the bones. Honestly. They broke and they mended. It's the burning I think about these days. Burning is awful, Joe. It hurts like hell – quite literally. Hell *is* burning. And it gives you nightmares so badly it's better not to sleep. And it's ugly as well.' And suddenly he pulled up his sweater and showed. 'See Joe?' he said.

The skin of his torso was criss-cross welted with skin grafts, and every colour from dead white to grape-like purple.

'I used to be quite pretty once', said Keith. 'Quite a lot of girls have said so. But now –' He pulled down his sweater and shirt, and tucked his shirt in, not very effectively. 'That's the reason I came here', he said. 'No cars. If there aren't any cars you can't have shunts and you can't get burnt. It's nice here, Joe.' He lifted his glass.

'I don't think much of your new hobby', said Cave.

'I didn't think you would.' Keith put down his glass.

106

'I don't expect you to sympathise, Joe – but I do have a good excuse... I'm scared. Of course I've always been scared, ever since I took up driving – only a lunatic wouldn't be if he did what I used to do – but now I'm scared of the fire, and that's different. Believe me. Like Everest is different from Snowdon.'

I can't answer him, thought Cave. I've never been burned. Not like Sandy.

'What do you want me to do?' he asked.

'Help me.'

'Well of course', said Cave. 'But how?'

'Another thing scares me', said Keith. 'And that's going on the way I am now. Look at me, Joe. What am I?'

He had to be told.

'You're an alcoholic', said Cave. 'Or you will be if you don't knock off the booze.'

'That's right', said Keith. 'That absolutely right. But I need the booze to help me over the nightmares – so what did I do, Joe... I looked in the mirror when I was sober and had a hangover and I said to myself – you need your head examined.' He paused. At last Cave said, 'That's it?'

'Certainly that's it', said Keith. 'I need a shrink who can cure me of being afraid of fire – because believe it or not, Joe, I still want to be world champion – if only I wasn't scared. So I need a shrink called Joel Berman. Uncle Roderick says he's the best there is, except he's retired he's so rich, and gone to live in St Tropez. Only he'll see me because he's mad about motor racing, and if God loves me I'll be cured.'

A bit rambling, thought Cave. But still coherent. It won't last much longer.

'Fine', he said aloud. 'Great. But what do you need me for?'

'You don't listen', said Keith. 'Nobody listens any more... I said he's in St Tropez, Joe. How can I get to St Tropez when I'm afraid of fire? How can there be any kind of engine without the risk of fire?'

'But in that clinic in Switzerland', said Cave, 'when

107

they treated you – when you saved my life – you drove around in a car then.'

'In an electrified wheelchair', said Keith. 'Batteries, Joe . . . not petrol. It's petrol that scares me. Fossil fuel. It burns. . . Get me to St Tropez, Joe.'

'O.K.', said Cave, and Keith sighed and smiled and passed out cold. Cave carried him to his bed, then set about cleaning up the cottage.

Chapter 11

NEXT MORNING Cave ran up the flag. It was Sandy's own personal flag, and he'd flown it in the pits of racing circuits, from the masts of hired yachts, on the flag pole at his house in Sussex: his own personal snook cocked at the world. A silver elephant on a field of green; Ganesh, Sandy Keith's own personal lucky charm. He hoped that this time it was a good omen, too.

Getting Keith to St Tropez, thought Cave, was like trying to herd a rhinoceros into a pigpen. Mercifully there was never any shortage of booze. On Michael Walsh's boat it was poteen, and in the pubs on the way to Cork airport it was porter. On Nadir's private jet it was liqueur brandy, but they all achieved the same result. Used in sufficient quantity they kept Sandy Keith either numb or unconscious.

They put down at London Airport, which surprised Cave, and bothered him too. The Lear was perfectly capable of flying direct to Nice, and in fact he'd instructed the pilot that they should do so. Putting down at London was definitely not in the script, and yet, when he demanded an explanation, all that the pilot would say was that they must go to the V.I.P.

lounge, where the gentleman would explain. He seemed neither to know nor care who the gentleman was. But somehow, Cave got the idea that whoever it was, the pilot was afraid of him.

By that time Keith was a stretcher case, and it was the hostess who thought of having him put on a stretcher, then wheeled into the V.I.P. lounge. It was in fact the only way of getting Keith there, and Cave became the hostess's slave for life.

But on the way to the V.I.P. lounge the hostess was called away, and a large and muscular man took her place, a man Cave recognised at once: one of Sir Roderick Finlay's bodyguard, the group who were known as the Goon Squad. They went not to the V.I.P. lounge but to a room that only just admitted the stretcher, and Sir Roderick was already there, spry still, still with the hint of swagger he'd acquired in the Scottish regiment he'd risen to command in World War Two.

'Thank you, Martin', he said, and the heavy left. Sir Roderick went to the stretcher and looked down at his nephew, who slept as a baby sleeps, silent and vulnerable.

Sir Roderick took a silver flask from his pocket, unscrewed a couple of silver cups. 'A little malt?'

Cave looked at Keith.

'If you don't mind, sir', he said.

'Ah yes', Sir Roderick said. 'Quite so.' For the first time since Cave had known him he put away whisky untasted.

'Taking him to St Tropez?' he asked.

'You knew about this trip?' asked Cave.

'Certainly I knew about it', Sir Roderick said. 'Sandy's my nephew. I advised him to go.'

'He served you well enough in the past', said Cave.

'He served his country', said Sir Roderick.

Cave said, 'And is he serving his country now?'

'How can he?' said Sir Roderick. 'Look at the state he's in. No, Joe. You'll be the one who's serving his country. Sandy's just your excuse for being there.'

110

'I might have known it', said Cave.

'Of course you might', said Sir Roderick. 'Didn't I warn you we were busy?. . . I want you to look out for a man called Zaleski. He's a Pole. But he's just joined his niece – she's French. They're in St Tropez. Got a place in the rue Daudet. Zaleski's one of Lech Walesa's friends, and a nice man. That makes him a refugee. He was a very high ranking mathematician in Warsaw – experimental stuff – rockets mostly – and we think he got out of Poland with some rather choice bits and pieces. Very choice, in fact. He's worked in Russia and East Germany as well as Poland. I want those bits and pieces, Joe.'

'Just like that', said Cave.

'It's never just like that', said Sir Roderick, unperturbed. 'The Russians want their bits and pieces back too, and they sent a team to fetch them.'

'Why doesn't Zaleski just bring the stuff to us himself?' said Cave. 'Or the Yanks? Or the French?'

'I told you he's a nice man', said Sir Roderick. 'He offered them to the highest bidder – the money to go to Polish refugees. We'd never be the highest bidder – not with the Yanks bidding against us. And the Russians wouldn't dream of parting with foreign currency just to buy back what's theirs. Get it for me, Joe. There's a good fellow. Only – you will remember that you're on the K.G.B.'s list, won't you?'

From behind them there came a moan, and the two of them went over to the stretcher. The effects of the brandy were beginning to wear off and Keith was once again in the grip of nightmare. The sounds he made were heart rending.

'And what about him?' said Cave. 'Do I just leave him on his own in St Tropez while I rob a kindly Pole?'

'You will take care of him, of course', Sir Roderick said. 'But you won't let it interfere with the execution of your duty.'

It's no use, thought Cave. It never is. Not against him. Especially when he talks like that. I can't win. Nobody can.

111

Aloud he said: 'Let me have your flask, will you?'

It was time to wake up his friend and offer him a drink.

They flew to Nice airport, and once again the stewardess went for a stretcher, once again they decanted Keith. As they wheeled him towards Customs she said: 'We've flown with him before, you know. Mr Nadir often had him aboard before he had his accident. He was good, wasn't he?'

'He was the best', said Cave.

The hostess touched Sandy Keith's cheek. 'He was a very nice man', she said.

The hotel they stayed in was also the best because Sandy Keith was the sort of millionaire who, drunk or sober, prefers the best... It took two hall porters and Cave to get him up to their suite but all the same they did it: the suite cost five thousand francs a day.

Cave settled Keith on his bed then went to his own room. There was a basket of fruit with a welcoming note from the management by his bed-side, and a package from a men's boutique that Sir Roderick had warned him about. Inside the package was a sealed box, and inside the box were a bug with a mini-recorder, a file on Wladek Zaleski, and a Smith and Wesson magnum, twenty rounds of ammunition, and a silencer good for six rounds at least. The complete spy outfit...

Cave stretched out on the bed and studied the photograph, read the words again and again, until every detail stuck in his mind. Born Cracow, 1920, Warsaw University, the Sorbonne, where he stood out even among the super-stars there, despite the fact that he was dyslexic. Did it hurt? Cave wondered, or was it a religion?... Then came the war and the partisans, then the Russians and rockets. Cave took matches from an ash-tray and burned the file page by page, and flushed the remains down the toilet. It was time to force Sandy Keith to eat something, then get dressed

112

in a webbing holster and a 357 magnum and some clothes and suss out a kindly Pole.

Two birds with one stone. That was what the Americans always said, when faced with such a situation, Jason Bird thought. And a very ironic situation it was. Not the recovery of defector Zaleski – that was pure routine, and any adequate wet job squad could have handled it. The irony lay in the fact that Joe Cave was involved. It had taken many many roubles to secure the information that yielded that one fact. And once again it had all been thanks to Sandy Keith, now a drunkard, but still invaluable to the K.G.B. It did, however, necessitate a certain revision of plans. No ordinary, adequate wet job squad would be capable of handling this one. For this one they had to send the best there were. Jason Bird remembered Kalkov's agonising choice of heavies to send on this particular task. It had not been easy. Already Department V had suffered too many casualties in its attempt to rid itself of Cave. The general who haunted Kalkov's nightmares had already begun to talk of how boring the story of the Ten Little Niggers was. Not, Jason Bird remembered, that the Americans – or the British either, come to that – would allow such a phrase in this day and age. Ten Little Indians had long since been substituted. The substitution puzzled Jason Bird. Why was it that niggers were considered prejudicial and Indians were not? But the thought was an irrelevance.

He turned his attention back to the television set, where the race was very shortly about to start. The cameras roamed around the pits, and Sandy Keith was clearly visible, alert, clear eyed, red hair flaming. He didn't look like a drunkard at all. It was all a long way away, both in space and time, from St Tropez.

The rue Daudet had no five star hotels, no chic discos. It was a place where the people of St Tropez lived, and went to bed early, so that they could wake up in time to prepare breakfast for rich visitors. But the night he went there it didn't lack for entertainment, thought Cave. Three large and determined men were assaulting a pretty young woman and a white-haired man. The white-haired man was doing his best to cling on to a briefcase, the young woman was doing her best to defend him... And a very good best it was, thought Cave. She'd been to the right martial art classes. Then one of the three clipped the white-haired man with a hard right to the jaw and he staggered into a lamp post and fell to the ground, still clutching his briefcase. The lamplight showed Cave the face of Wladek Zaleski. It seemed it was time to get involved.

The first man was easy. Move up behind him out of the shadows, interlace the fingers, strike with the edge of both hands at the nape of the neck. The first man dropped as if he'd been pulled with ropes.

The second man wasn't so easy. In the first place he knew that Cave was there, and in the second place he was good, maybe better than good. He threw a fist strike, and Cave read it only just in time and leaped away, drew the magnum as he did so. It wasn't a competition after all... The magnum burped – there was no other word to describe it, and the second man went down to the ground and stayed there.

Cave turned then to the girl. She was doing all right, he noticed, but even in this quiet street which seemed to set so high a premium on privacy and non-violent intervention, someone might call the police eventually. He took the magnum by the barrel, swung the butt, and the third man fell.

The girl said in French: 'I could have handled him.'

Cave spoke French, too. Carefully, seeking the words, he said: 'Of course you could. I just thought I would hurry things along, that's all.'

Her hair looked rumpled, but that was the fashion that year. Otherwise there wasn't a mark on her.

She said in English: 'You were right, of course. Thank you.'

114

'What made you think I was English?' Cave asked.

'Only the English speak French in quite that way', she said. Cave gathered that she was being tactful. She held out her hand. 'Simone Vernier', she said.

Cave held out his own. 'Joe Cave', he said.

She looked at Zaleski by the lamp post. He was still dazed, still clutched his briefcase. The girl went to him, her body between him and Cave.

'We'll have to move him', said Cave, but first he went to the three attackers, went through their pockets. Nothing except money, lighters and cigarettes, and an assortment of weapons – except that number three had a book of matches marked Hotel La Grange.

'How are they?' the girl asked.

'Yours is O.K.', said Cave. 'Except he'll be unconscious for a while. One of mine is dead.'

Because of Sandy, he thought. Because of what Sir Roderick told me to do. I lost my temper. The bloke was a mugger at best. More likely – far more likely – the K.G.B. But all the same I lost my temper. Killing him wasn't in the script.

'We'd better get out of here', he said.

Somehow they got Zaleski to a café that was far enough from the rue Daudet, and Cave ordered cognac, told the girl to tip off the police. She didn't like the idea of leaving Cave alone with Zaleski, but someone had to do it, and it couldn't be Cave and she knew it: not with the French he spoke.

So she went, and Cave watched her go. A pretty girl, he thought. Shining dark hair, eyes brown and brooding, pert nose, generous mouth, the chin small, but very determined. Nice body, too, nice way of moving – and she could chuck a twelve-stone man clear across the pavement... Not only that, but she reminded Cave of someone. Unfortunately he couldn't remember who.

He turned to Zaleski. The Pole was still dazed, and worried, now that the girl had left. As Cave watched, he opened the briefcase and flicked through the papers inside it, counting anxiously. Among the papers was a book, Cave noticed, written in English:

115

Alice's Adventures in Wonderland. Zaleski went on counting and checking till the girl came back and spoke to him in French far too fast for Cave to follow, then shovelled the stuff back into his briefcase while the waiter brought the brandy.

'You must be wondering what all this is about', she said at last.

'It is a bit puzzling', said Cave.

She flushed. 'I agree', she said. 'It was a banal remark, but any remark would be banal after what has happened.'

Cave waited.

'This gentleman', she touched Zaleski's hand, 'is a friend of my father's. We were taking a little walk together when those men attacked us and you helped us so splendidly.'

'No', said Cave.

She flushed again, darker than before. 'What do you mean – No?'

'Those three goons were carrying more than twenty thousand francs between them. Why would they rob you?'

'They wanted more. Obviously', said Simone Vernier.

'And for what you've got they risked the police and arrest and prison – and a damned good hiding, once they saw you in action? They didn't want money, Miss Vernier. They wanted that.'

He nodded at Zaleski's briefcase and the Pole's hands tightened around it.

'Who are you?' the girl asked.

'All in good time', said Cave.

'My name is Wladek Zaleski', said the Pole, 'and I resent the fact that you speak of me as if I were not here... I also thank you for coming to our assistance.'

'It was a pleasure', said Cave, 'and as long as you join in the conversation we'll all know you're here... Now. What have you got in that briefcase that's so special?'

'Simone is right', Zaleski said. 'First you must tell us who you are.'

'It's obvious', said Simone. 'He's a detective.'

'Nothing so common', said Cave. 'I'm Sandy Keith's minder.'

Zaleski looked bewildered, but the girl didn't. 'Sandy Keith the racing driver?'

'That's right.'

'Then what are you doing in St Tropez?'

'Sandy's here', said Cave. 'At the Provence.'

'But you are in the rue Daudet', said Simone.

'If it's any of your business', said Cave, 'I had a date there. I doubt if she's waited. Especially since we called the Old Bill.'

'Old Bill?' said Zaleski. 'You have called someone? Telephoned?'

'The Old Bill's the police', said Cave. 'Simone here called them.'

Zaleski relaxed, and Cave turned to the girl.

'Tell me another story', he said. 'I didn't like the first one much.'

The girl shrugged. It was a very pretty, very French shrug. 'This man is my uncle', she said. 'I am French, but Uncle Wladek is Polish. You have heard of him?'

'Should I have done?' asked Cave.

'He is one of the greatest mathematicians in the world', she said. 'He is also a great supporter of Solidarity. Lech Walesa is his friend. It is only because he has also many friends in the West that he was allowed to leave Poland.'

'If he was allowed to leave', said Cave, 'why was he attacked?'

'I don't know', said Simone. 'Maybe there has been a change of policy.'

Cave gave her ten out of ten for that. Liars rarely say they don't know. Not that she had really lied, not yet. Merely told a small fraction of the truth. There was a stir of breeze from the sea, and the girl shivered.

Zaleski said, 'I'm still here – and I know very well why I was attacked.' He tapped the briefcase. 'In here I have some most important papers.'

'Uncle Wladek', the girl began, but he continued, unheeding.

117

'A life's work', he said. 'All that I have ever achieved on Einstein's General Theory of Relativity. With this I shall get an appointment at a university.'

'Nobody would attack you for that', said Cave.

'They would if they thought it was something else', Zaleski said.

'Like what?'

'The work I did for the Russians', Zaleski said.

Cave kept his gaze on the Pole. Simone Vernier's face was showing first delight and then dismay, and perhaps his was too, no matter how much he ordered it not to. 'What work was that?' he asked.

'Work on rockets', Zaleski said. 'Fuels, trajectories, electronics systems. Every aspect of rocketry needs a mathematician, Mr Cave, and I was the mathematician they needed.'

'Then why didn't you bring the stuff out with you?' Cave asked.

'Are you crazy?' Zaleski said. 'Do you think they would let me?'

Chapter 12

'AND THEN what happened?' Sir Roderick asked. The pips sounded, and Cave put more coins into the public telephone, the kind you can't bug unless you bug them all.

'He showed me the stuff', said Cave. 'It made no sense to me at all.'

'What about his niece?'

'She looked at it too', said Cave. 'It made her miserable.'

'Blast!' Sir Roderick said. It was the closest he ever came to swearing. 'Anything else?'

'I went to the Hotel La Grange', said Cave. 'Three geezers checked in two nights ago. Dupont, Duclos and Durand.'

'Smith, Brown and Robinson', said Sir Roderick.

'Yeah... Well... They were damned good men whatever their names were', said Cave. 'Except Dupont's dead and the other two have headaches. They claim they were mugged.'

'Then why weren't they robbed?' Sir Roderick said.

'They were robbed', said Cave. 'Twenty thousand francs' worth.'

'Good man', said Sir Roderick. 'That's marvellous.

Overheads are terrible just now. Twenty thousand
francs – that's about two thousand quid.'

'The desk clerk copped a fair bit', said Cave. 'Mind
you he earned it. He says another geezer registered at
the same time as the three stooges. Bloke called
Favières. One of the waiters heard him bawling out
Duclos and his mates – only it wasn't in French... He
thinks it was Russian.' He waited, but for once Sir
Roderick had nothing to say.

'I need instructions', Cave said at last.

'Stay where you are', said Sir Roderick. 'And do as
Mr Asquith did – wait and see. And take good care,
Joe. Take very good care.'

'You think those Ivans are on to me?' Cave asked.

'It's possible', Sir Roderick said. 'You said yourself
that they were good men.'

Cave sensed that he was about to hang up, and cut in
quickly.

'What about Sandy?' he asked.

'Let him see his psychiatrist.'

'We phoned him', said Cave. 'But there's no answer.'

'There will be', Sir Roderick said. 'Patience, Joe.'
This time he did hang up...

Cave went back to the hotel. Sandy Keith had looked
awful, but at least he looked awful in the kind of
clothes appropriate to St Tropez, instead of cord jeans
and an Aran sweater. Money, thought Cave. Just pick
up the phone and the boutique owners all come
running.

'How do you feel?' he asked.

'Ghastly', said Keith. 'What do you expect?'

'You try Berman again?'

'Every hour', said Keith. 'Still no answer.'

'What are you going to do then?'

'Drink', said Keith. 'Unless you're going to stop me.'

'Only you can do that', said Cave.

The night before, Simone and Uncle Wladek moved
from the rue Daudet, but that was O.K., he'd helped

120

them move, then he'd gone back to rent the room next door, and plant the bug he'd received on the dividing wall. The trouble was they spoke French far too fast – when they didn't speak Polish. So far as Cave could gather Simone kept asking her Uncle Wladek whether he was sure he had no rocket secrets, and Uncle Wladek kept saying he was absolutely certain. When at one point it seemed that he went to the toilet, Cave suspected that she searched the briefcase, and then he guessed that she was absolutely certain too. At least she stopped asking Uncle Wladek if *he* was certain.

But they didn't know about the Hotel La Grange, Cave thought. They didn't know about a man called Favières. How could they? He hadn't shown them the book matches. And Favières and two goons with headaches would be out combing St Tropez, looking for a Polish mathematician and his ever-loving niece.

'You're working, aren't you?' said Sandy Keith.

'You call looking after you work?'

'I didn't mean that and you know it', said Keith. 'You're working for Uncle Roderick.'

Cave said nothing. Sandy knew him too well for him to waste time in denial.

'I don't mind exactly', said Keith, and poured a drink. His third. It was ten minutes after noon. 'I just thought you were a pal of mine.'

'I'm the best pal you've got when your uncle allows me to be', said Cave.

'Yes. I suppose you are', said Keith. 'It's a pretty ghastly thought, isn't it?'

Then he banged down his glass.

'I want you to forget I said that. Please', he said.

'All right', said Cave.

'I'm still scared, you see', said Keith. 'And I still can't reach that bastard Berman – so take it out on my friend.' Cave said nothing, and Keith reached out his hand.

'Please Joe', he said. 'I mean it.'

'I know you do', said Cave. 'But I have to go to work for your uncle.'

'To hell with you both', said Keith.

'I thought we'd got there', said Cave, and then: 'You're an educated man they tell me.'

Keith drank. 'Look where it got me', he said.

'What does dyslexic mean?' asked Cave.

The place to hide from Favières and his goons was obvious, once you thought of it. The Plage de Tahiti. About two thirds of St Tropez went to the Plage de Tahiti during the hours of daylight. Row upon row the bodies lay, brown and oiled, like basted chickens under the grill. Body after body, so far as the eye could reach...

Uncle Wladek wore a hip length beach coat to hide his whiteness, and sat on his briefcase while he did sums on a notepad. Cave too wore a beach coat with pockets big enough to hold the Smith and Wesson 357 magnum. Simone wore a white bikini that Uncle Wladek disapproved of: her body was as elegant as her karate, but Keith wasn't interested. He wore shorts and a shirt to cover the burns, and a forty-ounce bottle of Scotch. He'd insisted on the Scotch: otherwise he wouldn't have come, and Cave refused to leave him on his own, even when he was working.

Simone rolled over to Cave, handed him her bottle of sun-tan oil.

'Rub my back, please', she said, and Cave obliged. It was a splendid back to rub.

'Mm', she said. 'Nice.' And then: 'Why are you still helping us?'

'I fancy you', said Cave.

She looked at Keith, sprawled in the sand, an arm round his bottle.

'Your boss doesn't fancy me', she said.

Cave was silent. His hands grew still.

'We can't stay here for ever, you know', said Simone and slid down the straps of her bikini top. 'Now my shoulders.'

All around him women were going about topless, and mostly they were women who should not have been going about topless. Simone's sliding down her shoulder straps was an infinitely more sexy move than that.

Cave rubbed her shoulders, smooth, scented, rounded. 'If we can't stay here we'll have to run for it', he said.

'Soon', she said. 'I hope very soon.'

So you haven't given up on the rocket information, thought Cave. But why try here? Why not take him off to Paris?

'Just give me the word and I'll do what I can', he said aloud. She looked over her shoulder to smile at him.

'I wish I could kiss you', she said.

Cave wished it too.

They were blown next day. Keith was asleep, and his shirt became undone as he turned. For the first time Simone saw the marks that the fire had made: sickly yellow, bruised red, livid white.

'Dear God', she said. 'Is that why –?'

'That's why', said Cave, and before he could stop her she reached out to fasten his shirt, and touched the grafted skin. It was the one thing guaranteed to reach through all the booze that Keith had consumed, and at once he began to scream and the whole beach knew it. Cave had to shake him awake, then cuddle him like a child. It was time to go.

But Favières too had heard the screams, and he and his goons came after them. For once it seemed they were in luck. They had put off the Plage de Tahiti until the last, appalled by the vastness of it, but that day they had arrived, determined to examine it all, glistening body by glistening body. And after only a couple of hours, the screams summoned them to their goal. They saw Keith and Cave at once, and Zaleski a moment or two later, and at once they broke into a run. What saved Cave and the others was the bodies. It is impossible to run fast down the Plage de Tahiti in the

season; there are too many people in the way. The
K.G.B. men stumbled and hopped over fat bodies, thin
bodies, ugly bodies, lovely bodies, while Cave hustled
Keith, Simone hustled Uncle Wladek, to where they'd
parked their car.

To reach it they took a short cut across land
awaiting development; a bulldozed café and a rock
garden run wild. Not even the K.G.B., thought Cave,
would start something so close to thousands of near
naked bodies. But he was wrong. He had not allowed
for the fact that these particular goons had been
ordered to destroy him, and they started in at once,
opening up as soon as they got within range, because
Keith and Cave and Zaleski were important, and
nothing else mattered.

Their first shots smashed Sandy Keith's bottle,
snatched up despite the agony which had returned to
him, their second punctured Uncle Wladek's briefcase.
The third hit Cave in the leg as he pushed Sandy flat,
and they wriggled for cover behind a pile of rubble,
then Cave opened up with the magnum. A goon spun
away in an arching dive, and when he fell, moved not
at all, but the other two took cover behind the rockery.

'We'll have to move', said Keith, and looked down at
his leg that was dark with blood.

Uncle Wladek found his voice. 'Then they will kill
us', he said.

'They'll kill us anyway', Simone said. 'Unless I get to
the car.'

Sandy Keith looked at the shattered remnants of his
bottle. 'I rather think', he said, 'that that's my job.'

Simone took off her bikini top and used it and a
handkerchief and a comb as a tourniquet on Cave's leg.
None of the three men even looked at her. Death was
too close.

'You think you can?' Cave asked.

'I know I can', said Keith. 'Unless I get killed. And
even if I do –'

He shrugged, got to his feet, and jogged towards the
car. It was the nearest he could get to running, thought

Cave, and opened up on the rockery, forcing them to keep their heads down till the hired car, an Audi, roared up and Simone ran to it, grabbed her gun from beneath the seat, and began blasting in her turn at the rockery, until Zaleski and Cave got aboard, and Keith gunned the engine and roared away. Only then did she have time to put on her beach coat, and only then did Cave have time to reflect that hers had been the best looking bosom he'd seen all day.

The road to Nice was the one to take, thought Cave. In Nice or St Raphael or Cannes they could disappear just as easily as in St Tropez. But Favières had a Porsche, the biggest, and Favières knew how to drive, and was gaining.

'We'll have to take the back roads', said Cave, and Keith nodded, and turned off the autoroute into Provençal France – vines and olive trees and sheep – and stole distance on every curve because even in the state he was in he was a master, but on every straight the big Porsche closed the gap, once more came near enough to permit a burst of firing, and bullets spanged on the rear bumper, ominously close to the tyres. And it was at that moment that Cave remembered who it was that Simone reminded him of, only last time the car had been a Peugeot, and the pursuers had been on motorbikes not a Porsche.

'Next bend', he said, and Keith nodded. Like Cave, he'd done it all before...

The Audi squealed around the corner and kept on turning, off the road and into a patch of vines. Cave hopped out clumsily and Simone followed as neat as a cat. The Porsche thundered round after them, and Cave fired and killed Favières as the girl put a bullet into the Porsche's front tyre, another in its petrol tank, and the car spun blazing like a giant Catherine wheel... Cave limped back to Keith, took the emergency flask from his pocket and offered it to Keith.

'No, thanks all the same', said Keith. 'I'm driving.'

Cave could have kissed him. Simone Vernier did.

'I think you're wonderful', she said. 'I really do.'

125

The girl that she reminded Cave of had been called Bernadette, and they had met her in Bordeaux, and later in San Sebastian. She didn't look in the least like Simone Vernier, but she too had been beautiful, and she too had worked for French Security, and she too had preferred Sandy Keith.

'So she didn't want to kiss you after that?' Sir Roderick said.

'If she did she hid it well', said Cave.

'Do you know where she is now?' Sir Roderick asked.

'Looking after Sandy.'

'We'll have to get him back to St Tropez', Sir Roderick said. 'That trick cyclist feller Berman's turned up.'

'He was never missing', said Cave. 'You had him hidden all the time, didn't you?'

Sir Roderick poured single malt, passed one to Cave.

'Why would I do that?' he asked.

'To keep me in St Tropez chasing Zaleski... You recommended Berman to Sandy after all – which argues that you knew him – which argues that you knew where he was.'

Cave pushed his drink away.

'Your own nephew', he said. 'We owe him so much, too.'

'And I'm paying', said Sir Roderick. 'He'll get his treatment. Though he may not need it now.'

He pushed the glass back to Cave.

'Drink, man', he said. 'You've earned it.'

Cave drank, and Sir Roderick picked up Zaleski's copy of *Alice's Adventures in Wonderland*. 'What put you on to this?'

'I asked Sandy what dyslexic means... It means you've got a sort of word blindness. What would a dyslexic Pole be doing with a copy of *Alice*? It's one of the most difficult books there is for a foreigner – even one who can read...'

'Did Miss Vernier see you take it?'

126

'She was too busy looking after Sandy.'

'And Zaleski?'

'The ride upset him', said Cave. 'He needed a drink.'

'We found what we were after in that bit about Father William', said Sir Roderick. 'You are old Father William ... that bit. Three microdots. You can get an awful lot of rocket stuff on three microdots. We'd have paid fifty thousand pounds for it.'

'Poor Polish refugees', said Cave.

Sir Roderick said stiffly: 'Not at all. We *will* pay them fifty thousand. Not as much as the Yanks – but a lot more than the French.'

'Talking of the French', said Cave. 'Why didn't he give the book to his niece?'

'Because she wasn't his niece', said Sir Roderick. 'I've seen a photograph of his niece and she's as ugly as sin. French Security lured her away and put your girl in her place –'

'Sandy's girl', said Cave.

'– just like I did with Berman. It looks as if poor old Zaleski got wind of it. Probably because she wouldn't take him to Paris... She couldn't. He knew too many Polish refugees there. That's why she had to hide him in St Tropez.'

He sipped his malt.

'As a matter of fact I put a call in to French Security just before you came in and they're furious', he continued happily, and topped up Cave's glass.

'Come on, Joe', he said. 'Drink up. You've got rather a lot to celebrate when you think about it.'

Cave thought to himself that Sir Roderick was probably right. At least he was still alive.

Chapter 13

THE CARS were on the starting grid now. Sandy Keith
was in the pole position, because he had done the fastest
lap in practice, and barring accidents Jason Bird was
absolutely certain that Sandy Keith would win. But how
could one bar accidents in a Formula One race?

The Detroit Grand Prix, all the commentators were
agreed, would have its share. Like Monaco, it was a
street circuit, and equally disliked by drivers, because
it totally lacked glamour, which meant that anyone
out in front had only to stay there and he couldn't lose,
which was why the drivers called it difficult. 'Difficult',
so Jason Bird had been told, meant dangerous, and the
danger was acute if you had to try to pass the car in
front. But Sandy Keith didn't. He *began* in front, a
perfect example of capitalist élitism, thought Bird.

His mind went back to St Tropez, and the death of
the man called Favières, and all the others whom Cave
had killed. Once again General Malkovsky had been
furious with Kalkov, and Kalkov had once again
resigned himself to a closer acquaintance with the
Gulag Archipelago. But once again it was not to be.
The man on the Central Committee still wanted Cave
dead.

Somehow the general had managed to persuade him that Sandy Keith's death would be an irrelevance. Much, much better, the general had cooed, if Sandy were simply used as the bait, and only Cave were to die. Not only much better, Jason Bird thought, but much easier too. A double kill inevitably led to complications, and if only one man were to die, it just might be arranged.

On the starting grid the engines revved up, exhaust smoke began to billow, and Jason Bird found himself thinking once again about the man called Sandy Keith, and how incredible he really was. He doubted if even the K.G.B. could produce his match, for this was a man who had even overcome the fear of fire, had even managed to undertake once more the fearful risks of sitting in his incredibly lethal car with its even more lethal fuel, and drive it at 180 or more miles per hour, hour after hour, when every second brought the menace of death. He had begun to do it on his own – the day he drove the Audi which escaped Favières's Porsche. True, after that the psychiatrist Berman had helped him, but the initiative had been Keith's and Keith's alone. He was a really remarkable man, and would remain so until the day he died...

When he abandoned drinking, Keith returned at once to the life he had known. If the internal combustion engine was not to be feared, then it was to be exploited. He resumed his friendship with Nadir almost at once, and began to drive the Morton-Nadir as soon as he possibly could. It really was incredible, Jason Bird thought. On his very first race he finished sixth, and was obviously disappointed... With the resumption of racing, there came the resumption of parties, and the friendships with the beautiful groupies, and the life in the place in Sussex – all the paraphernalia of a successful racing motorist, and successful Keith was, from the very beginning. He remained successful right until the time when he fell in love again.

But none of this, Jason Bird thought, had been of the

slightest use to Kalkov, or the general, or the members of the Central Committee. Because once again Sandy Keith had gone one way, and Joe Cave quite another, and wherever the other way was, not even the most talented of the squads of Department V had been able to discover. Sir Roderick valued Cave's talents highly, and had no intention of putting them at risk. He more than anybody made sure that Keith and Cave, friends though they were, were kept apart. Until Keith's love affair.

After Trudi Jannot, Keith would have believed it impossible that he should ever have fallen in love again, and so would Jason Bird, but they had both been wrong: Jason Bird had seen the evidence – the photostats of letters, the tapes taken from the bugs that had been planted, and he knew. But Cave had not repeated his infatuation: this time it was no blue-eyed blonde, but a very different kind of girl. Keith had met Janet Tang at a party given by Iskandar Nadir, and that should have been ominous, but he didn't find it so.

The party was like all Iskandar's parties, an obvious success because all the girls were pretty, and all the drinks were both good and plentiful. Keith sipped at his glass of mineral water and wandered so to speak from flower to flower, the most welcome of bees, but Nadir, watching him, saw how wary he was.

At last he went up to Keith, and put an arm around his shoulders.

'Sandy, my dear friend', he said, 'surely there must be one jewel that merits the attention of such a connoisseur as yourself?'

'Do I seem as churlish as all that?' Keith said. 'I didn't mean to be.'

There was a hint of warning in his voice, and Nadir knew it, but he was far too good a friend to take it.

'In this life, we all make mistakes', he said. 'Not least with regard to women. But we don't always make mistakes. The lucky ones – they hardly ever make mistakes. But even the unlucky ones – they will be rewarded, if they are brave enough. Believe me.'

130

Keith looked up at him and grinned.

'You've got a jewel lined up for me to see, is that it?' he asked.

'I have indeed', said Nadir. 'A jewel who could well be beyond price.'

The orphans were enchanting. Row upon row of them in white T-shirts and blue jeans, honey-gold skin glowing, brown eyes bright. They looked straight at Cave, and sang a song in their own tongue he couldn't even begin to understand, and yet he had no doubt it was a happy song, and that they were happy singing it. The youngest orphan was perhaps three, the oldest no more than seven...

The soldiers were appalling. They had lined up the villagers in a row and proceeded to butcher them as if they were sheep in a slaughter-house. To accomplish their task they used pistols, machetes, the muzzles of rifles, and sometimes the butts, as if ammunition were infinitely more precious than the lives they took, thought Cave. The youngest of the villagers was perhaps twelve, the oldest seventy at least, perhaps eighty, perhaps even more. It was difficult to tell: the film was grainy and lacking in clarity; it had nothing of the sharp definition of the film of the orphans...

Sir Roderick Finlay pressed a button on the side of his chair and the film stopped and the screen went blank.

'That's quite enough of that', he said, and pressed another button. Curtains parted, sunlight flooded in, and yet Cave still saw nothing but death: savage, agonising, inevitable.

'Who were they?' he asked.

Sir Roderick took his time in answering, reached out first to a decanter, and poured out glasses of single malt. God knows we deserve a drink, he thought after that.

'They're the Khmer Rouge', he said. 'Jolly little chaps, aren't they?'

'They're scum', said Cave.

'Is that all you know about them?' Sir Roderick asked.

Cave sighed. 'It was', he said. 'But somehow I get the feeling you're going to tell me more.'

'They belong to Cambodia', said Sir Roderick. 'It lies between Thailand and Vietnam. It's a mess, Joe. It's been fought over for the last thirty years and more. Ever since the French lost Indo-China. Used to be a nice country, they tell me. It's a terrible place now... War always does that, if it goes on long enough.' He nodded at the blank screen.

'Only unending war could produce chaps like that. And yet a few years earlier they would have been just like the orphans ... all piping voices and cuddly innocence.' He sipped his Scotch.

'The Khmer Rouge call themselves Marxists, but really they're just pathological killers', he said. 'Homicidal lunatics. They kill because they enjoy it – it's the only thing they can do well. Recently their war has been declared officially over, but nobody seems to have told the Khmer Rouge that. The massacres still go on, whenever they can find somebody to kill. They're running rather short these days.' He sighed, and sipped once more.

'As I say, it's a mess', he said. 'But for once it isn't our mess, thank God... At least it wasn't.'

He poured more whisky into both their glasses.

That means it's going to be rough, thought Cave. Especially for me.

'I got the massacre film from the C.I.A.', said Sir Roderick. 'They did some complicated deal with the Ivans. It was a K.G.B. cameraman who took the pictures... The quality isn't all that good because he was being sick most of the time. All the same – it was good enough to show there was something missing among the victims... Did you happen to notice what it was?'

'Kids', said Joe Cave. 'Kids the orphans' age. The ones who were killed looked about twelve or more.'

Sir Roderick nodded.

'So they were', he said. 'The Khmer Rouge sold the younger ones ... to a fellow called Timothy Shu.'

'The bloke who runs the orphanages?'

'You've heard of him then?'

'He's pretty famous', said Joe Cave. And indeed he was. A devout Christian, an ethnic Chinese born and brought up in Cambodia, he'd devoted his life and the not inconsiderable fortune he'd made to the care of orphaned Cambodian kids.

'He and his assistants roam Cambodia and buy up kids like the ones you saw', said Sir Roderick. 'They bought the kids who escaped that massacre.'

'A good thing somebody cared', said Cave.

'For some reason the Cambodians trust him – and his assistants', Sir Roderick said. 'They don't trust anybody else.' He sipped his single malt once more. 'I had a signal from the C.I.A. yesterday', he said. 'By hand of messenger. Most Secret. Somebody in Timothy Shu's organisation is a spy... It's a nice set up when you think about it, Joe. They place orphans in Singapore, Hong Kong, all over South-East Asia. Australia too. And now they've come to England. An enterprising agent could pick up a lot of stuff, and orphans as a cover would be just about perfect. Who's going to query those poor, deprived little children?'

'But why did the Yanks call you in?' said Cave. 'Can't they handle it?'

'Of course they can', said Sir Roderick. 'They're perfectly competent – despite what we read in the newspapers. The thing is I want you to handle it *first*.'

Cave thought of the C.I.A. – the tens of millions of dollars, the thousands of operatives, the incredible complexity of hardware.

'There must be a good reason', he said.

'There is', said Sir Roderick. 'My nephew's involved with one of Shu's assistants – a young woman called Janet Tang.'

Cave studied the photograph Sir Roderick handed to him. Three quarters Chinese, according to what Sir

133

Roderick was saying, and one quarter French. Perhaps it was the French grandmother who had given her that touch of chic which enlivened the very plain dress that she wore. For the rest she was very Chinese – olive skin, gleaming black hair, slanting, hazel eyes, the small bud of a mouth – and very beautiful. But then the girls that Sandy Keith attracted were always beautiful, thought Cave. It was something in the nature of the man: that combination of courage, shyness, and an unquenchable will to win. Cave smiled. Sandy Keith was the only diffident egomaniac he had ever encountered.

Keith had rented a flat in South Kensington. It was both spacious and expensive, but the fact wouldn't worry him, Cave knew. He was growing richer by the minute. So it was no surprise that Cave should be welcomed enthusiastically, taken into an elegant drawing room, and supplied at once with a Campari and soda. He lifted his glass.

'Cheers', he said.

'Cheers', said Keith. His hands were empty. A question had to be asked and Cave asked it. There was no sense in shilly-shallying.

'You're not drinking?' Cave asked.

'I don't', said Keith. 'Not just at the moment.'

Cave winked at him, and looked about him.

'Very nice', he said. And indeed it was.

'Janet fixed it up', said Keith. 'You've heard about Janet?'

Cave hardened his heart.

'No', he said.

'She's from Cambodia', said Keith. 'She works with Timothy Shu's orphans... As a matter of fact so do I.'

'I thought you wanted to get back into Formula One racing – be world champion?'

'I thought so too', said Keith. 'But this is more important.'

This information was staggering. For all the years

that Cave had known him, nothing had been more important than the need to be world champion. He must be smitten indeed, thought Cave.

'What do you do exactly?' he asked.

'I help them raise funds', said Keith. 'Write letters, make speeches.'

'You're good at it?' Cave sounded incredulous, and Keith grinned

'I'm terrible', he said. 'But I'm also famous... People give... I give too, you know... I'd give them even more – if she'd let me.'

'She must be a wonderful woman', said Cave.

'She is. But that's not the point', said Keith.

'What is the point?'

'They're wonderful kids.'

Keith got up and went up to a desk, produced pictures of the new Timothy Shu Orphanage in Surrey. Dutifully Cave oohed and aahed at the schoolroom, at the dining room, the adventure playground. That his friend was intensely committed was obvious. But he was also nobody's fool.

'Does Sir Roderick know you're mixed up in this?' Cave asked.

'As a matter of fact he does', said Keith. 'I've touched him for a donation.'

'You did?' Cave was impressed. 'How much did you get?'

'Fifty quid.'

Cave wished he could have seen it done, and Keith looked at him warily.

'Why should Uncle Roderick have to know?' he asked.

'You know why', said Cave. 'Because you're his nephew.'

'Yes', said Keith. 'All right. But Uncle Roderick's business is with the guilty, Joe. Mine is with the innocent.'

And then the door opened and his girl came in: quiet, contained, very Chinese, and even more beautiful than her photograph; her air of French elegance, of chic, even more pronounced.

135

She accepted Keith's introduction to Cave as one of his oldest friends, a freelance photographer-journalist, and replenished his drink, listened to their memories of times past, the cars Keith had driven, the pictures Cave had taken – but no mention at all of the jobs they had done together for Sir Roderick Finlay. They were a secret Sandy Keith would never betray, and Cave knew it. All the same Keith was restless, his hand fidgeted with the silver elephant on its silver chain. Perhaps he was thinking of his father, and how he'd survived the Battle of Britain, Cave thought. Because Sandy was a survivor too, but only just. The K.G.B. had devoted all of their considerable expertise in an attempt to kill him: come to that that expertise was still being devoted in an attempt to kill Joe Cave, according to Sir Roderick. But at least, Cave thought, Sandy was out of it. Unless Sir Roderick was right, of course, and the use of orphans was also a cover for the use of espionage.

Cave compared and contrasted Janet Tang with Trudi Jannot. Once again it was obvious that they shared nothing but their beauty and a kind of determination. He had no doubt that Janet Tang had that; her chin, so neat, rounded and beautiful, was also very, very determined.

He looked from the girl to Keith. He was looking at her exactly as he had once looked at Trudi Jannot, with a devotion that gave away all too clearly the vulnerability that lay behind it.

There was sadness in his look too, because she was saying that soon she would be leaving for Hong Kong to join Timothy Shu and his other assistants, picking up more orphans, and didn't know when she'd be back. If the statement hurt Keith, she made no sign that she was aware of it. So Joe Cave thought it was time to go, and more than time.

Sandy Keith walked with him to the door, and took twenty quid off him on the way for the Orphans' Fund. When he got back she was collecting together the photographs of the orphans, stacking them neatly and returning them to their drawer.

'You didn't have a drink?' she asked.

'No', said Keith.

In exactly the same tone of voice she asked: 'Would you like to go to bed now?'

'Is that a reward for me?'

'No', she said. 'It's a reward for me.'

On the bed she lay beside him, and looked at his body, still scarred, still marred by the effects of fire, as it would be until he died.

'I've decided to give up entering beauty contests', Keith said.

'You shouldn't', she said. 'Those colours are really very pretty.' And her hands wandered over the scars.

'About as pretty as a patchwork quilt knitted by a gorilla', said Keith.

'If I say they are beautiful then they are beautiful', said Janet Tang, and her olive gold body entwined with his. Sandy Keith began to believe her.

Hong Kong, Sir Roderick thought, was bad news. Things were still quiet there after Cave's last visit, pleasant too: the mainland Chinese content to let the island's money flow in and help their flagging economy. The last thing the British government wanted was trouble in Hong Kong, especially with a State visit of a Communist Party Vice-President in the offing.

'You'll have to go there, Joe', said Sir Roderick. 'Keep an eye on things. I've got a chap there who should be able to help you – as a matter of fact I've had him working on this orphanage business. Chap called Yat Sung. He's rather good.'

'Not one of those mechanics we had when Sandy raced in Macao?' Cave asked.

'No', Sir Roderick said, and sighed. 'They were blown quite soon afterwards. I had to let them go. Not that they minded all that much. They started up a business in New Brighton and they're making a fortune. But Yat Sung is pretty good. You'll find he can cope.'

'And the C.I.A. won't mind our butting in?' asked Cave.

'The C.I.A. haven't got a State visit coming up', said Sir Roderick, 'and anyway, they want this thing cleared up as much as we do... What did you make of Sandy's girl?'

'Very beautiful', said Cave. 'Very bright. And absolutely dedicated to those kids of hers.'

'All Chinese are dedicated to something', said Sir Roderick. 'That's their strength as well as their weakness. Let's hope all her dedication is for the orphans.'

'Sir?' Cave asked.

'All Shu's helpers are dedicated to the orphans', Sir Roderick explained. 'But one of them is dedicated to something else as well. One of them is a spy.'

Chapter 14

CAVE FLEW out Cathay Pacific to Hong Kong, a freelance doing a piece for a colour supplement. The flight was long, and he'd seen both the movies, but all the same he enjoyed it. It gave him a chance to sleep.

He'd been booked in at a hotel in Kowloon. Nothing spectacular: the Carlton was if anything rather cheap for a journalist with an expense account – but it had one big plus: Timothy Shu and his assistants, including Janet Tang, were all staying there.

Cave showered and took a nap, woke in good time to dress and shave, and walk, with a bag full of cameras, to the Green Star ferry. In the first class saloon, a Chinese jostled him very slightly, at once apologised and moved away. Cave looked out at the Hong Kong skyline, then fumbled with his bag, which had become unzipped. It was heavier by the weight of a Colt magnum 357 revolver. Sir Roderick didn't like his operatives to go about without the means of protection. Neither did Joe Cave.

The ferry docked, and he took a cab to the Tiger Balm Gardens. It was late and they were almost empty, ready to close when Cave walked in. They were the setting for a nightmare. Tiger Balm is a kind of ointment which made a fortune for its inventor, and he used some of the fortune to build the Gardens, which are like a Disneyland for LSD addicts. Grotesque animals, gnomes, spirits, mythological figures loomed up on him from every side. They were at once comic and dreadful. Cave walked on. There was no sign of a human being. And then suddenly there was, the comedy receded, and fear took over...

Yat Sung lay at the feet of the Giant Laughing Buddha, a creature twenty feet high that was seated in front of an improbably painted sky. The Buddha continued laughing, despite the fact that Yat Sung, Cave was sure, was dead.

He went up to him, knelt beside him. The Chinese, middle aged, slender, tough, had been hit by a kung-fu expert, and hit hard. There had been three blows, Cave thought. A spear strike, a fist strike, and a kick. Any one of them could have killed him.

The body had been searched, too. On the ground, spilled out around him, were money, keys, a packet of chewing gum of the kind Cave had been told about before he left England.

He picked it up and spun round. There was a sound of movement behind him. Up the steps that led to the Buddha four men were running. Two carried axes and two carried guns. One of the axe men paused, and produced a string of fire crackers: the gun men took aim at Cave, who dropped flat in the Buddha's shadow, grabbed for the gun in the camera bag.

Suddenly the fire crackers exploded – in Hong Kong a sound as common as car engines revving – and the two gun men began firing, the axe men sprinted in for the kill.

Carefully, deliberately, Cave fired at the axe men, and the magnum bullets struck home, knocking them sprawling as if they'd been hit with sledge hammers. Cave rolled over as he fired, to the shelter of a flowering bush, then loosed off a shot at one of the gun men, missed, then fired again. The gun man dropped. Cave rolled over again, away from the second gun man's line of fire, but the second gun man was already running for cover. Cave got to his feet, held the magnum two-handed, and squeezed the trigger. The second gun man dropped.

Cave put the gun back in the camera bag and walked away. Tiger Balm Gardens was the place for nightmares all right, he thought. From now on they'd be the setting for a lot of his.

At the Carlton, Timothy Shu and his group were having a meeting. Shu had made a fortune, the fact was common knowledge, yet he stayed in a hotel which was scarcely more than a hostel: the reason for that was common knowledge too. Every penny he saved was spent on his orphans.

Cave paused on his way to the lift and looked in on the meeting. There were seventeen of them, eight men, nine women, and one of them was a spy. At that moment they were singing. They sang in Cantonese, and yet somehow the tune was familiar, and at last Cave spotted it. *There's a home for little children.* He'd sung it himself, at Sunday School, years ago. All piping voices and cuddly innocence, Sir Roderick had said. He'd been like that, too. He looked at Janet Tang. Her mouth was opening and shutting, but it was a bluff, thought Cave. She didn't know the words.

Then the hymn ended and the meeting broke up, the singers streamed out. Cave stood where he was, and Janet Tang looked at him, started in surprise, then came over to him. She was as chic, as elegant as ever.

'Mr Cave', she said. 'What a pleasant surprise.'

Either she means it, Cave thought, or she's a hell of a good actress – but then she would be.

'What are you doing here?'

Cave told her.

'But how exciting', she said, and turned to Timothy Shu, who had come out to join her.

'Mr Shu', she said. 'May I present Mr Cave? He's a journalist.'

141

Cave found himself looking at a medium-size Chinese, squat, powerful, and with a personality he knew at once would be formidable.

'It's always a pleasure to meet the press', said Shu. His voice was low pitched and soothing; there was no hint of a Chinese accent. 'Give us a mention when you can. We need the money.'

He smiled and was gone.

'Are you working now?' the girl asked.

'For a little while', said Cave.

'Can we meet later?'

Cave said, 'I'll buy you dinner.'

'I'd like that', said Janet Tang.

Cave wondered if that were true. The work he was about to do consisted of two things: first, to try to figure out who had murdered Yat Sung. To decide, in fact, whether it was the mainland Chinese, or the Hong Kong Chinese, or the K.G.B. or a *crime passionnel* come to that. And after he had failed in that, as he knew he would, he would have to send a message to Sir Roderick. Top Secret.

'You're not supposed to come here', said the man from the Governor's office.

'I am if there's an emergency', said Cave.

'There isn't an emergency', the man from the Governor's office said.

Cave looked at him: young, ambitious – and terrified of doing the wrong thing, such as being in the same room as one of those terrible thugs of Sir Roderick Finlay's.

'There will be if you don't belt up', he said, and the other man was silent. 'You send a diplomatic pouch every day back to London', said Cave.

'I'm afraid I can't answer questions like that', the other man said.

'I'm not asking questions', said Cave. 'I'm telling you. I want something sent back by the next pouch.'

'I'll do what I can', the other man said.

'You'll do what I tell you', said Cave, and handed him a packet of chewing gum. 'Get this off at once, you hear? It's urgent.'

The man from the Governor's office began to develop a migraine.

They ate in a Szechuan restaurant on Hanoi Road that was cheap, cheerful, and noisy: the slamming of tiles from the mah-jong school next door adding to the uproar. There was absolutely no chance of their being overheard, Cave thought, as the girl's chopsticks moved deftly among the hot spicy food.

'You are enjoying yourself in Hong Kong?' she asked.

'I'm working', said Cave.

'Yes of course. You told me. But surely work can be enjoyable?'

Cave wondered if she was having a little fun at his expense.

'Sometimes', he said. 'Have you heard from Sandy?'

'I phoned him yesterday', she said. 'The orphans in Surrey are well.'

'And Sandy?'

'He also is well. Happy too, I think.'

He'd certainly looked happy, thought Cave, but he'd looked happy once before with a woman, and she'd tried to kill him and almost succeeded.

'How did you meet him?' he asked.

'Mr Nadir gave a cocktail party', she said, 'and invited Mr Shu. And Mr Shu asked me to go with him. It was for the orphans.' She smiled. 'It usually is. But Sandy was also there and came up and asked me to go out with him and I did. Mr Shu was very pleased.'

'He was?'

'Sandy donated a thousand pounds to the orphans', she said and smiled once more. 'I was pleased, too.'

'You're doing a marvellous job', said Cave, and if she thought he was being ironic in his turn it was just too bad. 'Conditions must be terrible in Cambodia, even now.'

143

'They are', she said. 'They say the fighting is over, but it is not. It never will be, I think. And believe me, Mr Cave, I know much about Cambodia. I was born there.'

'But you got out', said Cave.

'Eventually', she said. 'But it wasn't easy ... it never is.'

And then Timothy Shu hurried in, and shouted in Cantonese above the uproar of the restaurant. The girl stopped eating, her hand trembled slightly as she put down her chopsticks.

'A most terrible thing has happened', she said. 'Some people have been murdered.'

Shu said in English: 'I am very sorry. What I have heard has upset me... I hate violence, you see ... it makes me –' He waved his hands. They were battered, work hardened hands. 'It makes me forget everything. Even my manners. I have seen too much of it, you see.' He turned to Janet. 'Explain please what I have said.'

'It was at Tiger Balm Gardens', she said. 'Four men were shot. But they carried weapons too. Axes and guns.'

'Gang war?' Cave asked.

'We must suppose so', said Shu.

'One of the men who was killed worked for us – with the orphans. He was a driver.'

'That sounds bad', said Cave.

'For me it is very bad', said Janet Tang. 'He came from my village.' Her head bowed, she lifted her hands to her face.

'He was her cousin, you see', said Timothy Shu.

'Lucky they didn't take the chewing gum', Sir Roderick said.

'Those four knew there was something, but they didn't know what it was', said Cave. 'So they staked the place out and waited for me to pick it up... Funny.'

'I'm always happy to share a joke', said Sir Roderick.

'Yat Sung was killed with hands and feet. Nothing

144

more', said Cave. 'But this lot came at me with axes and pistols.'

'You're a lot harder to kill than poor old Yat Sung', said Sir Roderick.

'They weren't to know that.'

'I think they did', said Sir Roderick. He straightened the blotting pad on his desk that had got perhaps an eighth of an inch out of alignment.

'A lot of these helpers are Cambodian Chinese, including Janet Tang', said Sir Roderick. 'But they all belong to what you might call the Russian Zone of Cambodia. They've all had a chance to become K.G.B. recruits – and it looks as if one of them has... Janet Tang got to Sandy. That's much too big a coincidence for either of us to swallow. It's a known fact that Sandy's my nephew – at least it's a fact known to the K.G.B. So are you known to them, Joe... That's why they came at you with weapons. They knew they'd need them.'

So it wasn't a *crime passionnel*, Cave thought. He'd never supposed it would be. It was only the K.G.B., as usual. Still it was part of his trade and he accepted it – but his trade wasn't Sandy Keith's.

'So Sandy's at risk too?' he said.

'I shouldn't think so', said Sir Roderick. 'The girl knows her business, I've no doubt. She'll know he's harmless by now. They'll be far too busy taking care of the ones who might harm them. That means you and me, Joe. And as I don't get about all that much I'm afraid it means you. Again.' He opened a desk drawer, took out the chewing gum wrapper. 'I'm keeping this', he said. 'Souvenir. Yat Sung used the dot over the letter i for his microdot... So much trouble and such a little space.' He waited, then:

'Things are still not good between Russia and China', said Sir Roderick. 'But they've never been better between China and the West. Especially with the British. We've signed two billions' worth of contracts with them already, and there's more to come. Everything's lovely for us. For China too. They don't

145

have to worry about fighting us. We get on. But they do worry still about fighting the Ivans – so that's where all their arms resources go – to the Russo-Chinese border. That means that the Russians have to pile up arms on that border too. And arms cost money – money they could spend better elsewhere.

'It'd be a lot easier if the Ivans could make trouble between us and the Chinese. Take the pressure off the Manchurian border and put it on Hong Kong instead.'

'I daresay it would', said Cave. 'But how could they do it?'

'The Chinese are sending a Party Vice-Chairman on a visit to England', Sir Roderick said. 'I believe I mentioned the fact.'

'That's right, you did', said Cave. 'Da Ming. He arrives tomorrow.'

'Da Ming', Sir Roderick repeated. 'The most loved and respected leader they have... Yat Sung reckoned that he'd be assassinated as soon as he gets here.'

'By who?'

'The evidence will show that it's some loony group of British Fascists backed up by the British Secret Service – that means me, Joe. In fact it will all be set up by the mole working with Shu's orphans... Would that be trouble enough, do you think?'

'Can't you cancel the visit?' Cave asked.

'Not possibly', said Sir Roderick. 'Da Ming would lose so much face he really would have to go to war.'

'Move the orphans out, then.'

'For God's sake', said Sir Roderick. 'These are *Chinese* orphans. Da Ming's asked especially to see them.' His hands fidgeted once more with his desk blotter, then were still. He said tonelessly: 'I hate to ask this of you, Joe – but I'm afraid I must. Sandy's at the orphanage just now – working as a janitor or some damned thing. I want you to phone him and say you're coming on a visit.'

You want me to be bait, thought Cave, but he kept the thought to himself. He had no alternative to offer.

146

The orphanage was set in downland, ringed with conifers, bright with flowers. Like the orphans it was clean and fresh and innocent, a symbol of hope. A good place to visit, thought Cave, and probably an even better place to live. Certainly Sandy Keith had seemed to think so when he'd phoned him. He'd never sounded happier in his life. But then Janet Tang was back in Surrey too. Sandy had reason to be happy.

Cave drove into the orphanage's car park, got out and looked about him. Just as it looked on television, he thought. The brightly painted bungalows, the Chinese looking gardens, the school flanked by the adventure playground. And that would be where his friend was waiting, shovelling fuel for the school's boiler. The only school in Britain with a millionaire for a boilerman, thought Cave, and knowing him he'll have another shovel waiting for me.

He set off through the gardens, and crossed the road that led to the adventure playground. There was no noise except that of a score of children having fun – on swings and roundabouts and helter-skelters: tiny children, absorbed totally in what they were doing – which was sliding and swinging and yelling as they did it. Cave made his way through them, and they were far too busy, too happy, even to know that he was there.

Suddenly there was the sound of an engine behind him, and he looked round warily. A car was moving slowly towards him, a dark green Range Rover with dark tinted windows. Sandy Keith's car. Cave stopped and waited and the car drew nearer. Then suddenly its horn blasted, silencing the shouts of the children, and the car came on to the playground, picking up speed as it came. Its windows were so dark that it was impossible to see who was behind the wheel, but Cave was quite sure it wasn't Sandy Keith. The children scattered before it like leaves before a wind – which was what the driver intended. The target was Cave, and nobody else.

Cave knew it, and turned and ran, swerving round the children – too young, too slow – who couldn't get

147

out of his way in time. But even they were able to find safety before the Range Rover reached them. All except one.

Cave's hope of refuge was a roundabout, the kind of circular swing that revolves on its own diameter if enough weight is thrown at it, and tilted as it revolved. It was like being aboard a North Sea trawler on a choppy sea. The kids loved it... Cave ran for it and kept on running, and behind him the little children scattered, screaming, the Range Rover gained on him, its horn still blasting the children out of the way. Except for that one.

Ma Li was blind. It wasn't that she didn't know there was a cause for panic – any survivor of Cambodia would know that, even if she was blind, even if she was only seven years old – it was just that, being blind, she didn't know which way to run.

And then suddenly this iron hard arm came around her, and yet it didn't crush or hurt her, and the voice she knew to be of the kind they called English said 'Upsadaisy' and she was swung high in the air, and the sound of the car horn grew louder.

And still she wasn't frightened. The arm that held her was kind: the body she pressed against was the body of a friend. Suddenly she felt herself flying through the air, still held by the Englishman, to land on the roundabout, to feel it tilt and spin. 'Upsadaisy', said Ma Li.

Cave held her close, and lunged out with all his weight, making the roundabout tilt and swing. Up and round it swung, and the blind little girl giggled in excitement as the roundabout began its descent, and a solid mass of iron shod wood slammed into the Range Rover, a side window shattered.

The blind child's arms tightened round his neck, and Cave forced himself to speak calmly.

'Upsadaisy', he said again, and again she giggled.

But the Range Rover had had enough. As he swung his weight again, levering the roundabout for a second blow, the car swerved from him, then reversed back

148

onto the road, drove away. Cave stayed on the round-about, waited for it to stop swinging, so that he could put his new girlfriend back on the ground.

Janet Tang said, 'I don't know why you should think it had anything to do with us.'

'I never said it had', said Cave. 'All I said was I told you I was coming to see Sandy... Where is he, anyway?'

'I don't know', she said. 'He got a phone call from Godalming. Somebody wanted to talk about giving a donation – so of course he went at once.'

'He didn't take his car', said Cave.

'Mr Shu lent him his', said the girl. 'It's quicker than the Range Rover.' She looked at Cave: his face, his eyes, told her nothing. 'Don't you believe me?' she asked.

Cave studied her: the smooth, unblemished skin of her face, her immaculate sweater and slacks. Arms and hands too were unblemished. Cave sighed. 'Did Sandy say where he would meet me?' he asked.

'He said he'd go back to the boiler room', she said.

Timothy Shu was waiting for him: he'd even taken the shovel and was shovelling fuel into the boiler, his body powerful, the gnarled, battered hands accurate and sure. When Cave came in he put down the shovel in the corner, carefully. Shovels cost money, after all, and the orphanage had no money to spare. There was blood on his hands, quite literally, Cave thought. Blood from a network of fine cuts, the kind you get from flying glass.

'You know then?' asked Timothy Shu.

Cave nodded. 'I know you killed Yat Sung', he said. 'And I know how. You say you don't like violence – and yet you have the hands of a karate fighter.'

'I prefer to call it kung fu', said Shu. Cave shrugged. 'Whichever it is, you have to punch hard every day on a bag of dry sand just to keep your hands as they are.'

149

He held out his own hands. 'Just as I do. You killed Yat Sung.'

'He was a spy', said Shu. 'He came and stole my secrets from me, and so he had to die. It was necessary that it was I who should kill him.' His body had slumped into a fighting crouch. 'You also, Mr Cave.'

'Don't be stupid', said Cave. 'You've lost.'

'Not if I kill you', said Shu. 'If I do that there will still be time to go to the airport and kill the deviationist Da Ming.'

'And who on earth are you going to blame it on?' Cave asked.

'The hireling of the Secret Service', said Shu. 'Sandy Keith. It has all been arranged.'

'But that's ridiculous', said Cave.

'I don't think so. After all – Keith is the nephew of the head of your section – and yours is the section that deals with death.'

'But why should he kill Da Ming?'

'Because he loves the orphans', said Shu, 'and he holds Da Ming responsible for their misfortunes.'

'All right', said Cave. 'It's plausible, I admit. But once anybody talks to Sandy –'

'Nobody will talk to him', said Shu. 'Once Da Ming is dead, and I have left the evidence to show Keith did it, then Keith too will die.'

Cave leapt for him, a great flailing dive that aimed his body like a projectile, straight at Shu. But the Chinaman swerved, and Cave sailed past him, landing on the pile of fuel, swerving in his turn to avoid the kick that would have finished him. From that moment he knew that Shu was too good for him, would beat him every time, but what could he do but fight on?

He rushed forward to grab Shu's arm as the hand came down in a karate chop. He hauled back, tilted his body, levered and pulled, waiting for the feel of Shu's body helpless in his hands before he went flying through the air. Except it didn't happen. Shu just stood there, holding Cave in check by sheer strength alone, then his free hand swung, aiming the killer blow at the

150

neck, and Cave ducked, but not enough. Shu missed the nerve but the force of the blow sent Cave sprawling.

He rolled over in the fuel to avoid the follow-up kick, but Shu recovered at once and kicked again as Cave swerved. And as he did so, a shadow moved between him and Cave, making Shu hesitate, so that the kick aimed for Cave's head slammed into his ribs, and Shu spun round, too late, to face a man holding a shovel who let fly before he had a chance to attack, using the shovel's edge like a blade. Shu crumpled and fell, to lie beside Joe Cave.

'I had a puncture', said Sandy Keith. 'And the spare was no good – so I had to walk back... Just as well, really.' He let the shovel fall. 'You'd better come inside and lie down for a bit, Joe. You look awful.'

'I'm glad Sandy didn't kill him', said Sir Roderick. 'He's got an awful lot to tell us. Of course he wasn't too keen at first – but we tried a few things and one of them worked. And now we simply can't shut him up.'

Cave tried not to think of the things they might have tried, and around him the Formula One cars in the Brand's Hatch pits howled like lost souls in hell.

'He was K.G.B. of course?' he said.

'Of course', Sir Roderick agreed. 'He says they got to him in the sixties when he was a teenager. Six months. That's all it took... Even quicker than the Jesuits... They found he had a talent to make money and a passion for good works... Best cover they could ask for, because most of all he wanted to put the world right and they sent him off to Lumumba, taught him how. Only they can do that... And if blood had to be spilled – well – you can't make an omelette without breaking eggs. He said that, Joe. He really said that. All that political philosophy culminating in a cliché.' Sir Roderick looked up to where Da Ming sat in a place of honour surrounded by a bodyguard Sir Roderick had picked himself.

151

'Better get up there, I suppose', he said. 'Odd that his nibs should have a passion for motor racing. Rather nice for Sandy, though. If he wins he might even finish up with the Order of something or other, what with cars and orphans as well.' He moved away, then turned. 'Enjoy yourself, Joe – and take care of those ribs', he said.

Cave said he would and walked off, and wondered if Sir Roderick would ever find time to look up the meaning of the word 'tact'.

Sandy Keith was geared up for the race, flameproof overalls, anti-flash mask, helmet, already in place. He looked like something from another universe, thought Cave, except that he had one arm round Janet Tang, and it was perfectly obvious that both of them were enjoying the embrace. It was equally obvious, Cave thought, that fire held no terror for Keith at all.

'So you're back where you belong', said Cave.

'I will be when I've won', said Keith.

Cave listened once more to the howl of engines, looked at the sleek menace of the car that Keith was driving, and remembered yet again the day in Las Vegas. That too had begun with a pretty girl's embrace: ended in the stench of burning flesh. Suddenly he couldn't help himself.

'Why, Sandy?' he asked.

Keith gestured to the car, then his overalls. Every available space was plastered with the names of sponsors: tyres, cigarettes, insurance, cars, even his old friend the meat pie man's name was there. But this time there was one more. Keith pointed to the place of honour – across the top of his helmet: 'SUPPORT JANET TANG'S ORPHANS', Cave read.

Chapter 15

SO ONCE again an attempt on Joe Cave had failed, Jason Bird thought, but the Member for the Central Committee didn't count that one, and even Kalkov hadn't worried unduly, Jason Bird remembered. The point was that Chinese had been used, and the Chinese were notoriously unreliable, not only deviationist but downright wayward. The four whom Joe Cave had shot in the Tiger Balm Gardens weren't even that – except the one who had been related to the girl Tang. He himself had recruited the others; gangsters who would do anything from hustling heroin to committing murder – and capitalists to a man.

Timothy Shu of course was different: not only a Communist, but one of the very earliest graduates of Lumumba University. And yet he too had remained unsatisfactory. He killed well, of course, and his mastery of the martial arts was almost absolute, but there had been a wayward streak in him that not even the Lumumba instructors were able to get rid of. There was his obsession with doing good. Nothing wrong with that, in general terms – it provided first rate cover for his real activity – except that Timothy Shu had not regarded his K.G.B. work as his real activity.

153

To him, the welfare of his orphans was as important as the welfare of the K.G.B., and that would never do. And so, when he failed to kill Joe Cave, the fact was not held against Kalkov, and Kalkov knew it.

Jason Bird looked at the screen once more. The race was progressing now, and Sandy Keith was still in the lead. Nobody had passed him, which was to be expected. Sandy Keith was a born winner, a man without complications. Not like Timothy Shu. Why, even Timothy Shu's Christianity was real, and not an extra cover for his K.G.B. activities. All in all, Shu had been a long shot, Jason Bird thought, and nobody had been in the least surprised when he failed. But the next attempt – that was not one to be labelled 'for amusement only'. The next attempt was serious, and everybody involved knew it: the Member of the Central Committee, the General, and Kalkov: Kalkov most of all...

The next attempt was to be Australia. Kalkov, like the others, had high hopes of Australia. It was a country of tremendous possibilities: enormous mineral wealth, enormous farms full of cattle and wheat and sheep, enormous cities full of – or so it seemed to Kalkov after he had read the briefing – homosexuals who spent their days jogging, and snarling in a manly way from behind closely clipped moustaches. Yes, a lot might be done in Australia, perhaps even enough to atone for previous failures.

The only thing wrong with the assignment, the only thing that had worried Kalkov, Jason Bird remembered, was that once again it was a defensive action. Once again the K.G.B. was trying to recover lost property, before British Intelligence could reach him, and once again, spear-heading the British effort, would be – or so they hoped – Joe Cave. So far as the K.G.B. were concerned, this for Joe Cave must be a positively last farewell performance.

'I want you to go to Bathurst', Sir Roderick said.

154

Cave kept quiet. He and Sir Roderick both knew he hadn't the faintest idea where Bathurst was.

'Not the one in Canada', Sir Roderick said. 'You'd hate it there – much too cold. And the one in Gambia's changed its name to Banjul and you're not going there. No no. The one I'm sending you to is the one in *Australia*.'

He sat back, beaming, like a jolly uncle who'd just presented his favourite nephew with a Raleigh bicycle.

'They had a gold rush there once', Sir Roderick said helpfully, 'and there are over seventeen thousand people. They make mining equipment. Boots and shoes, too.'

And that's not all they'll make, thought Cave. They'll make trouble, violent, dangerous trouble. Because that's what Sir Roderick specialises in – finding trouble. Just as I specialise in dealing with it.

Sir Roderick poured more single malt. 'Oh, you'll have lots of fun in Bathurst', he said.

'Making boots – or looking for gold?' said Cave.

'Looking for a girl', said Sir Roderick. 'It's never been a problem for you in the past.'

'Girls are always a problem', said Cave. 'That's part of their charm... Which particular lady boot-maker had you in mind?'

'This one', Sir Roderick said, and opened the file, flicked a photograph across the sofa table he used as a desk to where Cave sat.

Cave found himself looking at a girl wearing very little, and most of what she did wear irrelevant. A girl who really was a girl, he thought, and shapely, even elegant. Dark brown hair, eyes that were even darker, a mouth warm and full, and all that shapely elegance, that elegant shapeliness.

'It's what I believe is called a publicity still', Sir Roderick said. Cave kept on looking. 'You'll be issued with a copy', Sir Roderick said. Cave returned the photograph.

'Her name is Emilia Guardi', said Sir Roderick. 'What is known as a starlet. Mostly television, I

155

understand. Italy doesn't make many films these days. Even so – she had quite a promising career.'

'I believe you', said Cave, remembering her photograph.

'Until she was obliged to give it up.'

'Why was that?'

'She saw Cardona shot... As a matter of fact she did rather more than that. She saw who did it.'

'Cardona?' said Cave.

Sir Roderick snorted. 'I do wish you'd read right through your newspaper instead of just the sports results', he said.

'I usually stop at page three', said Cave.

'Cardona was Minister of Justice in the last Italian government but two', Sir Roderick said. 'He was a brilliant man – really quite brilliant. And a likeable one – both as a politician – and on a personal level.'

'You knew him?' Cave asked.

'I did. The fact is not relevant, except that we were involved in a scheme together – a scheme that failed to materialise.'

'If he was all that likeable – why was he killed?' asked Cave.

'He was catching terrorists', said Sir Roderick. 'He persuaded the people that they no longer need be afraid of Red Brigades and Red Army factions and the like. And the people believed him. And terrorists were caught. Small fry, then ones who were more and more important – bigger and bigger fish till he was close to the very top – and then he was murdered.'

'What's it got to do with Bathurst?'

'I've heard a whisper – a barely audible whisper – that she may be living there.'

'But why on earth should she? I mean – surely she'd stick out like a sore thumb.'

'I doubt if she plays cricket', said Sir Roderick. 'But there are thousands, perhaps hundreds of thousands – of Italian immigrants in Australia. One more wouldn't be noticed.'

'And yet you expect me to find her?'

'Of course. It's what you're for... Finding people.'
And killing them, thought Cave.

'This barely audible whisper', he said. 'How reliable
is it?'

'Reliable enough to send you there', said Sir
Roderick.

'You're paying for it?'

'Small fortune', Sir Roderick said.

'You must trust whoever it is very much', said Cave.
He'd known Sir Roderick far too long to bother asking
who.

'Of course I trust them', said Sir Roderick. 'I'm their
only hope. If they fail me – or if they are found out –
they'll die. And they know it.' He shuffled the pages of
his file together.

'I'll arrange for someone in Australia to work with
you – and my nephew will help, too, of course', he
continued.

'*Sandy?*'

'He's the only nephew I've got.'

'But surely – they don't have Grand Prix racing in
Australia – do they?'

'They have other kinds', Sir Roderick said. 'Especially at Bathurst. Sandy will be there.'

'But what's it got to do with Emilia Whatsit?'

'Guardi', said Sir Roderick. 'Like the painter. A
perfectly competent Venetian – though Canaletto was
much better.'

'Oh decidedly', said Cave.

Sir Roderick permitted himself one small smile. 'I
digress rather a lot, don't I?... Indulge my declining
years. The thing is, Joe, that Miss Guardi has a
brother who is very fond of her. He's a mechanic. A
rather good mechanic. One who specialises in racing
cars. And he's just about to go to Australia too.' He
shook the file and passed it to Cave.

'Go away and read it', he said, 'and then have a chat
with Sandy. Then go to Australia and fine me this
young lady.'

The file told him everything about Emilia Guardi, yet at the same time it told him nothing. Thanks to the photograph he knew where her mole was: photostated receipts told him where she bought her dresses, shoes, underwear. Birth certificate told him she was twenty-seven, and born in Naples. She liked Spaghetti Puttanesca, but what Neopolitan doesn't? She had also liked Alessandro Cardona. She had been in his bed when the Minister of Justice was shot.

What was more, she'd seen it done. They'd been together at the flat they'd rented under a false name, Signor and Signora Bianchi – Mr and Mrs White. And what a lot of fun the world's press had had with that one, when the story broke. The knock had come at the door, Cardona had gone to answer it because it was her birthday, and her present was due to be delivered, and a man had stood in the doorway holding a funny looking gun and it had gone 'pop' twice, like a champagne cork, and she'd seen it all through the bedroom door. Seen Alessandro fall and the man push him inside with his foot and shut the door...

She'd dressed in a panic and run, stepping over Alessandro's body, trying not to see the neat circular hole between his eyes, the bloody mess on his bare chest, and failing utterly. She had phoned her brother and told him these things, then she had run. Italian Security had of course known all about her. Alessandro Cardona was an important man, so naturally they knew, thought Cave. But he was also a man they liked. Even so, they'd failed to keep him alive.

Still they knew about her, and they knew about her brother. Domenico Guardi had nothing to hide. He told them all he knew. But that didn't include his sister's whereabouts. He'd wanted to find her as much as the police did. And for a few months he'd searched for her, searched hard. But in the end he had run out of money, and of hope, and gone back to pampering Ferraris... Until one day he'd rung the number Italian Security had given him, and told them he had a chance to go to Australia and would it be O.K.? The man in Italian

Security had said it would, and passed the information on to Sir Roderick, because Sir Roderick had liked Cardona too.

The file had a picture of Alessandro Cardona. Another publicity still inasmuch as he was making a speech, and had adopted a stance. Cave thought it must be typical: head thrown back, both clenched fists upraised. There was a cockiness about him, the kind of witty aggressiveness that came through even in a black and white photograph. No wonder people liked him, thought Cave. I like him myself. It was time to visit Sandy Keith.

Cave drove to where Sandy and Janet Tang lived: the Janet Tang Home for Orphans, a cluster of buildings designed for children, a paddock full of donkeys and ponies. A very impressive enterprise, the Janet Tang Home, and an expensive one.

Cave drove to Janet's house, passing children playing in the thin October sunlight. He'd phoned ahead, and Janet for once had sounded quite ready to talk to him, and told him how much Sandy too was looking forward to a chat. Cave had had no warning that he'd arrive in the middle of a row.

It had been a real up-and-downer. They could just about manage to say 'Hallo'. Keith went at once to the whisky bottle.

'Isn't it a little early?' Janet Tang said.

'No', said Keith; then to Cave, 'You want one?'

Janet would be annoyed if he said 'Yes', Keith if he said 'No'. Better compromise. 'Just a small one', he said. Oh great. That way he'd annoyed both of them.

Keith took him at his word, and handed over a damp glass.

'So you're going to Bathurst', he said.

'That's right', said Cave.

Keith said, 'I'm supposed to be going to Bathurst –'

'You *are* going', said Janet Tang.

'To drive in a race I don't like in a car I don't know – a dollied up production car.'

'That's never stopped you before', said Cave.

159

'Joe', said Keith. 'I'm getting on.'

He was thirty-two, but for a racing driver that was hardly the first flush of youth, and Cave knew it.

'You're getting twenty-five thousand pounds appearance money', said Janet Tang. Keith ignored her.

'This morning I had a call from Bob Harris', said Keith. 'The bloke who's modified the Morton-Nadir-Yummy.'

'The what?'

'The Morton-Nadir-Yummy. It's a Formula One car. Nadir put the package together with Penny Morton, Bob Harris did a revamp of poor old Charlie Morton's design, and Yummy Bars paid for it... You must have heard of Yummy Bars?'

'Pubs?' asked Cave.

'Chocolates, you bloody fool', said Keith. 'You know: "Please Mummy – buy Yummy".'

Cave knew. He also watched the telly.

'Their sponsorship's worth millions – and poor Bill Speers, he's Morton-Nadir Number One driver now – broke his toe in a disco.'

Cave snorted.

'It's not funny', said Keith, then grinned. 'Well Nadir doesn't think it is... He wants me to go back and be his replacement.'

'So?'

Keith looked at Janet Tang.

'You tell him', he said.

She had never looked more beautiful, thought Cave. Her olive skin flawless, black hair glowing, her carriage graceful yet alluring even in anger and frustration as she was now. When at last she spoke she was fighting to be calm, and her voice trembled.

'Nadir has made us an offer', she said. 'A very good offer. If Sandy wins –'

'Of course I'll win', said Keith. 'It's a marvellous car.'

'– then you'll make a lot of money. But not enough. There will be no more from sponsorship than we get now –'

160

'There will be when I'm world champion.'

'That may not happen', said Janet Tang.

Keith winced at that, winced as if she'd cut him with a whip, thought Cave.

'I didn't know you had such faith in me', he said. 'I'm touched.'

She said wearily: 'It's not a question of faith. It's a question of reality. If you sign for Nadir he will be in control. He has no need of anything except his cars – and winning. He will not think about the orphans – why should he? But when *we* are in control – we can think about them all the time.'

'When we are in control', said Keith, 'I never get to drive a Formula One car ... and what do you mean by "we" anyway? It's when *you* are in control. "We" doesn't come into it.'

It was her turn to wince then. Fifteen all, thought Cave, but she got up and walked out. Match abandoned.

'Let me get you a proper drink', said Keith, and Cave handed over his glass. It was either that or walk out in sympathy, and Keith knew it. 'Why does Uncle Roderick want you to go to Bathurst?' Keith asked.

'To find a girl.'

'You're good at that.'

'That's your uncle's joke.'

Keith shrugged. 'Don't waste it then. He doesn't make many... Does he want me to find her too?'

'No', said Cave. 'He wants you to go there and take me with you as your P.R. man.'

'What for?'

'Five thousand quid.'

'Plus the twenty-five thousand already on offer. Thirty g's... This must be important, Joe. Uncle Roderick never parts with money unless he has to.'

'It's important all right', Cave said. 'You'd better go, I think. It was your uncle who got your Bathurst sponsor to come to you in the first place... He really does want you to go, Sandy. And you know how he hates to be disappointed.'

Sandy Keith ran his hands through his hair, and as

161

always it changed from copper colour to angry, flaming red.

'You know what Uncle Roderick can go and do', he said. Then: 'No – Tell him not to bother... We'll go to Bathurst and I'll drive their bloody car. But not for you – and certainly not for Uncle Roderick. Janet signed on ten more orphans last week. We need the money. Every penny. That means I have to go. I haven't any choice, have I? All the same, sometimes I can't help bitching about it.'

Chapter 16

IN HIS FLAT Cave took up the Domenico Guardi file, and settled down to read. A lad in demand, our Domenico. Ferrari, Alfa Romeo, Lancia, they'd all found a use for him in their time. A lad who worked hard and saved his money and dreamed of opening his own garage and never said a word about his sister: rarely said a word about anything. A taciturn Italian, thought Cave. Whatever next? But at least he was a taciturn good-looking Italian. With a sister like that, how could he not be?

Sir Roderick had added a note in his own hand: 'Guardi will act as mechanic for a person called Loridan. Suggest you ask S.K.' If S.K. was capable of speech, thought Cave, but he dialled the number anyway. Keith answered, and to Cave's enormous relief, he sounded sober.

'You needn't have bothered calling', he said. 'I haven't started all that again. I need to be sober to race, and I have to race.'

'It wasn't that', Cave lied.

'And I haven't changed my mind either. I'm still going to Australia and that stupid production car rally', said Keith.

163

'It isn't that either', said Cave. 'Who's Loridan?'

'Don't tell me she's going?'

'She?'

'Don't you ever read the papers?' Keith asked.

'You're still stealing your uncle's dialogue', said Cave. 'I'll tell you what I told him. I never get past page three. – And that's hardly what you could call reading.'

'She could be on page three, too, if she wanted. She's the Flying Contessa... Old Venetian family, new fast cars... As a matter of fact she's pretty good', said Keith.

He didn't even add the words 'for a woman', thought Cave.

'What's she like?'

'Like? She's a redhead. Green eyes. A bit shorter than me.'

'For God's sake', said Cave, 'I mean – what she's *like*? Honest? Tricky? Kind? Short tempered?'

'She's the trickiest driver I know', said Keith. 'Overdoes it a bit. Not short tempered, though, not behind the wheel.'

'I mean', said Cave patiently, 'when she *isn't* driving.'

'Oh', said Keith. 'Oh, I see... Kind, I suppose. She gave me some money for the orphans once... Not a lot, but it was all she had at the time, and it helped.'

'What about honest?'

'I doubt it', said Keith. 'She's a woman.'

'Are you sure you're not drinking?' Cave asked, and the question was serious. Keith's drinking had always been linked to betrayal and the memory of Trudi Jannot, and that assessment of the Flying Contessa sounded ominous.

'I'm going to race', said Sandy Keith. 'I told you.'

'You haven't answered my question', said Cave.

'Nor do I want to', said Keith, then his voice softened. 'I know you mean well, Joe', he said. 'And I thank you for it. But don't worry. When we get to Bathurst I'll be fit to drive.'

'You mean you're going to stop before we get there?'

'From time to time', said Keith, and hung up.

Cave depressed the receiver rest, and dialled the number he knew best.

'Oh, so it's *that* Loridan', said Sir Roderick. 'As a matter of fact we have a file on her.'

'You do surprise me', said Cave.

'Used to be one of the radical chic lot in her early days', said Sir Roderick. 'The Via Veneto Communists ... you know ... gold chains and Gucci shoes and Power to the People. – Then she took up driving instead.'

It sounds as if I've got more to worry about than drunken driving, thought Cave.

But on the flight over, Sandy started to sober up. It was Cave who drank the champagne: after a couple of goes at a Buck's Fizz Keith stayed with the orange juice. All his life he'd gone out to win, Cave knew, and boozers never won, not in his game. And Keith felt the urge to be a winner even more strongly than the urge to be a boozer, and so he drank orange juice, and Joe Cave thanked God for it.

They stopped over for one night in Singapore, to undo some of the damage of a whole day in the air, slept and ate breakfast, and went back to Changi Airport, and the First Class hospitality lounge, where they waited for the plane... A Do-It-Yourself bar that stretched as far as the eye could see: more orange juice for Sandy, and a Campari and soda for Cave. (No champagne it seemed, till you were airborne.) Keith hunched morosely in his chair, watching Japanese and European businessmen hunched in their chairs, scowling at their *Wall Street Journal*s and pocket calculators. It suited his mood. And then all that gloomy peace was shattered. A girl strode in, a redheaded girl in a yellow silk jump-suit, and even a stride didn't really describe it, Cave thought. It was rather more like a swagger. She was a little shorter than Sandy,

165

with a dark and handsome man scurrying beside her, and carrying her hand luggage and his own.

She yelled across to Keith, 'Hey Sandy. It's good to *see* you.' Then she talked in Italian to the scurrying man and strode over to Keith, held him lightly by the forearms, kissed him on the cheek. 'You going to beat me again?'

'I'm going to try.'

'Then you're going to do it', she said. 'Is that why you drink orange juice?' She turned to Cave. 'Are you a driver, too?'

Keith said, 'This is Joe Cave – the Contessa Loridan.'

'Claudia Loridan', the redhead said. She looked around. 'Domenico.'

The dark man came up, scurrying still. He brought two orange juices and two Campari and sodas. The Contessa waved him to a chair. 'This is Domenico Guardi', she said. 'Best mechanic in Italy.' Guardi bowed and grinned, as the Contessa took one Campari and soda, and gave the other to Cave.

'I like it too', she said. 'Cheers', then to Keith: 'Hey Sandy – you remember that time at Monza you couldn't get your car to start and I gave you a push and it still wouldn't start and I kicked it and it did?'

All around her calculators clicked indignantly, but she went on remembering, in that loud, well modulated voice, as Sandy Keith's scowl grew deeper.

'What's the matter?' she said. 'You don't like reminiscing?'

'I don't like reminiscing about the times when I used to drive Formula One cars', said Keith, and then their flight was called, and not before time, thought Cave.

On the plane she sat beside Cave, and drank one glass of champagne, and refused the meal.

'What do you do, Joe Cave?' she asked.

'P.R.'

'For Sandy? . . . He doesn't even drive Formula One any more.'

'He's got a lot of sponsors. I do the P.R. for them.'

166

'People still like him then?'

'People still think he's the greatest.' And that at least was true, he thought.

'Me too... But he shouldn't drive these kind of races. Grand Prix... That's what he should drive.'

'You tell him', said Cave.

'Well, of course', the Contessa Loridan said.

They stayed the night in Sydney, and the hotel was fine, the air conditioning just right for a warm, Spring day. Cave showered and lay down and slept, and then the phone rang.

'Hey', said the Contessa. 'What are you doing?'

'Trying to sleep', said Cave.

'Oh no you're not', the Contessa said. 'It's time to get up, Joe Cave. It's party time.'

He met her in the lounge. She wore green silk this time, and a yellow waterproof on top of it, a long yellow umbrella in her hand. There had been no threat of rain, but the colours were perfect for her. Like Italian icecream, Cave thought: colourful, rich and very edible. He was glad he was wearing his new light-weight suit. He stopped by the bar.

'You want a drink here?' he asked. 'While we wait for the others?'

'We are the others', she said. 'I mean there's only us. Sandy's watching a video-tape of last year's Bathurst race – and Domenico is too tired. I do hope you're not too tired?'

Inside the bar a squat and muscular man in a T-shirt put down his glass and stood up as if the floor show had just begun.

'I hope so too', said Cave. 'Where do you want to go?'

She ticked them off on her fingers. 'Look at the Opera House, look at the bridge, look at King's Cross.'

'What's King's Cross?'

'The red light district. At home everybody said I should see it. Damned if I know why.'

They took a cab to look at the Opera House and the

167

bridge, and the bay with scores of ferries and sailing craft. Being Italian, she preferred the Opera House to the bridge.

Then they walked through King's Cross: the only way to see it, all her friends had said. Not that there was anything to see she hadn't seen before. Strip clubs, blue movies, dirty bookshops, massage parlours, half clad girls all over the place. The Contessa gawped at them all like a tourist in a gallery gawking at a Van Gogh.

'Interesting – no?' she said.

'No', said Cave.

'You are right', said the Contessa. 'Let us have a drink instead.'

She walked into the nearest pub before Cave could stop her. It wasn't one he would have chosen for her, or even for himself. A pub stripped down to the essentials: a pub that could ignore the cigarette burns on its tables and the stains on its carpets because the glasses were cold and the beer was colder. All the men in the room were watching the T.V. screen, giving a cricket match the sort of reverent hush a nunnery might afford a visiting Pope, while what the Contessa called the ladies of joy waited patiently for their innings.

The Contessa's entrance achieved the impossible. It dragged the men's eyes away from the T.V. screen. Cave noted without surprise that he was sweating. Then the Contessa called for champagne, and Cave suspected that he was blushing, too. The men's eyes grew rounder and rounder, their faces expressed a mixture of bewilderment and rage. Cave couldn't blame them. The Contessa looked like a gazelle among a herd of bison.

The men all wore T-shirts, Cave noticed. All except him. He was wearing a lightweight suit that had been made for him in Hong Kong. A poncey sort of suit he thought, by the standards of this pub; a pommy sort of suit. The ladies of joy began to look a little more joyful, and Cave thought that he understood why. It didn't make him feel any happier. Alan Border cracked a four

168

through the covers and nobody even looked up, except one lean, rangy man who sat firmly with his back to Cave and stared unmoving at the T.V. set. Cave wished he could have seen his face: a cricket enthusiast so dedicated would be rare indeed, even in Australia. Then the barman came up and dumped a bottle of champagne and two beer glasses on the table, with the air of a man who has plumbed the lowest possible depths. Cave popped the cork, poured, and raised his glass to the Contessa.

'Cheers', she said, and sipped, and then: 'But it's *good.*'

If only she hadn't sounded so surprised, thought Cave. He'd paid a lot of money for that suit. A tall, well built man got up and came over to their table.

'What do you think you're doing here?' he said.

'Drinking champagne', the Contessa said. 'You should try it. It's good.'

'Not me', the tall man said. 'I'm not a poofta.' He turned to Cave. 'Are you a poofta?'

The Contessa also turned to Cave. 'What is a poofta?' she asked. 'A homosexual?'

Cave nodded, and she turned to the well built man. 'He isn't. At least I don't *think* he is.'

'Let him speak for himself', the well built man said. Cave drank more champagne.

'Come on, poofta. You going to let your sheila do all the talking?'

Cave drank once more. Really the Contessa was right. It *was* nice champagne.

'Cat got your tongue, poofta?'

Cave topped up his glass, put the bottle down, and as he did so two more men came up to the table: one barrel shaped, and so covered with tattoos he looked like a stamp collection and the other a sort of cross between a Greek God and Neanderthal Man, golden tan, golden hair, body like Apollo, but the face like an illustration from a book on evolution.

'Me and my mates is waiting, poofta', the well built man said.

'You and your mates are disgusting. Go away', said Cave.

'My oath', said the well built man, 'a *Pommy* poofta.'

That made it the last straw. The Neanderthal grabbed the champagne bottle and made to empty it on Cave's head, but Cave was already up and moving and if the Contessa got his share, she'd asked for it.

He stood facing the three, hands open at his sides.

'Believe me', he said, 'we don't need this.'

The barrel shaped man spoke for the first and last time.

'Get him', he said and charged at Cave, short, massive arms moving like pistons. Cave slipped his rush the way a matador slips a bull and kicked the Neanderthal God in the stomach. The God's stomach muscles were good – he'd obviously done the right exercises – but Cave's kick was good too. The toe of the Russell and Bromley moccasin smacked precisely into the right place and the God groaned and clutched where it hurt.

The tall man swung a punch, a loping right which carried all his weight behind it, and Cave ducked beneath it and hooked his arm across the tall man's, sent him spinning away into a tableful of ladies of joy as the barrel shaped man charged in again, swung a punch at Cave that he was a little too late in dodging, hitting the hard packed muscle of his shoulder.

Pain came at once, a searing pain that slowed him up as the barrel shaped man came at him again. This time he was too late to duck, and as the barrel shaped man swung, Cave struck with the edge of his hand that was as hard as teak, aiming for the biceps, feeling it bite into the flesh, and the barrel shaped man roared aloud.

Cave spun to face the tall man, who grabbed for Cave, caught the lapel of his suit and pulled him in towards him. Cave heard his lapel, the hand stitched lapel by Sam's of Kowloon, rip and tear, and struck with a spear strike at a point below the tall man's breast bone, then spun round for a high kick to the side of the barrel shaped man's neck. He had really liked

170

that suit. The barrel shaped man fell with a crash that shook the pub, but the Neanderthal God had got enough breath back to grab the champagne bottle once more. This time he smashed it against the wall before he charged at Cave, a dozen dagger points of glass swung at his face.

Cave swayed to one side, then grabbed the Neanderthal's wrist two handed, swung hard and twisted as he swung. The Neanderthal God screamed as his arm broke, and Cave clipped him on the side of his neck and he fell among the glass he had smashed.

Cave looked about him: all three of them were unconscious. He turned to the barman.

'What do I owe you for the champers?' he asked.

'On the house, sport', said the barman. He seemed rather nervous, but even so he added: 'Drop in again. Any time.'

Suddenly a man began to applaud, and the rest of the men joined in, and then the ladies of joy. As he and the Contessa walked out they all rose to their feet. A standing ovation, he thought. And the nicest lightweight suit I ever had. In the street he took off the jacket, looked at the lapel.

'Ruined', he said.

'Never mind. You were tremendous', the Contessa said. 'Are all P.R. men like that?'

'Some of us have to be', said Cave.

'Which ones?'

'The ones who let girls lead them astray.'

She made a face at him.

'We eat now', she said. 'Then maybe you can teach me how to fight.'

Later he said, 'You fight pretty well yourself.'

'Who won?'

'It was a draw', said Cave. 'Just.' She laughed and kissed him.

'Get some sleep', she said. 'We have to be fit at Bathurst tomorrow.'

Then she left him and he lay back on the pillow. No
word from his Australian contact, and Sandy was all
right. Still watching tapes of last year's race. Maybe he
could get some rest at that, he thought, and closed his
eyes...

The phone rang just as sleep came: the most mad-
dening time of all for a phone to ring. Cave grabbed it
and grunted.

'We've got to talk', said a voice that belonged to a
squat and muscular man. Cave groaned again.

'Come on up', he said, then checked his mini fridge to
make sure that there was beer.

'You know who I am then?' the squat and muscular
man asked.

'Your Department sent photographs', said Cave.
'They didn't give a name.'

The other man looked defensive. 'It's Norm', he said.
'At least my chief says it is.' He swallowed beer. 'My
chief's got a sense of humour.'

At least I'm spared that, thought Cave. Aloud he
said: 'You find anything?'

'Yeah', said Norm. 'After you left with that sheila,
Guardi decides he's going on the town, too. Only he
doesn't want to see the opera – or the bridge.'

'What does he want to see?'

'Bit of life', said Norm. 'He goes straight to King's
Cross... He's had a few lessons somewhere, that joker.'

'You mean he was on to you?'

'Would've been – only we had a team. Three of us.
We kept switching. It was the only way we could keep
up with him.'

'Where'd he go?'

'Pub', said Norm. 'As a matter of fact you went there
yourself... That was quite a floorshow you put on.'

'One does one's poor best', said Cave. 'Were you
there?'

'In the doorway, watching', said Norm. 'I didn't
think you'd want me to interfere.'

172

'Right', said Cave. 'What happened after I left?'

'He got sort of restless. Kept looking at his watch. Then another bloke came in and handed him a note.'

'And then?'

'He went to look at a blue movie. I went too. Ugliest lot of sheilas I ever set eyes on.'

'And after that?'

'Hamburger', said Norm. 'Tomato relish and onions. Icecream to follow.'

'And then?'

'Hotel... Not like this place. He talked to a girl there.'

'What kind of girl?'

Norm struggled for words. 'The blue movie could've used her', he said at last.

'We'd better go and take a look', said Cave.

'Too right', said Norm. 'She talked like she was in the coffee business – but I reckon it's Emilia Guardi.'

Cave headed for the shower.

Chapter 17

THE BIDAWHILE was rough, but it was also ready. Rooms by the day, the night, maybe even by the hour, thought Cave. The sight of two men together gave the desk clerk the jitters: it was definitely not that kind of place. But Norm explained that they weren't that kind of fellers and that they'd come to meet a mate called Bluey Green. He was told he wasn't there, which was not surprising, as he didn't exist. And as they left the girl came down to pay her bill, and at the sight of her the desk clerk was so overcome that he was polite, and lost all interest in two men together.

She'd gained maybe a couple of pounds, thought Cave, but she'd had room for it. Now she didn't have room for another ounce. She was perfect. Cave almost had to drag Norm outside to the car.

Emilia Guardi had had a taxi ordered, and went in to the Ansett Bus Terminal.

'Now where's she going?' Norm asked.

'Bathurst, where else?' said Cave. 'Did she spot you at the hotel?'

'No', said Norm. 'It was her brother who was the leery one.'

'You're going to Bathurst, too', said Cave.

174

'No worries', said Norm.

'In the bus', said Cave. Norm began to swear.

Emilia Guardi was followed on to the bus by a couple of Italian-looking characters who seemed pleased to see her, but then what man wouldn't? thought Cave. He strolled over to stand behind a woman in a loose fitting coat, a scarf about her head, who watched the bus draw out.

'Can I give you a lift, Contessa?' he asked.

The Contessa Loridan went up in the air about a foot, but landed with dignity.

'No thank you', she said. 'I have my own car.'

'I hope it's a nice one', said Cave.

'It is a Rolls-Royce', she said. 'I find it adequate.'

The cars for the Bathurst race had been built for speed and endurance: Holdens and Fords. Technically production models, which meant that at least two hundred of them had been made, they had a thousand kilometres to cover, and a course around the foothills of the Blue Mountains that dipped and swooped five hundred feet up – and down. From time to time, to add spice to the competition, the course went round an abyss: a sheer drop of hundreds of feet, with nothing to keep you in except an Amico crash barrier.

'What do you think?' Cave asked.

'Do you know', said Keith, 'it's more interesting than I thought it would be.'

'It does look exciting', Cave agreed.

'That's what it's for', said Keith. 'Fast too ... and long. One hundred and twenty-seven laps.'

'I might have known you'd enjoy that', said Cave.

Keith fingered the little silver charm called Ganesh that hung by its silver chain around the neck.

'It isn't Formula One', he said. 'It never will be. Still, if the car holds together, I just might do it.' He was driving a Higgins Special: Mr Higgins, who had many millions, had caused two hundred cars to be built so that Keith and the Contessa could drive two of them.

175

In the pits engines revved, T.V. and radio commentators poked mikes at drivers who had better things to do. A covey of them descended on Sandy, and Cave left them to it. Not very good P.R. but he had to look for Norm, not seen since the bus stop in Sydney.

He still wasn't visible, but Emilia Guardi was. She wore a very tight, very short dress, and was handing out cups of coffee under a sign that read: 'Emilia's Espresso. Only The Best Ingredients'. A T.V. interviewer took a cup from her and went to try his luck with the Contessa, and Cave kept on looking... Near the Contessa's Higgins Special, Domenico Guardi was talking to two Italian-looking men and they were listening hard. For once Guardi seemed to have things to say. Cave looked again. They were the two men who'd got on the Ansett bus behind Emilia... Still no sign of Norm. He looked towards Sandy Keith, who was submerged beneath a tide of microphones and signalling frantically. Time to get back to work, to bodyguard his man to the starting line.

As a race, thought Keith, it was more like a gigantic game of chicken. You took your line and held it, and if the bloke in the way stayed in the way – then it was dodgem cars at 120 m.p.h. plus. And to add to the fairground motif, there were the switchback effect of the up and down slopes, and the wall of death sheer drops. You could never call it boring, but then you couldn't call it racing either. Not the kind of racing he knew and loved. More like a very good point to point when what you wanted was the Derby.

But he had skill and he had nerve, and he needed them. Without them he hadn't a prayer. Those Aussie drivers drove for keeps. No quarter. But first they had to catch you... Craftily Keith eased out of the pack, tucked himself in behind the leaders... Ninety-three laps to go, if the Higgins held together.

Cave watched the race on T.V. in the V.I.P. tent, and drank soda water as he watched. It wasn't yet time for

176

champagne. Emilia Guardi was still handing out her coffee, still proclaiming the best ingredients, but there was now no sign of Domenico. In the pits where he belonged, thought Cave. Still no sign of Norm, either. But the two Italian-looking men were there, still staring at Emilia Guardi. Surely to God they can't start anything in front of this mob? thought Cave...

Seventy laps to go. Keith was still tucked in behind the leaders, and they didn't like it, were doing their considerable best to lose him. But they couldn't. It was a race, and Keith had a chance of winning. He was taking it... Towards an uphill slope he spotted the second Higgins. The leaders lapped it; soon it would be his turn. Well at least the Contessa wouldn't give him any trouble, he thought. They were team mates.

But suddenly the Contessa proceeded to go out of her mind. Keith drew level with her as they reached the top of the slope, became briefly airborne as they crested the ridge on to the downhill stretch – and the Contessa steered deliberately at him, and Keith sheered off enough to take a glancing blow that sent him skidding crabwise as the Contessa smacked into the steel railings, then bounced away to come at him again. Keith flicked a glance across at her. That last crunch must have knocked her out, he thought, and steered gingerly into her car, knocking it away from him. But she made no move, remained slumped onto the wheel as her car sped on. They swooped on to level ground, and he flicked her car again and again, easing her away from the Fords and Holdens that thundered by, until for a moment he'd jolted her back into consciousness, and she reached for the automatic control, eased it back, and passed out again. Keith eased back too. This time he could nudge her car to a halt...

Cave saw it on T.V. They'd even managed a zoom lens close up on the Contessa, slumped over her steering wheel. And suddenly he *knew*, and left the tent at a run and headed for the crash wagon, leapt aboard. The crew looked at his Higgins T-shirt and let him stay.

177

Keith had switched off both ignitions and held the girl in his arms as the crash wagon drew up and Cave came running. He called out: 'She's asleep... It's crazy. She won't wake up.' Then the crash wagon crew scooped her out of the Higgins Special, wrapped her in a blanket, and went off with her towards a doctor. Cave looked at the survivor.

'Will your car go?' he asked.

'Of course.'

'Let's go then.'

They got in and roared away, off the track, back to the pits, to find Domenico Guardi. He was in the Higgins pit, where he should have been, but he too was unconscious. Norm, with a bump on his forehead the size of a goose egg, stood looking down at him.

'It isn't him we want', said Norm.

'I know', Cave said. 'Get in.'

Norm turned to Sandy Keith. 'Are you sure it's all right?' he asked.

'Of course', said Keith. 'I had no chance of catching up anyway. Glad to help.'

Norm got in and they roared off again, their quarry a coffee coloured van with cream coloured lettering: 'Emilia's Espresso', and beneath, again in cream, 'Only The Best Ingredients'. One of the Italian-looking men was driving it, the other sat in the back with Emilia Guardi. With them was another man that Cave would have given much to see, but he kept his face turned away from them, never once looked back at his pursuers. But the Italian-looking man who drove knew that they were there, all right. As soon as he spotted the Higgins he headed, quite literally, for the hills. And it was their best option at that, thought Cave. Scatter out in the open, and pick us off one by one. That they had guns he had no doubt... But Sandy Keith aimed the battered, dented Higgins like a missile, and they never made the high ground: pulled up in scrub instead, and started running.

Norm had picked up a gun from somewhere. He began blasting before the car stopped. Cave, more

178

cautious, dived into the scrub as one of the Italian-looking men turned and fired, the bullet spanged off a stone by his foot, as he squeezed off a shot in his turn. The other man fell, twitched, was still.

Emilia Guardi yelled at the man who had kept his back to them, and he kept on running, but she turned away, in her hands a repeating rifle, the sort you use on kangaroo hunts. She aimed at Cave and began blasting. Cave rolled to the shelter of the car and Norm took one in the shoulder, cursed and fired back, and Emilia Guardi ceased to be beautiful. The surviving Italian-looking man crouched like a sprinter and ran at them, gun blazing, in the suicidal courage of despair. Deliberately Cave aimed for his legs and fired, and bowled him over like a rabbit.

Norm said, 'You want me to finish him?'

'He has to talk', said Cave, and looked about him once more. But the man who had valued his anonymity so highly, the man who Emilia Guardi had given her life to protect, had reached high ground and disappeared.

A phone call from a safe phone, and Sir Roderick tetchy because of the hour it was.

'I can't help it', said Cave. 'It was you sent me here.'

'Just tell it', said Sir Roderick.

'All right. It was Emilia Guardi shot Cardona. She'd been a Red for years – and anyway she paid for it well enough. All those banks the terrorists robbed.'

'Who told you this?'

'The bloke we took alive. He was a terrorist too. He swears she was the one who killed Cardona. It makes sense when you think about it. She was the closest. There never was an unidentified male killer – only her... She ran away in case she was found out. And she was.'

'Who by?'

'You know very well who by', said Cave. 'Italian Security – they sent the Contessa Loridan after her.'

'Was she any good?'

'Indeed she was', said Cave. 'Good cover, that radical chic past. And she used Emilia's brother to nose out Emilia. That was good.'

'What about the brother?'

'Nice enough feller. Went to Australia to ask his sister to give herself up and got knocked unconscious... Same thing happened to Norm, when she spotted he was tailing her and he thought she hadn't. She tied him up, too. Took him a day to get free.'

'Weren't you attacked?'

'Emilia set another lot of heavies on me. Hired muscle. To tell the truth I thought the Contessa had done it at first. But she was only keeping track of Domenico.'

'So it's all wrapped up rather neatly?' Sir Roderick asked.

'Not quite', Cave said. 'There was another man involved whom I didn't get a look at. Tall and lean, but I only ever saw him from the back. He was very good at keeping his face hidden.'

'You've no ideas about him at all?' asked Sir Roderick.

'None.'

'Pity', Sir Roderick said. 'But I can't discuss it with you over the phone. It costs too much.'

'What do you want me to do?' Cave asked.

'Stay there', Sir Roderick said. 'See if you can get a line on whoever it is. I'll be in touch soon', he added, then: 'Try to keep the expenses down, Joe. Things are terrible here at the moment.' Then he hung up. Cave put down the receiver very gently. Sir Roderick, he thought, always hung up as forcibly as he possibly could. He looked at his watch. It was late, but there still might be time for a chat with the Contessa.

She wore an awful lot of white nylon that somehow did very little to cover her, and she yawned a lot, but she was awake.

180

'They tell me it was the Guardi cow', she said. 'She put something in my coffee.'

'Only the best ingredients', said Cave, and then: 'She won't do it again.'

'Oh', said the Contessa.

'That's right', said Cave.

'Sandy saved my life. Came to see me and I thanked him. He says he's fed up with this kind of racing. He's going back to Grand Prix. At least he says he is, once he's phoned Janet to tell her so. Poor Sandy...' She lay back on the pillows. 'Come and teach me some more of your holds', she said. 'It might help to keep me awake.'

Cave saw Sandy Keith next morning at breakfast. He looked ghastly, but that wasn't surprising. He had been drinking most of the night. Cave watched as he wrestled with the coffee cup that he could only manage two-handed.

'So you've given up the idea of racing any more?' he asked.

Keith swallowed coffee, gagged, then put the cup back more or less in its saucer, slopping coffee as he did so.

'No I damn well haven't', he said. 'I admit I had a lot to drink last night, but that was medicinal. I had to tell Janet that I wouldn't do something that she wanted me to do, and for that I need medicine. Every time.'

'And what did you tell her?' Joe Cave asked, knowing the answer only too well.

'I told her I was going back to Grand Prix racing', said Keith.

'And what did she say?' Cave asked.

'She said goodbye', said Sandy Keith.

Sandy Keith didn't go back to England, and Grand Prix racing, and the Morton-Nadir-Yummy, Jason Bird remembered, at least not immediately. He had wired Nadir at once, of course, as soon as he was free, but Nadir had races for the car to enter, and schedules to be met, and Sandy Keith was too late, at least for the time being. Formula One would have to wait, yet again. But, Keith found, there were compensations. He went off to Hawaii with Domenico Guardi, and enjoyed the sunshine and breakers of Oahu, while he sat with Domenico and together they drank, and swam, and talked about racing cars. Guardi liked it so much that he had all but decided to open a garage there, and Sandy Keith stayed on to help him choose a suitable one, and continued his acquaintance with Mai-Tais.

Of course Cave went back to England at the first possible opportunity. The anonymous looking man had been a hopeless cause, thank God, tall, rangy geezers were ten a penny in Australia, and without being able to supply a reason for his being with Emilia Guardi, other than the obvious one, the whole exercise was pointless. He told Sir Roderick so in a telephone conversation conducted at breakneck speed because of its high cost, and flew back home, and sat in the sauna, and was happy for all of two weeks. And then Sir Roderick sent for him once more...

Chapter 18

'I'VE GOT something here that might interest you',
Sir Roderick said.

Interest, thought Cave. That's a new word. What's
he up to? He sipped his single malt and waited.

'Thought it would be just up your street', Sir
Roderick said heartily. Sir Roderick was rarely hearty.

'Oh yes?' said Cave.

'You don't sound very enthusiastic', said Sir
Roderick.

'I don't know what you want me to do', said Cave.

'Look for a feller', said Sir Roderick. 'Bring him back
to me if you can. Bring me a tape-recording if you
can't.'

'Why shouldn't I bring him back?' asked Cave. 'Will
he not want to come?'

'The K.G.B. are after him', said Roderick.

He'll want to come all right, Cave thought. The trick
will be to get him here in one piece.

'His name's Peltzer', said Sir Roderick. 'Mean anything to you?'

'No', said Cave.

'East German. Born in Leipzig. About thirty-five.
Good engineer. Better than good. Brilliant. So brilliant

that the Russians took him away to work on their space programme.'

'Did he mind?'

'I don't think so', said Sir Roderick. 'He was a Party member because at his level of achievement he had to be. No hope of promotion without a Party card. No other reason. But at least he knew the patter when he trod the sacred soil. Then he had all the special food and allowances, too. Holidays in a dacha in the Crimea. Lots of pretty girls. He didn't mind joining the party at all.'

'Then why –?'

'Just a moment, Joe', said Sir Roderick. 'I'm trying to think.'

Cave waited, and looked about at the material objects that Sir Roderick used instead of friends. When you sat in Sir Roderick's chair friends were a luxury you weren't allowed. A little Degas painting of a dancer on the wall, a Sheraton desk, a William IV carver used as an office chair, some old Waterford crystal, and about ten thousand files. No friends. And that'd about be me, too, thought Cave. Except that I haven't got enough money to buy paintings and antiques and I only get to read the files one at a time.

'He defected', Sir Roderick said at last. 'That much is obvious. He went home to visit his sick mother but she died while he was there and he legged it.'

'How?' Cave asked. It was never easy to defect from the Soviet Union, or even East Germany.

'What they used to call the Lindemann Route – after the bloke who invented it. The K.G.B. closed it last year.'

Cave asked the next, inevitable question: 'Why?'

Sir Roderick shrugged. 'My guess is disillusion.'

'Is that why I'm going after him?'

'Good Lord no', Sir Roderick said. 'It's him I'm after – or failing him that tape of his.'

Then why the big build up? Cave wondered. Why don't you just show me the file, tell me where you think he is, then turn me loose?

'Where is he?' Cave asked.

Sir Roderick sipped his single malt. Glenmorangie that week. 'Do you see anything of my nephew these days?' he asked.

The man's inside my mind, Cave thought. Here I sit thinking that I have no friend, and all the time there's Sandy Keith. He was perhaps the only man that Cave could call his friend and he was a good friend indeed.

'Well', Sir Roderick said. 'Do you?'

Cave got back to the present.

'Not for a while', he said. 'You've been moving me around rather a lot recently.'

'I want you to look him up.'

'Be a pleasure', said Cave. Sandy's converted farmhouse in Sussex still had the best sauna Cave had ever used. It was nice to know that Sandy was back in England...

'He's not at home just at the moment', Sir Roderick said. 'He's been living in Hawaii.'

'You want me to visit him there?'

It would be no hardship, no hardship at all, to spend a little time in Hawaii, Cave thought.

'He's left Hawaii', Sir Roderick said. 'Making a little trip. As a matter of fact I fixed it up for him. It's not entirely unconnected with this job of yours.'

'Where is he?' Cave asked.

'He's gone back to Australia', said Sir Roderick.

I might have known, Cave thought, and I *do* know the reason for all this heartiness and jollying along. Australia's the last place I want to go, and he knows it... Full of thousands of miles of nothing at all. What they call the outback... Cave hated the countryside: felt at ease only in cities, the larger the better.

'I won't go', he said.

'Pity', said Sir Roderick. 'I was rather hoping you would. After all Sandy's marvellous in a car, but he's not frightfully good at the rough stuff, is he? He might need a bit of help with that.'

And there the old so-and-so had got him. Sandy was hopeless with his hands and worse with a gun, but he was his friend. His mucker. His mate. Cave sighed.

'Let's have the file', he said.

Sir Roderick passed it to him, and lifted his glass in a toast.

The Lindemann Route had always been trouble, Jason Bird remembered. Even before the K.G.B. had discovered its existence, the defections had been going on. And these weren't just little men, Party members and the like, who had suddenly developed a taste for the bright lights and embezzled enough marks to raise the price of a diamond or two on the Black Market: the defectors who used the Lindemann Route were the big boys, the important boys, the ones that the Democratic Republic of Germany and the Union of Soviet Socialist Republics could least afford to lose. And perhaps among them all, Peltzer was the most valued. What he had on paper, and what he had inside his head, were beyond price.

That was why he was allowed to use the Lindemann Route. It was far too important to be risked for anyone who could bring with him only a modest fortune in diamonds. After Peltzer of course, the K.G.B. had really gone to work, and the Lindemann Route had inevitably been uncovered, and its perpetrators, or most of them, either shot or sent to the Gulag Archipelago, or given a fortune if they survived the investigation, and a face alteration job in that clinic in Zurich. But it was all too late, the damage had been done, and mere punishment of its perpetrators was not enough. The K.G.B. wanted Peltzer back. And this time it was the general, Malkovsky, who was put in charge of the operation. In other words, Jason Bird thought, it was Malkovsky's head that was on the block. But Kalkov had still been there with him. He had been made Malkovsky's first assistant. In other words, he was right there alongside Malkovsky, his head on a smaller block, but one that would make sure that in the event of failure the head still left the body even so.

On the plane, after the usual bitter haggle to get a business class seat, Cave thought about Peltzer. No rush. He had twenty-eight hours in which to think about him before they got to Sydney. (No time even for a two-day stopover in Singapore to cope with the jet lag, Sir Roderick had decreed. This was a rush job.) . . . Franz Joachim Peltzer. Aged thirty-six next birthday. Educated at Leipzig Gymnasium and Dresden University. Doctorate in engineering. Unmarried. Father and mother dead. One sister, Hildegarde, aged twenty-eight. A translator employed by the East German government.

And that was about it. Franz Joachim Peltzer had gone to Russia, done his work, eaten well, drunk well, chased the girls, then come home, sat by his mother's deathbed – and defected. For no reason at all that the file could provide. But Sir Roderick was convinced that he was in Australia, and Sir Roderick's information was usually sound, especially when it involved K.G.B. contacts. Sir Roderick, Cave thought, must have had pretty useful contacts himself.

There was one other piece of information. Besides wine and women, Peltzer had liked motor cars, fast ones, to the point where the Russians had actually dug up an elderly Ford Mustang and an E-type Jaguar for him to play with – then taken them away again because he drove too fast. He must have done good work for them, thought Cave, and began to realise too why Sandy Keith should be involved.

But there was no point in wasting time worrying about Sandy, not yet. That could only be done when he had arrived and was with him. For the moment Cave had to concentrate his mind on Franz Peltzer. Not a bad looking bloke, he recalled. Fair hair, blue eyes, looked as if he took a lot of exercise. . . But if he had to remember faces Cave would sooner it was his sister's. Hildi Peltzer was a knockout: a blue-eyed blonde with a short straight nose and a mouth that really should be doing other things than translate political speeches. On the other hand it wasn't Hildi he had to look for: it was her brother.

He carried on with the agenda. Fast cars. That, he already realised, was what explained Sandy Keith's involvement. Sandy, according to Sir Roderick, was doing a guest appearance at something called the Sydney Veterans' Grand Prix. Thrills and Spills. All Action. None But The Brave, the publicity handout said, and much more. Much, much more. But it didn't tell you exactly what was going to happen, except that a lot of ageing motor cars would be driven at impossible speeds. It didn't tell you that Sandy Keith was bait. It didn't even begin to explain why Sandy Keith was involved in the first place – his one true love was Formula One, and always would be. But there was a clue, of course. Sir Roderick had been twisting his nephew's arm.

The jumbo came down on time, and Cave was greeted by Customs and Immigration with the snarling hostility that seemed to be international, then took a taxi to a hotel overlooking the harbour, then bed for twelve hours. When he woke he didn't feel completely well, not yet, but at least he could face the day. A chambermaid brought coffee, and a messenger brought a package labelled 'Books. With Care'. He phoned the number Sir Roderick had given him to say thank you and was told to get a move on. There was a lot of unusual activity in the East German Embassy at Canberra, but nobody knew why. Not yet. And there was a rumour, it appeared, passed on by Sir Roderick himself, that some of the East Germans were more Slav than Teuton.

Cave opened the package of books to find that he was once more the proud owner of a Smith and Wesson 357 magnum revolver, a webbing holster, and twelve rounds of ammunition. He yawned hugely, then loaded the magnum, strapped on the holster, and practised that savagely fast, clawing draw that might within the next day or so be his only chance of survival.

It was Spring in Sydney, a cool, crisp October day, and a jacket would in no way seem eccentric. The holster could be used when he went out. Cave practised one last time and left at last. The weight of the gun against his ribs was a comfort that he welcomed.

He paid his bill, picked up a hire car, and went to a seafood restaurant in Rushcutters' Bay. The seafood, he thought, is at least some consolation for all this, and he ordered another helping of Moreton Bay Bugs. Then it was time to go to work, look at the road map, start up the car, and find his way to Cutler's Creek. There was an awful lot of outback to cover before he found it, scrub and eucalyptus and hard dry earth, and hardly a living thing anywhere, except parrots overhead, and kangaroos – but the kangaroos were not living. They lay dead by the roadside, mown down by cars, like rabbits or hedgehogs in England. At the end of it all was Cutler's Creek.

The creek itself was all but dried out, waiting for rain, and struggling alongside it was a scattering of houses and more-or-less public buildings: a motel, four pubs and a church. The whole place was packed. As Cave left the car in the zone marked 'Officials Only' he became at once aware of the frantic need that pervaded the whole place: need for a meal, a bed, a drink. All around him men scurried in search of one or other, or all three.

The car park attendant came up to him. 'You official?' he asked.

'It says so here', said Cave, and produced credentials. The attendant peered.

'Oh, publicity', he said. 'You better go and see Tim Whelan. He's over in Bennett's pub.'

Bennett's too was packed, but Whelan had a room to himself, and enough clout to get Cave a cold beer straight away. Pushing forty, Cave thought, but not too hard. Tall and slim. He'd have looked ten years younger if his hair hadn't turned grey. 'Chief Promotions Officer' his little desk board said. What was he promoting? Cutler's Creek?

189

Whelan folded up Cave's papers neatly and handed them back.

'Glad to have you with us, Mr Cave', he said. 'So you're with Sandy Keith?'

'I'm with his sponsors', said Cave, and reeled off the list: the cigarette firm, the insurance company, the yogurt maker. It seemed that the pie man hadn't been interested... 'They wanted to make sure he's handled right. That's why I'm here.'

And you can check it all you like, he thought. Sir Roderick's fixed it.

'We got word about all that ', said Whelan. 'Seemed sort of funny.'

'Oh really?' said Cave.

'I love it when you Poms say that', said Whelan. 'What I mean is Sandy Keith told me himself he hasn't done any big racing for a while. Real Grand Prix I mean.'

'His name still sells things', said Cave, and it was true enough.

'Of course this race is a charity affair', said Whelan and Cave thought, I might have known. When it came to charity Sandy Keith was in a class apart. He even supported a whole schoolful of Vietnamese boat orphans out of his racing earnings, a fact of which Sir Roderick was well aware.

'I'm hired to see he gets as much publicity as possible – and as much money', he said aloud.

'Great', said Whelan.

'Tell me something', said Cave. 'Who gets the money?'

'Orphaned kids', said Whelan.

And that makes it just about perfect, Cave thought. The whole set-up could have been designed for Sandy Keith.

He went off to find him. Over by the cars, Whelan had said. In the big paddock by the back road. Cave walked because it was quicker, and found himself transported back fifty years in time, for on the field's hard packed earth were the sort of racing cars that

190

Cave had seen only in photographs or old movies: racing cars that really looked like *cars*: bonnets, mudguards, even the occasional running board. Cars immaculately maintained, elegantly painted, each with a proud owner who fussed over it as if it were his firstborn, while a professional entourage did all the real work.

Cave spotted Sandy and went towards him. He was leaning against the chassis of what Cave vaguely took to be a Bentley in British racing green, watching somebody else fuss over its innards. Then he spotted Cave, yelled 'Joe', and came running.

And he can still run, thought Cave. His leg had been fractured in three places, his pelvis and hip joints smashed, but he could move all right. And some of it was good surgery, the best: and some was a body that healed quickly; and some was Sandy Keith's absolute certainty that he couldn't – wouldn't die before he became world champion. At least Cave hoped that was it. When last seen heading for Hawaii, Keith had seemed more interested in becoming world drinking champion than world racing champion, that was if Domenico Guardi didn't beat him to it. He looked around for Guardi, but there was no sign of him. He must be the man with half his body inside the Bentley's engine.

Then Keith reached Cave and looked up at him: the long, lean man towered at least six inches above him, but the lack of height was no disadvantage to a racing driver.

'Joe – how are you?' Keith asked.

'Tired', said Cave. 'But glad to see you. You're looking well.'

'Purely social', Keith said at once.

'What is?'

'My drinking', said Keith. 'Didn't you know that Nadir had flown out to see me in Hawaii?'

'You mean didn't Sir Roderick tell me?' Cave said. 'The answer is he didn't.'

'No doubt he had his reasons', said Keith. 'He always

does. But Nadir and I had quite a chat. And in the end I listened to him. He wants me back driving the Morton-Nadir-Yummy as soon as I've finished with this race. It seems the guy he hired in my place didn't quite measure up. Tough for him, but my good luck.'

'Congratulations', said Cave. 'Did you bring Guardi with you?'

'No', said Keith. 'Nadir snapped him up as soon as he saw him. Took him back to England to dry him out and look after the car until I'm ready.'

'Lucky old Guardi', said Cave. 'I thought that was his backside I was looking at behind you?'

'No', said Keith. 'That's somebody else entirely. You'll meet him quite soon, but I don't want him interrupted. Not when he's working on my car.'

'Sir Roderick put you on to this meeting?' Cave asked.

'Who else?' said Sandy Keith. 'He even warned me that you'd be along, too. And as I say, it's nice to see you, Joe, but he promised me that all I'd have to do was drive. You'll do the rough stuff.'

'To each his own', said Cave.

'Exactly', said Keith. 'And after all it is for charity. Besides – I honestly think I would have done it anyway.' Cave looked at him, incredulous. Sandy Keith had *always* insisted on driving Formula One only, unless and until Sir Roderick insisted that Sandy worked for him. And Sir Roderick, and Janet Tang, had been the only ones who ever could insist with Sandy Keith.

'Don't look at me like that', said Keith. 'This isn't just any old production model. This is a classic. A work of art.' He gestured round the field. 'So are they all. They're all absolutely bloody marvellous.' Then he turned back to the Bentley. 'Come and meet Willi', he said, and led Cave over to the Bentley, yelled at the figure still at grips with the car's insides. A head emerged like an ostrich's from the sand.

'Willi Scheule – Joe Cave', said Keith.

A youngish man. Fit. Well built, with close cropped

black hair and a black moustache. Cave had no doubt at all that he was looking at Franz Joachim Peltzer: but he didn't like it. He was getting too lucky too soon.

Scheule-Peltzer bowed and smiled; his teeth very white against the oil smudge on his cheek.

'I do not offer to shake hands', he said, 'because mine are so disgusting.' He showed them, broad, strong-fingered hands, engineer's hands, coated in oil.

'Any luck?' Sandy Keith asked.

'Ja, I think so.' There came a flood of technicalities. 'Give me just one minute –' He dived back into the bonnet.

'Your mechanic?' Cave asked.

'Nothing so common. He's a driver. That's his car over there.' He gestured to a weird looking lump of flame red metal of undoubted antiquity. 'My mechanic's terrified of this thing – so Willi is just giving us a hand.'

Cave looked at Keith's car. 'It's a Bentley, isn't it?' he asked.

Keith snorted. 'Yes', he said. 'It's a Bentley. The 1929 Short Chassis Red Label three litre Bentley as a matter of fact.'

'And you're going to drive it?'

'I'm going to win in it', said Keith.

'You are?'

'Why not?' Keith said. 'It won at Le Mans in 1929.'

'But it's a what-not – a touring car. Some of the others are racers, aren't they?'

Keith winced at the word.

'We've got all sorts', he said kindly. 'G.T.s, Specials, racing cars – that thing of Willi's for instance.' He nodded to the weird lump of metal like a vast abstract sculpture. 'It's a converted World War Two scout car. Now it does 130 on the straight.'

'But even so', said Cave. 'Against that Bugatti for instance –' He nodded at an elegant racing machine that looked ready to go to the moon and back, despite its age.

'We've got a handicap system', said Keith. 'But don't

193

ask me to explain it. They have to use a computer to do that.' He grinned, and Cave saw at once how happy he was. A bone-breaking car crash, a heart-lifting love affair that finally failed, a drink problem bitterly conquered, but somehow despite all three he had achieved happiness. And earned it.

'You're looking pleased with yourself', said Cave.

Keith looked at the weird collection of museum pieces that lay about the paddock. 'I'm back', he said. 'Oh I know I managed a few Formula One drives once I got off the booze, but I never believed it would last. But now I do. I honestly believe that I'm only here on a visit. It's all a bit comic compared to what I'm used to – but I'm doing it, because I can afford to. Because I'm going back to the real thing.' He grinned. 'Next year you can come and do your P.R. for me at Monza.'

Willi finally emerged from the Bentley, stood alongside Keith, and grinned just as Sandy had done. Another happy man. I hate to spoil it for them, thought Cave, but it's what I'm here for. It's why Sir Roderick sent me.

'Maybe when you go to Monza I come too', Willi said. 'Maybe you need a good mechanic.'

'Wouldn't that be great?' said Keith. 'I mean I've already got one good mechanic, but two is better.' He looked from one to the other of them. 'Who's for a beer?' he asked.

'I've got to wash up first', Willi said.

'Me too', said Cave. 'You go and order the first round, Sandy. You're rich enough.'

Keith left them, and Willi led the way to a washroom still raw with newness. As he used solvent on his hands, Cave rinsed his and dried them carefully, then eased his left shoulder, feeling the magnum move precisely into place.

'Have you known Sandy for long?' Willi asked.

'I've known him for years.'

'He's a very nice man', said Willi. 'Also he is a *great* man. At least I think so. To drive like that – it takes a kind of genius.'

194

'It takes courage, too.'

'More than I have', said Willi, and reached for the towel. Both hands occupied. Now was the time.

'Oh I don't know, Franz', said Cave. 'I'd say you had your share.'

The hands twisted in the towel, then too late resumed their drying.

'What did you call me?' he asked, but his voice shook.

'Franz', said Cave. 'Franz Joachim Peltzer.'

'I know no such man.'

'We none of us know ourselves', said Cave.

'Please', said the other. 'No philosophy.'

'I haven't come to hurt you', said Cave.

'That is what the wolf always says to the lamb.'

'I am not K.G.B.', said Cave.

'That is what *they* always say.'

'I'm from British Intelligence', said Cave. 'I've come to offer you asylum.'

'Please?'

'To help you disappear.'

'I thought I had... I was wrong.'

Cave said, 'You came out on the Lindemann Route.' Peltzer nodded. 'That was run by the West Germans ... the Defence of the Constitution boys. Surely they wanted you to stay with them? To work in West Germany?'

'Of course they did', Peltzer said. 'But I'd had enough of working for a country ... any country... I made up my mind that I was going to make it on my own. I was wrong there too.'

'Of course you were', said Cave. 'It just can't be done. You've got to have an organisation behind you. Surely you realise that now?' He looked at Peltzer, but the German made no move. 'We can do it for you – honestly we can', he continued. 'We've done it dozens of times and never failed yet.'

'What can you do?' Peltzer asked.

'Give you a new identity, a new face, a new place to live and money to live there, work if you want it – but only if

195

you want it.' That last was a lie, of course, but he could safely leave it to Sir Roderick to sort out that one.

'And what must I do for all these goodies?' Peltzer asked.

'Come back and talk. Bring your tape-recordings', said Cave.

Peltzer showed no surprise that Cave should be aware that he had tape-recordings.

All he said was, 'And that's all?'

'That's all.'

'I think I accept', Peltzer said. 'But I'm not quite sure.'

'Don't play games with me', said Cave.

'No games... But there is one thing – one very important thing – that I must know. It will be soon. Then I accept – I hope with one more condition. Give me a day. Just a day.'

Cave said, 'All right. One day. And that's all you can afford, believe me.'

'You think the K.G.B. are getting close?' Cave nodded. 'I think so too', said Peltzer, 'but then I have been thinking that ever since I ran.'

'Why did you run?' said Cave.

'Ivanov', said Peltzer.

'The poet?'

'Ja', Peltzer said. 'The poet. I am an engineer, but even an engineer can like poetry. He lectured once at Dresden when I was a student. I think he is a great man. Greater even than Sandy. Maybe a saint... I never forget him... Then they put him in the camp and he died there... Then I go home and I watch my mother die, and I have time to think. Really to think. And I know I can't work for the Russians any more... Then I heard about Lindemann – I will not tell you how I heard about Lindemann.'

'That's all right', said Cave. 'We don't need to know.' And indeed they didn't, not any more. Lindemann was dead; the route he had devised no longer existed.

Peltzer hung up his towel. 'If the K.G.B. are so close, you will protect me?' he asked.

196

'Of course', said Cave.

'How please?'

Cave's hand made its short, abrupt movement, and the magnum was pointing at Peltzer.

'All right', said Peltzer. 'Put it away.'

The gun disappeared.

'You are good', he said. 'Just as your friend Sandy is good. It is very sad, you know.'

'What's sad?'

'That Sandy should travel all that distance from Hawaii just to betray me.'

'Sandy doesn't know a damn thing about you', said Cave, 'except that he was lucky enough to find a good mechanic.' Peltzer said nothing. 'Please believe that', said Cave.

Peltzer looked surprise. Perhaps it was the use of the word 'please'.

'Very well', he said. 'I believe you. Now let us have that beer. I have still work to do on Sandy's car.'

'What about your own?'

'It's as good as I can make it', he said. 'But it has no chance at all. I know my limits. But it is an honour to have been in the same race as Sandy Keith – and I shall treasure it wherever your people hide me. Treasure it until I die.'

He means it, thought Cave. Another racing nut. And they went for their beer.

Chapter 19

IT HAD been a defensive operation, Jason Bird remembered. It was Sir Roderick Finlay who was on the attack, setting out to steal Franz Peltzer. The K.G.B. were only there to defend what was theirs, and to take it back to Russia where it belonged. General Malkovsky, like all K.G.B. operatives, great or small, hated being on the defensive. He and all the others had been taught from the moment they joined that the proper role of the K.G.B. was to attack, ruthlessly, brutally if need be, and above all else, successfully. To defend was alien to them... It was perhaps for that reason that they had hired outside talent for the first attempt...

Sandy and Joe Cave and Peltzer had their beers in Whelan's office, the only place where there was room to stand, and even then with four men in it the room was full. Whelan opened another pack of stubbies, passed them round and grinned at Sandy.

'On the house', he said. 'Cutler's Creek is grateful to you. You packed the place out.'

'There's rather more than me', said Keith.

'There are just two things', said Whelan. 'There's the

198

race itself – and there's you. All the rest are just walk-ons. Right, Mr Cave?'

A hundred per cent, Cave thought, but you don't have to say it with a walk-on standing next to me.

'Yes and no', he said. 'Sandy can't race against himself.'

'True enough', said Whelan, 'but there are blokes offering thousands to get into this race just because your boy's in it – and we're having to turn them away. – There are too many entries as it is. A banana bender offered me fifty thousand.'

'A what?' Keith asked.

'A banana bender. It's what we call a Queenslander. That's because it's the place where they grow the tropical fruit. They're all mad up there.'

Keith put down his stubby.

'I want to try out the Bentley if that's O.K.', he said.

'Sure, go ahead. She's fine', Peltzer said. They all three rose.

'Could I have a word, Mr Scheule?' Whelan asked. 'That scout car of yours – there must be a story in there somewhere. Who did the conversion on her?'

Peltzer hesitated. 'I think it must have been the man I bought it from', he said at last, as the others left him.

Outside, Keith said: 'Why does he have to be so modest? He converted her himself. He told me.'

The K.G.B. had got so close, Jason Bird remembered. It had not been easy. Indeed it might have been impossible, had the computer in Dzerzhinski Street not reminded them that Peltzer was so enthusiastic about driving and racing fast cars, and that Sandy Keith was about to enter a race, and that Sandy Keith was the only Westerner for whom Peltzer had ever professed admiration... They had got close, all right. They had got right up to him. But then somebody had made an error of judgment, which was why neither General Malkovsky nor Colonel Kalkov any longer worked for the K.G.B. Why they no longer worked at all, in fact.

They had had it made. The contact was in place, and all they had to do was immobilise Cave and lift Peltzer. They had even put in place the men capable of achieving both those objectives, Russians disguised as executives with the East German Trade Mission, and a couple of East German experts who were every bit as good at killing as any wet job experts of the K.G.B.'s own, and yet they had had to go and call in outside help...

Sandy had a caravan: or rather he had an American camper about the size of a modern semi. It was parked away from the town, with nothing to look at but more outback, but Sandy Keith was a nature freak, Cave knew, and anyway he had given him the guest room. Which was just as well. There wasn't a bed to be had in Cutler's Creek... Cave parked his car on the edge of a hard path, then hefted his bags and trudged over to the camper. As he did so a pick-up truck shot out from a clump of trees, slowed enough for a man to drop from it, then accelerated again, only to squeal to a halt across his path. Two more men jumped from the truck. The caravan wasn't as isolated as Cave had thought. Maybe there was something to be said for unadulterated outback after all.

'You're not wanted here, sport', one of the two men facing him said. 'Get back in your car and go home before we spoil your pretty clothes.'

They were pretty at that, thought Cave. And expensive. His own money. Sir Roderick would never pay for that sort of gear. It seemed to be a recurrent misfortune that every time he got into any form of strife in Australia he was wearing clothes that cost a lot of money, and his own at that.

'I'm afraid I don't understand you', he said. But he understood all too well. If he turned his back on those two to get in his car and go home they'd jump him anyway, and hold him while the third man did whatever nasty thing he had been told to do. Cave

200

edged to one side: just enough to hear what the man behind him was up to.

He could shoot them, he thought, but that wasn't the way to start a charity race. It wasn't very good P.R. either.

'Go back to Pomland', the spokesman said, then: 'Seeing you don't want to – we're going to show you why you should –'

His voice droned on, masking the fact that the man behind Cave was beginning his run. At the last possible moment Cave swerved to one side, swung one suitcase to connect with the runner's leg, tripping him so that he went over in a flying dive. Cave followed it up with a karate kick, the side of his lightweight moccasin connecting neatly with the man's neck as the other two charged and he swerved, swung both suitcases at them and let them go as he swung. The impact of the suitcases split them apart which was what he wanted, and the gabby man fell, which was the kind of luck he needed, because the other geezer had produced some kind of antipodean cosh and looked as if he knew how to use it. It would have to be the gun after all.

Cave's hand moved in its short, abrupt arc, and was filled with the magnum. He fired and the cosh was shattered, the owner's hand numbed. Cave reached out to slam him with the magnum's barrel then turned to the gabby man, who was now pinning his faith on immobility, apparently in the belief that if he stayed perfectly still Cave would go away. He was wrong. Once again Cave reached out, to clip the gabby man behind the ear with the gun, and he fell.

Dimly Cave became aware during the fight of a kind of growling and scraping noise. He realised now that it was the pick-up truck, and that its driver was about to leave, but he couldn't go forward because gabby was in the way and for some reason he was reluctant to drive over him, so he decided to reverse instead, but his hand was shaking so much he couldn't engage the gear.

Cave went forward in a standing leap, and his right hand reached through the truck's open window, splayed finger and thumb finding pressure points just below the jawline. The driver whimpered, and Cave's other hand reached out for the ignition key, turned off the engine.

'Out', he said, and opened his hand. The driver scrambled obediently, and Cave grabbed him again.

'Who's in charge?' he asked. 'Who's the boss?'

'Me', the driver said at last.

'Do you always lead from behind?'

'Muscle's cheap', the driver said.

'Who hired you?' Cave asked.

'I don't know.'

'I don't believe you', said Cave, and the splayed fingers reached out again. This time the driver yelled aloud.

'I don't know', he said, but the pressure went on. His voice rose to a scream. 'Please mister, I don't know and that's the truth.' The last word sounded like one he didn't use very often and Cave relaxed his fingers a little.

'Tell me about it', he said. 'And don't lie. I don't like liars.'

'This joker rings me up, back in Sydney. Says he's got a job for four blokes and there's ten thousand dollars in the post. I ask him if he thinks he's Santa Claus, but next day there's a letter with ten grand. I get another phone call. Same geezer. Take your bunch of larrikins to Cutler's Creek, he says.'

'Larrikins?' Cave asked.

'You know. The mob', said the driver. 'I might have a bit of work for you, he says. So we come here and stand by the phone like he tells us —'

'How did you get accommodation?' Cave asked.

'All arranged. Then we get a call to come after you.'

'How did you know where to come?'

'Your car', the driver said. 'He had the number and everything. Sydney car hire, he says. Somebody in Sydney must have got a bit chatty. You want to watch that.'

The fingers pressed again: again the man made noises.

'No advice', said Cave. 'Not from you. You're the

202

bloke who let his mates take a hiding.'

He got names and addresses, and he'd frightened the gabby one enough to be sure that they were true. But they were only Sydney crooks after all. Bone-headed muscle that went where it was aimed and never asked why. He told the gabby man to take his mates and his truck back to Sydney and stay there, and felt sure the advice would be followed. Then he helped him load the fallen into the truck and watched him leave, carried his cases to the caravan.

It even ran to a shower – and he needed one after all that exercise. His muscles ached, but the hot water soothed. Just as well he hadn't had to kill anybody, he thought. Made a nice change. Suddenly he began to sing in the shower. This time his new gear had scarcely a mark on it.

When Sandy came back to the caravan his smile had gone.

'You didn't tell me Willi Scheule was the man you were after', he said.

'Did he say that?' Cave asked.

'He didn't have to', said Keith. 'Before you got here he hadn't a care in the world. I leave him alone with you for five minutes and he's frightened to death... I've seen it so many times.' He moved closer to Cave. 'I'm right, aren't I?'

'Yeah', said Cave. 'You're right... But we had no reason to suppose he'd be a friend of yours. Anyway – I'm trying to help him.'

'Oh sure. I've seen the way you and Uncle Roderick help people.' Then Sandy's face softened. 'Joe – why do you do it?'

Oh no, Cave thought, I'm not going to play motivations, not even with you. My psychiatrist says it's bad for me.

He picked up a copy of the *Sydney Herald* from the table, and page two told him why Peltzer needed twenty-four hours. It also told him why the East

203

German Embassy in Canberra was so lively. A nice photograph. Clear. Two columns. 'East German Trade Mission meet for talks in Canberra' said the caption. And there they all were – Aussie politicos, East German primates – if they all *were* East German. And on the extreme left, a dazzling blonde. Even a press photograph showed it. She looked as if she'd wandered in from another group photograph entirely.

Oh dear, thought Cave. Oh dear oh dear. What is he up to? Then a fist banged on the door, it opened, and in he came.

'I am so sorry to disturb you', he said to Sandy, 'but please – may I speak to Mr Cave alone?'

He's terrible, thought Cave. Really terrible. Aloud he said. 'It's all right. You can trust Sandy.'

'Of course', said Peltzer. 'Of course I trust him.' He even smiled... Terrible, terrible... Then the smile vanished.

'I think I better be with you all the time now', he said to Cave.

'Something's happened?' There was a pause.

'No', Peltzer said at last. 'But I see in the paper –'

'Your sister's in Canberra', said Cave. 'I saw the paper too.' He passed it to Keith.

'But why –' Keith began.

'You want your sister out', said Cave. 'That was the other condition. Right?'

Peltzer nodded.

'Do you realise what it's going to take to get your sister out of there?' Cave asked. 'From the East German Embassy crawling with their own security men – and maybe a few K.G.B. for reinforcements? Do you know how good that kind of security is?... A battalion of S.A.S. might do it. I don't think I could manage it with much less.'

'She won't be in Canberra', Peltzer said. 'She will come here.'

'You're joking', said Keith.

'No please', Peltzer said. 'The organisation who got me out –'

204

'They're blown', said Cave. 'Ages ago.'

'Ja – but before they got Lindemann he arranged for me to be in touch with her... We talked sometimes... I think she wants to get out. There is a plan... I am almost sure she will come.'

'Why not just ask for asylum?' Keith asked.

'I am here illegally', Peltzer said. 'I have done things... Illegal things... Papers and so on. Better my sister and I go with this man.' He nodded to Cave.

It was pathetic, thought Cave. With his abilities Peltzer could have asked for asylum no matter what he had done short of murder. But how could he say so, and explain it to Sir Roderick?

'I'll give it a go', he said, talking Australian. 'How soon can she get here?'

'It will not be long', said Peltzer. 'It is Friday. She has permission to go to Sydney till Monday. To do some research in the University. Instead she will come here.'

'She told you this?'

'No one knows she phoned', said Peltzer.

Oh sure.

'Won't she have to report?'

'Only by telephone', said Peltzer and Cave shrugged. There was nothing else to do. Peltzer's sister was perfect bait, and both the K.G.B. and the East Germans know it. On the other hand, to get her to Cutler's Creek was the only chance Cave would have of lifting her, and without her, Peltzer would never go back with him to London. Of that Joe Cave was utterly sure.

It was a defensive action, Jason Bird remembered again, and one that should have been easy enough, apart from the temperamental dislike of acting defensively that all those involved felt. But there was a complication, and that was Joe Cave. All the textbooks said that the men of the West were inhibited when it came to involvement in physical violence, and that left the edge with their opponents, the natural victors, the

205

K.G.B. Unfortunately, Joe Cave did not appear to have read the textbooks.

They had their advantages, of course. Inside information, numerical superiority, the most beautiful stalking horse that they were able to devise, but even so the man in charge was worried. And not without cause, Jason Bird remembered. General Malkovsky had been ordered to Canberra in sole command, but when it came to going into the field, actually to go to see Joe Cave die, and Peltzer return to the fold, permission was refused. This time the Member of the Central Committee held the general so responsible that he was not to be allowed outside the safe prison of the embassy. As for poor old Kalkov, Jason Bird remembered and grinned, he wasn't even there at all.

The problems this time were the general's – and also those of the Member of the Central Committee. He was in too deep now. The operation to dispose of Joe Cave had cost too many lives, too much money. And even Members of the Central Committee can be held personally responsible, if they don't learn how to cut their losses. Unfortunately, thought Jason Bird, that is a capitalist ability, which the theoreticians in the East had yet to learn. . .

She was a blonde who could have stampeded a monastery, even in the Russian two-piece she wore by way of disguise – that looked as if it had been cut with a knife and fork. She carried a holdall Cave knew he'd have to look at. Then he took another look at Hildi Peltzer and knew that the guest room was no longer his.

Cave and Peltzer had met her at the bus, and brother and sister had begun talking German at once, were still talking as Keith and Cave prepared a meal. News, old times, memories of their parents, Hildi's unending stream of boyfriends: an old family joke.

After they'd eaten Cave interrupted. It was nice to see Hansel and Gretel united, but there was work to be done.

206

'Are you coming with us, Miss Peltzer?' he asked.

'Of course she is', Peltzer said.

'Let her answer', said Cave.

'I —' she gestured. 'It is all so complicated.'

'No it's not', Peltzer said.

'Please listen', she said to her brother. 'For you there is no difficulty. You have nothing to lose. But for me —'

'Those swine', Peltzer said.

She interrupted him. 'They are swine, certainly', she said. 'But there is also my life, and my friends. And there is a man I have met — I don't know. I just do not know.'

Cave said, 'I have to know. And soon. There's been a leak from the Sydney end it seems. A bunch of blokes attacked me this afternoon.'

'Poor blokes', said Keith.

'What a softie you are', Cave said. 'But they were only the B team. Rent-a-muscle. I don't think they'll talk, because they took the money and failed — but we haven't much time.'

'Let me talk with her', said Peltzer, and brother and sister went into the spare room. Cave knew they would, and that the next time they referred to it it would be her room. They were gone for quite some time... But when they returned Peltzer said they would go together, and his sister said nothing at all. Cave went outside and overhauled the magnum.

Next day was race day, and Cutler's Creek was crowded even more with people who had come up for the day. Hildi Peltzer wore a pair of jeans, and a T-shirt she'd borrowed from Keith, but she still looked as dazzling as ever. Cave told her to stay with Keith, and put on sunglasses. Successful drivers inevitably attracted gorgeous groupies.

The race was to be run on sealed off public roads, and for miles round ageing racing cars and G.T.s were scrambling one last, frantic practice. Keith took out the Bentley and pronounced himself satisfied. He looked like something straight out of a twenties movie, Cave thought. Leather helmet, goggles, gauntlet gloves – and the little silver elephant called Ganesh hung round his neck by a silver chain. Then Cave remembered that it had belonged to his father, too, when he had flown a Spitfire in the Battle of Britain. He looked again at Keith, and realised that that was exactly how his father must have looked when he climbed into the cockpit.

Enthusing over his car he looked about seventeen. Her four massive cylinders seemed to fire about once every alternate second, he said, but she knew how to move, and it was still possible to change gears without using the clutch – if you got your timing right...

Whelan came over to where Cave, Keith and Hildi waited to see Peltzer on his practice run.

'Gooday Joe', he said. 'Keeping well I hope?'

'In the pink', said Cave, and wondered how long it would last.

'And you Sandy? You going to surprise us?'

'No', said Keith. 'I'm still going to win.'

He was absolutely serious. Whelan looked at Hildi. 'I don't believe we've met', he said.

'No more you have', said Keith, and put his arm round her shoulders. She was as stiff as a board, but his hand squeezed a warning and she yielded against him. 'This is an old friend of mine', he said. 'Charlene. Charlene, this is Tim Whelan.'

'Gooday', she said, and said it perfectly. She should give her brother some lessons, thought Cave.

And then Peltzer thundered past in the flame-red Maybach Scout Car, went into the corner far too fast, and survived it only because it wasn't his time to die yet.

'Thrills and spills is right', Tim Whelan said, and Sandy Keith's hand squeezed the girl's shoulder once more.

The general's last mistake was to try to economise on

K.G.B. lives and send a couple of East German experts instead, thought Jason Bird. True, the East Germans really were experts, and totally reliable, despite their sexual tastes, but for a job like this only the very best of wet job specialists should have been sent. To imagine that one could curry favour from a Member of the Central Committee by pleading that one had saved Russian lives was naive in the extreme, and indeed the general had paid for it. Paid in fact as much as a man can pay. It had all been so unnecessary, Jason Bird remembered. And yet how could one blame the general? Two expert killers with back-up from an inside man should have been more than enough. The trouble was that the general had under-estimated Joe Cave – an unforgivable mistake considering the amount the computer had told him about Cave. Nevertheless, he had done it, and then he had paid for it. The Member of the Central Committee, after all, was at considerable risk himself.

Chapter 20

GETTING them lined up according to the computer's theory of handicapping was the worst part, but at last it was done and the flag went down, and the resultant noise sounded like Day One at El Alamein. There was a twelve-litre Sunbeam Napier Railton that made noises like a whole battery of artillery all by itself. Cave watched them go. Sandy, for some computered reason, had been placed seventeenth out of forty-three. As the flag went down he at once began weaving his way through the opposition like a darning needle through the threads of a sock.

Peltzer at number nine got off pretty briskly as well, Cave thought. But the mood he was in he had nothing to fear. All he had to do was put his foot down and everyone else moved over...

Thirty laps, and a longish time before anyone would need a pit stop. Cave looked over to Hildi. She was in the middle of a solid phalanx of enthusiasts from Melbourne, who divided their time between her and the circuit. Time to take a look at that bag of hers... But before he could get to work on it there was a surprise for him – there on the floor of the camper. A racing tyre that belonged it seemed to a Maybach

210

Scout Car, and a note.

Dear Mr Cave, (he read)
Please take care of this for me. They are very rare, and thieves are so cunning.

Yours sincerely, 'Willi'.

The girl's bag too was in plain sight in the middle of the guest room, and he went to work on it anyway. There was nothing. He'd gone over it the way he was taught and he was absolutely sure... Better phone Sydney... But that was where the muscle had come from... Time was something he didn't have. And yet he had to be sure... He walked down the steps of the caravan, wishing he were computer enough to sort out all the imponderables, concentrating so hard he tripped on the bottom step.

That was what saved his life. As he pitched forward, a bullet split the air above him, slammed into the camper's door. Cave allowed himself to go on falling, and when he hit the ground the magnum seemed to have got into his hand all by itself.

There were two of them, with him forming a letter 'V', of which he was the point. Cave loosed off a shot at the man on his left, missed, and rolled over like a dog. Two bullets slammed in to the spot where he had been. Cave kept on rolling, then as he came up fired again, and the man on his right, gun lifted, checked for a moment, his answering shot hit the ground in front of him. Then the man on Cave's left took off suddenly, running towards his mate, and Cave admired him for it, but shot him nonetheless, head and heart. He fell like a full sack dropped from a cart, and Cave moved in towards his pal who had sunk to his knees, but had raised his pistol two-handed even so, while the blood jumped from the hole in his shoulder. The automatic and the magnum fired together: the automatic's bullet missing by a yard but the man who fired never knew it. He was dead.

Cave went over them. Anonymous men in anonymous suits. Anonymous guns come to that. West

German Walthers. Ubiquitous as Volkswagens... No means of identification... Were they lovers, he wondered, that one should run to the other so? It was possible. It takes all sorts to make security: even East German Security.

He drove them off into the outback and left them there together, then raced back to the improvised pits. When he got there, Tim Whelan was waiting for him. Cave opened the esky and gave him a beer.

'Your bloke's doing well', said Whelan.

'He usually does.'

'I'm setting up a private reception afterwards. I'd like him to come – and his mate of course. You and the sheila and the German bloke.'

'Glad to', said Cave. Whelan emptied his tinny and strode away, tall and rangy, as Australian as a kookaburra. Cave watched him go.

Peltzer came in at last, yelling for water and fuel, and while the mechanics worked, Cave went towards him. Then on his way, suddenly, he remembered. He leaned over Peltzer, yelling against the noise of the elderly tearaways as they went screeching past, and Peltzer nodded his head, and said, 'Ja, ja. I believe you.'

'Then get out of the car', Cave yelled. 'It's time for you to go.'

'Time for Hildi to go', Peltzer said. 'Take her please. But as for me, I must come later. This has been the greatest happiness of my life.' Then the mechanic nodded, the Maybach eased its way back into the maelstrom.

He did two more laps and Sandy Keith was already back in the pits when it happened; chequered flag down, champagne corks popping. The Maybach came up for its penultimate lap, doing far better than the computer had forecast, and Keith raised his glass as it thundered by. Peltzer grinned, and Cave was quite sure that he was still grinning as suddenly his car seemed to go out of control, the whole solid mass slammed into the P.R. Cabin and detonated like a bomb. Both he and Tim Whelan died at once.

'I should have known earlier', said Cave. 'It was after your brother stayed alone with Whelan that he –'

'Began to be afraid', Hildi Peltzer said.

They were in the camper. There had been no celebration after all.

'Right', said Cave. 'He told me why... In the pits. Just before he died. When they were alone Whelan said to him: "You should be careful. You survived a Mustang and E-type Jaguar – can you survive this?"'

'I don't understand', his sister said.

'The Russians gave him the Mustang – and the "E"-type', said Cave. 'No one else was supposed to know.'

'I'm sorry', said Keith. 'I blamed you.'

Cave shrugged, and looked at Hildi. 'What's it to be? Your people know you're here, don't they?' She said nothing.

'Whelan gave *him* a choice, too', Cave continued. 'Either he would go back to Russia – take up his work again – or you would suffer.' He turned to Hildi. 'Even if I got him away – you would still be at risk – unless you came too. That's why he died, you know, so that you could get away...'

'But surely –' Keith began.

'Oh come on, Sandy', said Cave. 'A Party member, top interpreter for an official delegation – just walks out and nobody cares? Nobody even follows her? Come *on*.'

'Nobody did follow her', said Keith.

'Two blokes', said Cave. 'One five feet nine, slim, blue eyes. The other a bit shorter. Thick set. Brown eyes. Mole on his cheek. They could have been queers.'

'Oh my God', said the girl. 'What happened to them?'

'They're dead', said Cave.

Again she said it.

'Oh my God.' Then: 'Get me out of here. Get me away... Please.' And she turned to Sandy Keith, lay sobbing in his arms. It was always the way, thought

213

Cave. *Thank you very much for all the risks you took, Mr Cave* – then off to Sandy Keith for consolation. All he could do was go back to Sir Roderick. Precious little chance of consolation there, but maybe he could take a sauna afterwards.

'Whelan was a sleeper', Sir Roderick said. 'The K.G.B. recruited him at university, then sent him on a tour of Europe, so that he could do his postgraduate work at Lumumba. Just like all the others. He spotted you as soon as you arrived, you say?'

'Yes sir', said Cave. 'Of course he'd seen me in Sydney at that fight in the pub. He was the only one who didn't watch. He was with Emilia Guardi, too. All the same – it wasn't just that he recognised me. I know it sounds strange, but I honestly think he was waiting for me.'

Sir Roderick said: 'Of course he was. He was tipped off.'

'But how could he –?'

'Sandy's sponsor', said Sir Roderick. 'The chaps you were supposed to be working for. Never underestimate East German Intelligence, Joe. Especially when they've got the K.G.B. yapping at their heels. They may not be imaginative, but by God they're thorough.'

'There were three sponsors – cigarettes, insurance, and yogurt. For some reason Sandy's meat pie man's a Grand Prix snob. He wouldn't play. Just as well. I had to have a contact in them all – and of course I told them what to say – only the blasted idiot in insurance went off to New York and forgot to tell me.'

'Well the East Germans rang all three and some chap in the insurance company said he'd never heard of you – and there you are.'

'I'm lucky to be here', said Cave.

Sir Roderick poured a single malt and raised it in a toast – to Cave? to himself? to good fortune? If there was any justice, it would be to all three.

'The girl's useful of course', Sir Roderick said.

'Interpreters are always useful. But it's the tape I really like. Where was it?'

'Inside the hub of a spare tyre', said Cave.

'Trust an engineer', said Sir Roderick. 'He really was brilliant, you know. That's why the Ivans wanted him back alive. The Yanks would give their eye teeth for this little lot.'

'What is it?' said Cave.

'Ultimate space', Sir Roderick said. 'How to get there. Away beyond the solar system.'

'Peltzer's there already', said Cave.

On the television screen the cars still shrieked round the circuit, but for Sandy Keith the chequered flag went down, the champagne gushed like foam from a fire extinguisher. The man who called himself Jason Bird abandoned his memories and came back to reality. Sandy Keith had made it at last. This was the victory he needed. He was world champion, and nobody could stop him now. Thanks to Joe Cave, Jason Bird thought. It would be nice to have a drink on that. But not vodka this time.

There was, of course, nothing easier. All he had to do was walk to the cabinet, and take out ice and scotch — single malt — and water, and mix all three. Sir Roderick Finlay would have been appalled had he been there to see him do it, but Sir Roderick was not there. Sir Roderick would never see him again. It was a pity, thought Jason Bird. Sir Roderick Finlay had been a very pleasant man to do business with, one capitalist dealing with another.

It was true that Sir Roderick had given Jason Bird a small fortune, but on the other hand, Jason Bird thought, he had earned Sir Roderick a larger one. And he owed it all to the Member of the Central Committee, or perhaps to General Malkovsky. More likely to both of them. Because it had been evident once the hunt for Joe Cave was up, that whoever succumbed and whoever survived, Kalkov was marked for death.

Whoever won, Kalkov would lose. He knew too much, and had not enough power to protect his knowledge.

And therefore it had been the logical thing to make contact with Sir Roderick Finlay. Sir Roderick in fact had been his only chance, and Kalkov had taken it. In order to do business with Sir Roderick he had been forced to take the most hair-raising risks, but after all he was doing that anyway simply by being in Dzerzhinski Street, and there was no money in that, beyond a K.G.B. colonel's salary. The risk had not only been worthwhile, it had been essential.

And the wonderful thing was that it had worked. He had got the information out about the Lumumba University graduates, Trudi Jannot, the Chinaman obsessed with orphans, and all the rest. Sir Roderick had listened, and believed him – a rare ability among spy masters – and had acted as and when opportunity had arisen, and never once told anyone else in his Department, not even Joe Cave. A man to do business with, as the British Prime Minister had said of quite a different kind of Russian. And it had worked. Keith had survived, and Cave had survived, and Kalkov had survived.

He was Kalkov with a different face, and a different life-style, and a different name, but he was Kalkov even so. Alive and well and living in luxury in St Petersburg, Florida. Light years away from the Gulag Archipelago where General Malkovsky, so he had heard, had died of all kinds of things, including frostbite and a beating by guards.

Jason Bird-Kalkov lifted his glass in a toast to Sandy Keith. Thanks to his uncle, he was here, but thanks to Sandy he was here too. If the Member of the Central Committee hadn't opted uncharacteristically for vengeance the best Kalkov could have hoped for was a lifetime of service to the K.G.B., with little hope of ever progressing beyond the rank of colonel. Being Jason Bird in Florida was much, much better.

He became aware, almost imperceptibly, of a gnawing pain, a pain like indigestion. Somehow it related to

216

the investments he had made a week ago. The investments had been good so far, and there was no need for
him to sell – not according to his interpretation of the
Dow-Jones Index. And yet the pain persisted, and even
increased, as he sipped at his malt whisky and water
and ice. And then the irony of it hit him. Jason Bird,
otherwise known as Kalkov, was the first K.G.B.
colonel in history to be developing an ulcer because of
his investment in the capitalist stock market. That,
surely, called for another drink. But it would have to
be milk.